ENTANGLED IN TIME

ENTANGLED IN TIME

A Jason Falcone Technothriller

BOOK 1

LYNN M JAKOBS

This is a fiction book that references actual historical events. The dates and details in the historical accounts were adapted to suit the story. With that exception, the characters and the events in this book are solely the result of the author's imagination. Any resemblance to persons, living or dead, is coincidental.

Email the author at lynnjakobsauthor@gmail.com

DEDICATION

I dedicate this book to my daughter-in-law, Karyn Jakobs (1977-2016),
who coined the term "night naps"

TABLE OF
CONTENTS

ACKNOWLEDGMENTS

I extend my heartfelt gratitude to Eva Jakobs, Torrie Lauer, and Ashley Wursten for their invaluable assistance in the creation of this novel. Their contributions have played an instrumental role in shaping and refining the narrative, making this journey an enriching and collaborative experience.

PART ONE
THE PACKAGE

PROLOGUE

Sara kept her footfalls quiet; even the faintest sounds reverberated in the rocky gorge. She moved cautiously, not wanting to trip or step on something slithery. Despite the fear threatening to consume her, she resisted, determined not to succumb to it. She knew she was breaking scientific protocol but kept going, knowing she must act swiftly to safeguard her discovery.

Taking careful but determined steps, she neared the mouth of the cave, her heart quickening with each passing moment. The small opening, barely visible in daylight, was nothing more than a dark shadow. Her flashlight, whose beam would have been a beacon to anyone following her, was stowed in her backpack. In its place, she opted for night-vision goggles, a trick she learned from Jason.

Sharp rocks dug into her thick clothing as she slid through the narrow opening. The momentum propelled her forward, landing her roughly on the cave floor. While taking stock of herself, she heard a faint sound. "What was that?" she thought. How foolish of her not to bring a weapon. She didn't hear it again; maybe it was just her nerves.

She stepped forward cautiously; the inky darkness at the periphery of her goggles made navigating difficult. At the opposite end of the cave was a nearly invisible passage that someone had carefully cut it into the rock to form an optical illusion. Anyone who entered the cave would not have seen it. She only knew of its existence from the cave drawings in Akrotiri.

She stopped as a distant sound caught her attention once more. The place was like an echo chamber, making it impossible to determine which direction the sound was coming from. A chill ran down her spine, "Was it fear, excitement, or the coolness of the cave?"

She followed the passage deep under the ridge, passing by several small corridors she had already explored. With each step, she noticed the ground beneath her feet shifting from a rough, uneven surface to a remarkably smooth one. She ran her fingers along the walls, feeling the texture change; she was close. A few minutes later, she stood at the entrance to the room where she had made her first discovery.

As she stepped inside, the sound echoed once more, now closer, and more unsettling. Her mind raced with possibilities; was it an unusual air current in the cave system or something else entirely. Her thoughts were violently interrupted as a hand seized her from behind, muffling her cries with a cloth. Struggling in vain, the grip only tightened. As darkness enveloped her, she knew she would never find it.

CHAPTER
1

I T WAS LATE summer in West Virginia; the trees were starting to turn, and the nights were getting colder. Jason Shaw was splitting firewood near his secluded cabin outside Yellow Spring. He chose the surname Shaw for its meaning, a clearing in the trees, where he chose to live. With each swing of the axe, his muscular body worked in perfect harmony to accomplish the task.

His cabin was off-the-grid and sat in the middle of a 100-acre plot of land dotted with White Ash, Red Spruce, and Hemlock trees. Power was provided by a hydroelectric unit on a small river flowing through the property's edge and his only connection to the world was a private satellite dish that supplied internet and cell service.

He caught movement in his peripheral vision and saw a herd of deer munching on ground cover about a thousand feet away. There were two does, each with a fawn born last spring. Usually, you couldn't see them clearly from that distance, but he could. He brought his gaze back toward the cabin and surveyed the property. There were several outbuildings visible through the autumn leaves. The largest was a red barn that appeared deceptively old and neglected.

He glanced toward the driveway where his two vehicles sat. The first was a customized black Land Rover designed to defend and sustain him for several weeks should the need arise. It had a bullet-resistant exterior, snorkel, heavy-duty winch, and defensive weapons. He had purposefully outfitted the rig himself, lifting and augmenting the suspension, changing out the stock axle for a straight axle, and adding three auxiliary gas tanks. A large gun safe was stored under the back seat, while the rear compartment was divided into ammo storage, tactical gear, water, and MREs.

The second, more practical vehicle was a Toyota FJ40 he had restored himself. Neither rig had an electronic signal that could be tracked, but the downside was their dependence on gasoline. His current project was a vintage Land Rover that he was converting to a hybrid for long off-road excursions.

Having satisfied himself that no human intruders were near, he continued splitting wood. Remote mountain life required manual labor, which usually focused his mind on the present. But memories of the past had a habit of creeping in, especially when least expected. He tried to force them back into the deep recesses of his mind, but it was useless.

He was in Iraq, leader of Seal Team Six, listening to Commander Miller's voice through his com system. He and his team were attempting to extract an undercover operative who had been captured and was scheduled for beheading during a live television feed.

The FBI got lucky, or so they thought, when a team in New York raided the apartment of an extremist group. In addition to bomb-making paraphernalia, they recovered texts between members of a terrorist organization in Bagdad and one in New York. The U.S. group planned a suicide bombing in the middle of the Manhattan Bridge immediately after the televised beheading. It was like adding an exclamation mark to maximize the terror. The FBI contacted the military with intel on where the Bagdad group planned to film the beheading.

Jason's team was spun up for the extraction. They were at the target, and his demolition man, Jorge, was placing C4 on the door. The last thing he remembered was taking cover behind a metal cargo box, waiting to lead his team into the warehouse. He woke up in the techno-trauma unit at Landstuhl Medical Center a few months later. Their op had been a trap; he was the sole survivor.

Injuries from the thermal blast constituted an immediate threat to his life. The rescue team had placed him in a trauma pod, and the robotic medic kept him alive until he reached Landstuhl. After a year in the hospital undergoing experimental and technologically advanced procedures, he was finally discharged. It took another year of training before he was able to operate again.

After each successful mission, he increasingly felt he was just an expensive piece of tech. Admin would review tapes from his body cam and compare his performance to pre-established criteria. He felt like a guinea pig in some bizarre experiment. He became disillusioned with the Navy and tried to retire several times, but they always pulled him back with another crucial mission.

It took a painful romantic break-up for him to reject the situation and resign his commission. Now he was a wanted man, wanted by black ops for his unique abilities, and wanted by any foreign government that had the ability to reverse engineer him. There was only one person he could trust, Mike Miller. His thoughts were interrupted by the buzz of his cell phone.

CHAPTER
2

MIKE MILLER WAS in his office at the U.S. Naval Academy in Annapolis, grading assignments and wanted to finish before leaving. It was Labor Day weekend, and he and his wife were taking their two little girls to the Cape for an end-of-summer getaway. They would leave as soon as he got home.

Mike was a career Navy man and had remained single until his deployment days were behind him. After a failed mission in Iraq, he decided field work wasn't for him. He changed his career trajectory at thirty-eight and eventually accepted a teaching assignment at Annapolis.

Five years ago, he ran into his high school sweetheart while attending a home game with some old football buddies. After an awkward greeting, Nicole agreed to get a cup of coffee and catch up. They had been inseparable during high school, but she had been destined for an Ivy League university, then on to med school. He was destined for the military academy. Nicole wanted Mike to follow her to George Washington University, but his SAT scores didn't qualify him for a GWU scholarship. Annapolis was close to D.C., and Mike thought they could still see each other.

His scores might not have been high enough for an Ivy League scholarship, but the Navy felt they were high enough to offer him a spot at the Officer's Training School. Nicole was in med school by then, and he was working very hard to prove himself at OTS. They broke up not because they fell out of love but because of their respective career paths. Nicole eventually married a fellow physician, and Mike found himself part of an elite military intelligence group working with a task force in the Middle East. He thought he had avoided long-term commitments because of his job, but once he saw Nicole again, he realized it was because he had never really gotten over her.

It had been years, but when he saw her again, it felt like he was back in high school. She was as beautiful as ever, with long thick black hair that hung to her shoulders, intelligent brown eyes, and a tall, athletic body. He learned she had left her husband after discovering he wanted a lucrative career more than a family. The revelation was like music to his ears; he saw an opening and took it. A year later, they were married; two years later, their oldest daughter, Millie, was born, followed eighteen months later by their youngest daughter, Lydia.

A second knock jarred him back to the present, and he said, "Come in."

Seaman O'Hara saluted, then handed over a medium-sized package. "This just came for you sir; it was marked urgent."

He glanced down; it didn't look like a base communication, "Do you know who sent it?"

"No sir, it came through civilian mail."

He took the package and looked at it. The return address was odd; it looked like a code. Whoever sent it knew that one of Mike's hobbies was deciphering codes; it must be someone who knew him. He looked back at the seaman and said, "Thanks O'Hara, I'll take it from here."

He had a couple of hours left before signing off for the weekend. His interest was piqued, and he thought, "What the heck, why not?" and began working on the code. He wanted to know who sent it before deciding whether it was safe to open. Since 9/11, all mail entering the Base was scanned for incendiary devices, so at least he knew it wouldn't explode. An hour later, he had cracked it, although it wasn't a very sophisticated code. The sender was someone he knew all right, Dr. Sara Peterson, an archaeologist specializing in ancient languages.

He carefully opened the package only to find that it was a package within a package. Taped to the inner wrapping was a note that read:

Mike, I'm so sorry to put you in this position. I had to send this to someone who could not be connected to me. I need you to get this to Jason, preferably with no one knowing. But I can't be sure that someone won't find out who this package is addressed to. Watch your back; I have no idea what these people will do to retrieve it. Please don't open it! Jason has no family to worry about and is better equipped to handle the danger. Thank you so much, and again, I'm sorry to get you involved.

He walked over to his window and stared blankly down at Dewey Field. "What do I do now?" Jason had become reclusive after leaving the Navy. Mike didn't blame him; after all, Jason, or more accurately, the tech inside Jason, was worth a lot of money on the military black market. But he and Jason had developed an unbreakable bond and kept in touch. In the field, they could almost anticipate each other's reactions, and their ability to trust one another had kept them alive during many missions. He tried to put himself in Jason's shoes, to understand his mistrust of the military and the fear that if anyone came after him, the people close to him would get hurt. This fear and doubt ultimately caused Jason and Sara to split.

Sara's warning about the possible danger to his family jarred him from his thoughts and spurred him to action. He immediately called Nicole and made an excuse for her to drive the girls to the Base and wait for him. Once here, they would be safe while he and Jason decided how to proceed. He wanted to call Sara, but he didn't have her number and had no idea how to get ahold of her.

He returned to his desk, opened a drawer, and pulled out his encrypted phone. If Sara were this worried, he had to be cautious. In the unlikely, but not impossible, chance that he might be followed, he had to get Jason to come to him, not an easy task given Jason's mistrust of the military. He tapped Jason's number.

CHAPTER

3

J ASON SAW THE incoming number and answered on the first ring, "Hey man."

Mike curtly said, "We're encrypted on my end."

Jason, on high alert, replied, "We're secure." He had known Mike for over ten years. As a young Seal, he had been assigned to work with him during the Middle East campaign. Initially, the two didn't like each other. Jason thought Mike was just another career officer, arrogant and ignorant regarding the realities of fieldwork. Mike thought Jason was just another grunt, relying solely on combat training and weaponry with no intelligence or independent thinking. After a failed and deadly mission, their attitudes changed as they relied on each other for survival.

"Jason, I just received a package from Sara along with a very cryptic note. She wants me to get the package to you, says it's very important, but also very dangerous."

Jason was immediately suspicious; he didn't think Sara wanted anything to do with him.

Mike continued, "Nicole and I are headed to the Cape this weekend. I called her, said something came up, and asked her to pick me up here. Look, the package might be traced, so I don't want to take it with me and I don't want to leave it on Base." Mike paused to let the information set in. He then continued, "Can you get here as soon as possible? Sara sounded scared; she even encoded the return address."

Jason wiped the sweat from his brow and asked, "Were you able to crack it?"

Mike rolled his eyes as if to say, of course, I did, "Yes, it was sent from the Greek mainland three days ago. Look, I know what the breakup did to you, but I really don't know what to do here."

Jason tried not to relive the night that he and Sara parted. He loved her and regretted that his fears had torn them apart, "Yeah, I don't want to rip that bandage off."

Mike replied, "I know brother, hopefully this will turn out to be nothing, but the crypticism has me worried. And I really don't believe she would joke about my family's safety, so until we know more, I'm taking this seriously." Mike hoped he had presented a strong case, strong enough for Jason to come to the Yard.

Jason was uncomfortable with the thought of returning to the Base. Once there, he could be whisked into a briefing room and presented with a mission that would be hard to resist. That tactic kept him operating after recovering from the incident that almost killed him. In a sense, it *had* taken his life, the life he knew, the body he knew, and ultimately Sara. But since he'd take a bullet for Mike, he didn't hesitate, "I'll be there as soon as I can," then half-jokingly added, "Make sure the gate guard won't detain me."

Relieved, Mike said, "Thanks, brother; we'll sit tight until you get here."

Jason's mind was running through all kinds of strange scenarios. What was Sara playing at? He was also concerned about Nicole and the girls. Before Mike hung up Jason added, "Hey man, if you're worried about Nicole and the girls, why don't I swing by your house, and we can convoy to the Base. It will only be fifteen minutes out of my way, and it might ease your mind to know that I'll be right behind them."

Mike replied, "Thanks brother, but they should be on the road in a few minutes. You might miss her, and that would just eat up time. I would call her, but I don't want her distracted and delayed." He thought of an alternative and said, "I'll check the security system at the house and make sure everything is OK."

Mike ran his fingers nervously through his hair, trying to push back the sense of dread that was beginning to creep into his mind. With Jason waiting, he checked the phone app connected to their home's security system. The system had been set to *leave*, meaning Nicole must have locked up and left.

Jason continued, "OK, while you wait for us, why don't you do a search and see if you can find out where Sara has been working, last I heard she was in Egypt."

Mike was booting up his encrypted laptop and replied, "Already on it."

Jason hurried into the cabin and changed into a long-sleeve shirt that would hide his scars. As he moved quickly toward the bedroom, he glanced at the framed photo of Sara sitting on a corner table. It had been taken during their trip to Belize. Her long hair was pulled back in a ponytail; she was smiling and her eyes were full of love. Even though they were no longer together, he couldn't bring himself to put the picture away.

After a lightning-fast clean-up, he headed for his vehicles. Needing speed more than sustainability, he jumped into the Toyota and hastily maneuvered the vehicle down the long gravel road. He took Highway 259 to Interstate 50, then turned onto the onramp toward Annapolis. He wanted to get there fast but kept the speedometer just five miles over the limit. He didn't need the state police pulling him over.

While he drove, his mind kept drifting back to Sara. A few years ago, she had become involved in an incident near the ancient city of Ur, approximately 220 miles southeast of Bagdad. An American archeological team had been granted permission to excavate outside the city's previously known boundaries. The team had discovered ancient clay tablets but had difficulty deciphering the inscriptions. Sara, a highly respected philologist, was called to the excavation site as a consultant.

Unfortunately, radical Islamists took them hostage, threatening to torture and behead them. The Seals were called in to extricate the group as quietly as possible; no one wanted an international incident. His team managed to free the hostages without alerting their captors, but then things went south. Their ticket out of the country was shot down, and it took several days for another Blackhawk to rendezvous with them.

Sara did not fit his idea of what an archeologist should look like. With her long blond hair, athletic body, and smooth tanned skin, she looked more like one of the California surfer girls he gawked at in his teenage youth. She was also strong-willed and could be stubbornly independent, a character trait reflected in her emerald green eyes. Yet, it was her unique blend of intelligence and resilience that captivated him. He tried to resist his attraction, but their perilous situation made it impossible to avoid her.

Once back in the U.S., Sara had to undergo debriefing and medical clearance. Jason appointed himself her escort, and they gradually became friends. They had little in common other than the loss of both their parents and their love of history. Eventually, they became lovers, but each maintained a little distance.

Over the next couple of years, they stole a few days together every month or so. Ultimately, this wasn't enough for either of them, especially as Jason contemplated life after the Seals. Sara was creating quite a name for herself in archeological circles, and he knew that if they were together, he would never be off the radar. He also knew she would never give up her career and live a life off-the-grid with him. He became more withdrawn as the reality of their situation began to sink in, and Sara finally broke things off. He had not seen or spoken to her in over a year, but the wound was still raw. Again, he wondered, "Is she in some kind of danger?"

CHAPTER
4

Nicole was packing the car, making multiple trips in and out of the house, and did not see the vehicle as it snaked up the long maple-lined drive. Their dog, Oscar, had already been dropped off at the kennel, so he wasn't there to alert them of its approach.

The girls were excited about their trip to the beach. They were running around the house, trying to gather up as many toys as their little arms could carry. At age four, Millie relished her role as the big sister. She took after her mother, with thick dark hair and brown eyes. She was already reading and could write her name and an extensive repertoire of simple words.

Lydia was just shy of her third birthday and took after her father, with blond curls and big blue eyes. She liked to do everything her sister did and received the same formative education they provided to Millie. The girls didn't understand what their father did for a living, but they were starting to realize their mother was a physician. They weren't allowed to watch much television, but they watched the Disney cartoon, Doc McStuffins, and understood that their mom did something similar with people.

Millie asked again, "How long will we be gone mommy?"

Nicole replied, "Three night-naps," then laughed and added, "so we don't have to take *all* the toys. Pick out a couple of sleep stuffies and one of your baby dolls and I'll pack the beach toys. You can also take your iPad for the drive."

Just then, Lydia walked in carrying her little suitcase. "I helped pack Mama; I'm ready to go."

Nicole smiled at her two little helpers. She couldn't imagine life without the girls. They would have so much fun this weekend. No phones or laptops, just their little family having quality time together. She took Lydia's suitcase and said, "I need to finish packing the car; please go into the playroom so I can finish, then we can *leave*!" The girls giggled at their mother's funny expression and the way her voice squeaked when she said, "leave." They ran for the playroom as requested and tried to keep busy and not bother their mom.

Nicole was stepping out the front door, carrying the last of their gear, when she saw a black Suburban with military plates parked behind her Mercedes SUV. Three men wearing military police brassards on their uniforms got out of the car. She was immediately worried that something might have happened to Mike. Her concern for him took priority over her annoyance that they had blocked her car.

A navy lieutenant, face set in grim determination, approached her and flatly said, "Dr. Miller, my name is Lt. Garcia; your husband sent us to get you. We have a situation and need to get you and your family to safety." He flashed a badge and continued, "Please get the children and put them in the car."

Her breathing quickened, and she dropped the gear, "What is this about, lieutenant? My husband called and said we were to meet him on Base. Is he alright?"

He didn't react to her anxiety; he simply replied, "I'll explain everything once we get you to safety."

She knew the sight of strange men would scare the girls, "My little girls are inside and I don't want them frightened by the sight of you coming into the house."

Trying to deescalate the situation, he softened his tone, "Dr. Miller, since the children's car seats are in your car, why don't you go get them. You can make some excuse for us being here. I'll drive you in your vehicle, and we'll follow the Suburban."

Nicole shook her head and firmly said, "I'm not going anywhere until I've spoken with my husband, I'm calling him right now."

Lt. Garcia ominously leaned in, "Please Dr. Miller, we don't want to make a scene that would scare your kids."

Heart racing and eyes darting around, she desperately tried to find a way out of the situation. She took the cell phone out of her pocket, but Lt. Garcia grabbed it from her hand before she could stop him. Visibly shaking, she yelled, "What do you think you're doing? You have no right to take my phone away!"

In a menacing voice, he replied, "Dr. Miller, we're wasting time here. If you don't get your children and put them in the car, we will."

Desperately trying to reach her children, she ran for the front door. Before she got two steps away, he took out a Taser and hit the trigger. He caught her before she hit the ground. As he carried her to the SUV, he motioned to the others to go inside and grab the girls. His preference was not threatening women and small children, but anything was possible for a price, and his current employer was willing to pay handsomely for this job.

The girls were playing doctor with a stuffed bear when the men entered. Even at their young ages, both girls knew about stranger danger and started backing towards the wall. The men said nothing as they ominously approached them. Lydia began whimpering and put her thumb in her mouth. Millie hugged Lydia and cried, "Mommy!"

The men tried to coax the girls toward them with toys, but they continued to cry for their mother. Time was of the essence; each man grabbed a girl and covered their mouth with chloroform-soaked cloths, and in a few seconds, they were out. They carried the girls to the Suburban and placed them in the cargo compartment beside their mother. Nicole's hands had been zip-tied in front of her, and she was still out.

Before leaving the scene, Garcia entered the house and located the security controls, exactly where his employer told him they would be. He rewound the recording to the point just before he and his men drove up. He then turned the security system to "leave," walked out the front door, and locked it behind him. He got in the Mercedes and followed the Suburban out of the driveway. If anyone were to do a casual security check, everything would look normal.

CHAPTER
5

A KNOT FORMED in Jason's gut as he approached the Yard. It had been a year since he last drove through the gate, and he had planned never to return. But despite everything, he had good memories of his time here. He had entered as a boy, idealistic with high expectations, and left as a man. The reality of world politics had dampened his idealism, but his values of loyalty, honor, and commitment remained intact.

As a cadet entering the academy, he was in culture shock. He was raised as an only child, so having roommates and classmates constantly in his face was annoying. But over time, he came to think of them as family. He worked, played, laughed, and fought with them; through it all, they had formed a bond. He smiled as he thought of the good times they had together.

At Gate 1, he showed his civilian credentials. The guard confirmed his appointment, and he was let through. Driving through the complex, he saw cadets running between classes and remembered the anxiety some professors caused when you were late. One in particular, Professor Bacon, a short man who wore horn-rimmed glasses, gave twice the regular homework to any cadet who walked into his classroom late.

Mike's office was in Rickover Hall, overlooking the river. As he neared it, he saw cadets rowing in synchronous motion. He thought, "I hope they're in good shape, or their arms will be sore tonight!" He parked near the northeast entrance to the Hall and entered the building without notice. At the elevator, he was stopped by a guard, and after another ID check, he got in and pushed the button for the third floor.

He quickly tapped the office door then entered. Mike was alone, nervously pacing the room. Without a cursory greeting, he looked at Mike and said, "Where's Nicole and the girls?"

Mike's worried eyes met Jason's, "I don't know, I keep calling her phone but it goes straight to voicemail. I'm worried that she may have gotten into an accident or something."

Jason shook his head, "Once she got out on the interstate our paths would have crossed and I didn't see any sign of her." He quickly reviewed the possibilities, "Did you check the security feed at the house?"

Mike said, "Yes, it just showed Nicole and the girls getting ready. I didn't actually see them leave the house, looked like a glitch in the feed, but the system was set to "leave," and up to that point everything appeared normal."

They looked knowingly at each other; the odds of a glitch occurring at the same time as this mysterious package arrived were slim to none. Jason reassuringly touched Mike's shoulder, "We'll find them. This all seems to revolve around Sara, any intel about her?"

The color was draining from Mike's face as he replied, "I called the University and was told she was on a dig on Santorini. It took me a while, but I managed to get through to the dig site." He paused, then said, "They reported her missing over 24 hours ago."

Jason's stomach sunk. He walked over to the package sitting on Mike's desk. It was Sara's handwriting and the note was as Mike had described. He wanted to open the inner package but had to examine it thoroughly before doing so. With Nicole's whereabouts unknown, the package would have to wait.

Beads of sweat formed on his brow as he looked at Mike and said, "We need to get to your house and see if anything is out of place, maybe find something that can give us an idea where," he was interrupted by the ring of Mike's personal cell phone.

Mike answered it, praying it was Nicole and that everything was OK, but it wasn't her voice he heard. Jason was breathing a sigh of relief when he saw the horror reflected in Mike's eyes.

Despite his obvious distress, Mike had the wherewithal to put the phone on speaker mode. Jason heard a strange voice say, "I assume by now you realize that your wife and children are missing?" The caller used a digital voice changer that made it sound eerily ominous.

Mike gritted his teeth and demanded, "Who is this and where is my family?" Without waiting for an answer, he added, "If you hurt Nicole or the girls, I will hunt you to the ends of the earth. Getting them involved was completely unnecessary."

The voice replied, "Oh really Captain, if we had asked nicely how willing would your friend have been to hand over the package?"

Mike's gaze locked onto Jason, a mixture of surprise and fear etching across his features. How did the caller know about the package, specifically the note inside. And how did the caller know that Mike had just been promoted to Captain?

Jason analyzed the situation. First, the caller knew he was with Mike and the package was meant for him. The caller may have seen the message in the package, but why didn't he just grab the package then if that were the case? Maybe when he saw the note, the package was not with it. Second, the caller had not used Jason's name; he only referred to him as Mike's friend. Either the caller had not seen the note, or he did see it but didn't want to give that information away by calling Jason by name.

The eerie voice continued, "Your family is safe for now, but I want *that* package. Your family's lives depend on how well you convince your friend to cooperate and give it to me."

Mike clenched fists and looked at Jason, who nodded. Working hard to keep his voice calm, he replied, "OK, where are you? I'll give it to you right now."

The caller emitted an eerie laugh, "Do you take me for a fool Captain? If you underestimate my resources and resolve you will never see your wife and those sweet little girls again."

Mike bristled at the caller's seeming familiarity with Nicole and the girls. Images of their frightened faces flashed before his eyes. His mouth was now so dry he could hardly speak, "OK, looks like you're calling the shots, what's the plan?"

Jason could sense that Mike was losing it. He chose this moment to speak up, "Look, you might think you're holding all the cards here but this package gives us the edge. If you want it, you'll turn over Nicole and the girls immediately."

The caller replied, "So, the mysterious friend has a voice," then continued, "We have limitless means to get that package; this is just the timeliest. My men find Captain Miller's beautiful wife very tempting; I can only hold them off for so long. And his girls are worth a lot of money in certain circles, if you know what I mean. They are safe for now, but I cannot guarantee this will continue to be the case."

Although his mind was racing at incredible speed, reviewing all possible options, Jason resolutely replied, "If Mike's family is hurt in any way, you will *not* get this package. You want it more than I do. I will blow it to hell before you get your hands on it."

This took the caller aback, "Let's not be hasty. Once Captain Miller delivers the package and we are satisfied that you are not a threat, we will give you the coordinates where you will find the captain's family, safe and sound."

Shaking his head, Jason looked at Mike and replied, "Not a chance; looks like we're at an impasse. Let me make a counter-proposal, me and the package for Nicole and the girls. I will go to a public place where I can see the entrance and exits. I will wait there, in plain sight, with the package. Once I hear from Mike that his family is safe, I will walk away and leave it." For Mike's benefit, he added, "Obviously, you are watching us, so you will know that I have not exchanged the package for another one."

The voice replied, "Very well, but I will name the place."

While talking to the caller, Jason surreptitiously took out his phone and placed it within Mike's view. Mike saw the screen light up and knew Jason was accessing his neuronal interface. Mike covertly looked down at the screen. "If this goes down and they give you a location, don't go alone. Send in an advance team with a drone. Watch for snipers, tripwires, or explosives. I don't believe they will let them go. Leave your phone behind and grab a burner. Text me the new number. Send me a message as soon as you have Nicole and the girls in a safe location, and I'll do the rest." As Jason kept the caller occupied, Mike finished reading the message.

The caller continued, "There is a restaurant, The Briefing Room, just off the beltway. It should take you no more than forty-five minutes to get there. You will be seated in a rear booth, wait there for my instructions."

Jason did some mental calculations; he knew the place; he'd been there a couple of times, once with Sara. It was on the Virginia side of DC, in Old Town Alexandria, near the waterfront. The clientele was mainly DC types, uptight and full of themselves. He might look a little out of place with his kaki's, cotton shirt, sans tie, and no suit jacket. He always kept a plain windbreaker in his rig; it would have to substitute for a sport coat. The place was relatively dark and noisy, which could be to his advantage.

Jason said, "If you're only giving me forty-five minutes, I'd better leave now; traffic will be heavy on a Friday night." He and Mike knowingly looked at each other, shook hands, and then with a nod, Jason was gone.

CHAPTER
6

K ARL'S ARISTOCRATIC BEARING suggested a background of privilege rather than science. His presence was refined and distinguished, with a slender frame and impeccable grooming. His neatly combed hair exhibited a hint of grey at his temples, which only added to his dignified appearance.

He stood in an expansive room; tall, mahogany-paneled walls were adorned with classical paintings. They looked down at him as if to silently declare, "You don't belong here." They were right. He had confidentially leased the mansion from an old family that could no longer pay for the upkeep. Its proximity to the temple and secluded location was perfect for his needs. However, as private, and magnificent as the house was, he still preferred his lab.

He was a man of science who dealt with predictable results; he hadn't expected the complication of a third party. His plan had been derailed, but he would soon get it back on track. He had already taken care of the female archeologist; she had been under surveillance the minute she turned up at Akrotiri. But his men had gotten sloppy and let her slip out of her room one night, which is when she must have found it. She probably realized its significance and that others might be searching for it. She tried to mislead them by secretly sailing to the mainland to send it to Miller. Finding the Hellenic Post she used and the postal worker who accepted the package wasn't difficult. It also didn't take much persuasion for the postal worker to give them the address on the package. His body eventually washed up on shore, and his men ensured the death appeared accidental.

One thing still bothered him, why did she return to the cave? They were sure she had already removed it, so why risk returning? Maybe there were other relics, or she just wanted to ensure she hadn't missed anything.

If his men hadn't been so hasty, he might still be able to ask her. The questions unnerved him, and he began pacing the room.

He stopped in mid-step; members of the Fellowship practiced meditation and mindfulness. He had to readjust his thinking and maintain positivity. Once he took care of Miller, his family, and the mysterious friend, his plan would proceed undeterred. However, the identity of Miller's friend was not yet known, and this bothered him. He began pacing again.

They tried identifying Miller's friend through facial recognition without success. The man was most likely an undercover asset of some kind. Since he was close to Miller, he must be current or former military. Efforts to discover the man's identity were focused on Miller's military career, who he was close to, and who he had worked with before. An incoming call interrupted his thoughts; he tapped his cell phone and answered, "Yes."

The caller, Eric, was a digital technology wizard whose skills Karl often relied on. Eric reported, "I've done a cursory check of Miller's military career. I had to hack into some pretty sophisticated sites. Several of his missions were conducted with the Seals. One Seal in particular, Jason Falcone, worked with Miller on several operations but was killed during a mission in Iraq. To be thorough, I ran Miller's friend and Falcone's photo through facial recognition, but they didn't match. I'll continue to work on it."

Karl wasn't satisfied with Eric's efforts and harshly said, "Finding this man might be the difference in the failure or success of our entire plan."

Eric tensed at the sound of Karl's disappointment, "I understand. If he's in the system, I'll find him."

Karl didn't like this turn of events. Their plan was reaching a crucial point, and he would do anything to make sure it succeeded.

With a menacing voice, Karl replied, "I'm sure you will, Eric. Notify me at once when you do."

Karl walked over to the window, placed his hands behind his back, and gazed past the balcony to the courtyard below. He thought about their plan and how recent events could threaten its execution. That package held the last piece of information they needed, the information they had been searching for years to find.

The Order had financed numerous digs on Crete with the hidden agenda of trying to locate the cave but had no success. Now, after all these years, newly unearthed ruins at Akrotiri must have led Sara Peterson to it. He was pacing the floor again when his phone buzzed.

Eric wasted no time in saying, "We got him. I used some sophisticated filters on the photo of Miller's friend again. I got a ninety percent match with the facial structure of a deceased Jason Falcone."

Karl barked, "Ten percent still leaves room for error, I don't like it."

The enthusiasm in Eric's voice dissipated, "Yes sir, I understand. I think we're dealing with someone who either purposefully altered his facial features or perhaps had serious facial injuries." Eric continued, "There are rumors of an enhanced soldier program. The military experimented with men so severely injured in Iraq they had no hope of survival. They've denied it, but the rumors have persisted. Falcone's death in Iraq coincides with a spike in the rumors. Besides, Falcone's military records have disappeared."

Karl stopped pacing, "Do you know what type of enhancements this Falcone might have received?"

Eric replied, "No, but it's no secret that DARPA is working on a program that would not only increase a soldier's reflexes but enhance their strength. They're even going so far as to look at using telepathy on the battlefield."

Karl thought about this for a minute. He knew about DARPA, the Defense Advanced Research Projects Agency; their work was well-known within the scientific community. "Thank you, Eric. If you discover anything else about Falcone let me know immediately." He ended the call and gazed out the window again, "Could Miller's mysterious friend be the deceased Jason Falcone?"

CHAPTER
7

MIKE HAD EARNED several commendations for his exceptional intelligence-gathering skills, but his true passion lies in engineering, as reflected by his doctorate in robotics. His specialization is drones, specifically their potential applications in intelligence gathering. His research goal is to provide soldiers with a strategic advantage in battle. He's currently working with a top-secret drone prototype. With his family in danger, he thought, "Now is the perfect time to see if it is worth the millions of dollars spent on R&D." Of course, if he were caught taking it from the lab and off Naval property, he would, at the very least, be demoted, at the very worst, court-martialed.

As Jason suggested, having a team to back him up would have been better, but that would attract attention and take too much time. If the drone worked as expected, its surveillance and tracking abilities would substitute for an entire team. It would be at least forty-five minutes until Jason sent him the coordinates to Nicole's location. He used the time to prepare.

He always referred to the drone singularly. Actually, the prototype was multiple drones that were linked through infrared technology to work as one unit. They're called beetle bots because they look and act like live beetles. They look so real that with cursory inspection, they can't be differentiated from live beetles.

There had been distinct advantages to using live beetles as drones in the past. Their hard shells make attaching electrodes and sensors possible and they are very strong relative to their size. They can carry the weight of sensors and other equipment without interfering with their usual activities.

Test after test proved that live beetles could be directed to perform activities such as climbing poles or trees and flying grid patterns. While these feats are remarkable, robotic beetles have multiple advantages over the real deal. They don't have to be fed, don't have a mating instinct, are easier to work with, and, most importantly, don't omit an odor that predators can detect.

The first prototype, Beetle Bot 1, proved that electronics could be attached to the shell without affecting the beetle's organic movements. Additional refinements and modifications were made with each successive model. BB5 carried tiny cameras that allowed researchers to view the bot's surroundings, direct the cameras 360 degrees, and zoom in on distant objects.

When BB6 rolled out, researchers added tiny directional microphones. The cameras and microphones were astounding breakthroughs in nanotechnology, but they weren't enough. Careful inspection of the bots could reveal the hidden electronics inserted into their shells. Mike and his team were tasked with improving the bots while making the enhancements invisible to inspection.

His team decided to take a concept from bee research to enhance the beetle bots. Bee robots mimic the swarming activities of natural bees, a term called swarm robotics. Mike's team used the concept to improve communication among the beetle bots. An electronic message, such as search coordinates, would be sent to the swarm, and the bots would automatically veer off in the pattern that would best accomplish the mission. However, this required a computer-directed neural interface to calculate the most efficient approach.

To mitigate this need, his team integrated LiDAR technology, enabling the bots to detect their surroundings and identify obstacles in their flight paths. The bots were then capable of autonomous flight, a game-changer as the bots no longer needed a pilot. Anyone could program the flight coordinates into a laptop, and the bots would do the rest.

While the bots' ability to take real-time reconnaissance images without using satellites made them an invaluable field resource, Mike and his team took this further and developed another piece of tech. They developed BB goggles, similar to virtual reality glasses. The goggles were connected, via wireless technology, to one, several, or all of the beetle bots. The bots could then send real-time data, via the goggles, to soldiers who would follow behind them. Depending on the target's proximity, the bots could be feet, yards, or even miles away from the team. This would eliminate the possibility of walking into a trap or an ambush, both of which Mike had experienced in Iraq.

Mike and his team had spent the last two years on the beetle-bot project. Most of the robotic and nanotech work had been parsed out to individuals unaware of the final objective. It was up to his team to integrate the components into a whole beetle bot. Only he, three other engineers, and selected top brass members knew the entire project. Their final prototype, BB12, was ready for field testing, and there was no better time than the present.

He assumed Nicole and the girls would not be too far away. The kidnappers would need to allow Mike time to rescue them and signal Jason they were safe. Only then would Jason give them the package. With forty percent of Maryland and over sixty percent of Virginia covered with forest lands, odds were that Nicole and the girls were being kept in a rural wooded area, the perfect environment for beetle bots. Since he couldn't hedge his bets, he would also take an array of light helo-drones for distant reconnaissance and surveillance. But first, he had to get into the lab, basically steal the prototype, and leave the Base without being caught.

CHAPTER
8

URING THE DRIVE to Alexandria, Jason tried to ignore the clock ticking relentlessly toward Nicole and the girl's horrific fate. Even though he wasn't exactly sure what that was, he knew it wouldn't be good. "Don't get distracted by thinking negatively; work the problem," he told himself.

He turned his attention from Mike and his family to the caller. Jason knew he would not be meeting with him, but most likely several of his henchmen. The caller himself was probably in a control room orchestrating this entire ugly scenario. It was apparent he had access to an extensive surveillance network, probably via private satellites, which meant he had power and money. He also seemed prepared for Jason's suggestion to trade himself for Mike's family and didn't pause before naming a meeting place. "I'm walking into a trap," he thought.

He exited I95 and turned onto King Street. Alexandria is a mixture of old and new architecture, but Old Town is zoned a historic district, and King Street is the best example of historic preservation. He parked in a garage at the western end of the long street, close to the entrance to I395. Parking a fair distance from the restaurant meant an extended walk, but the space would give him time to lose anyone following him. The tree cover, congestion, and the garage roof would also make it difficult for someone to spot him using overhead surveillance.

He secured the vehicle and entered onto a crowded red brick sidewalk, package safely stowed under his left arm. Old Town reminded him of Main Street Disneyland, with its buildings bathed in the soft glow of gas lights and the scent of hanging flowers in the air. His parents took him there yearly for his birthday until he was twelve. Those trips were some of his best memories. His parents were always busy with their work, but he had them all to himself at Disneyland.

Just then, a blond ponytail appeared in the crowd a few feet ahead.

His heart raced. As he quickly moved to catch up, the woman turned her head. It was not Sara; this woman looked nothing like her. Sara's eyes were green, and their tint reflected her mood, like a mood ring. They had an aqua tint when she was happy but became emerald when she was intense or sad. This woman was older and had brown eyes. He worked hard at maintaining focus despite his disappointment. "Was that the plan? Did the caller place this woman here to distract me?" He snugged the package even tighter to his body.

He had forgotten how expansive the area was. You could walk a mile gazing into historic buildings full of shops, museums, and restaurants. The sidewalks were also part of the charm; lined with elms and horse chestnut trees, they enticed diners to eat al fresco during the midday heat.

As he walked past Lee Street, the aroma of barbequed ribs wafted toward him, and he realized that despite his anxiety, he was also hungry. Fortunately, the military taught him how to suppress the need for food. But even as this thought went through his mind, his mouth watered as he caught whiffs of seafood and remembered that the best crabcakes in America were sold in Alexandria. He then caught sight of the open food market in front of City Hall where families were sampling treats and bartering with vendors for the best price. "This is the wrong place to come if you don't want to think of food," he thought.

The streets were full of couples walking hand in hand, enjoying the festive atmosphere, and he couldn't help but think of Sara again. Once Nicole and the girls were safe, he had to find her. Maybe this crisis would bring them back together, then filled with regret, he remembered why they broke it off. "God, I hope she's OK."

The cacophony of people, music, and planes caused him to augment his hearing. A jazz band was playing down one of the side streets. He loved jazz; his grandfather played saxophone in a garage band, and he would sit for hours listening to him play. His grandfather always attributed his mathematical acumen to his early experiences in music class.

He positioned his directional sound detector upward but didn't detect any drones. It didn't matter; he knew he was under surveillance. The caller couldn't risk losing the package, a weakness he could use to his advantage. While he walked, he scanned the area taking GPS readings of the surrounding streets and structures via his cell phone. This data could be easily retrieved if he needed it for an escape.

He checked his watch; he still had plenty of time. As the restaurant appeared, he again wondered why the caller chose this location. It was in a bustling historic district bound by two interstates and a busy waterway. "Could the restaurant's proximity to the river be why it was chosen?"

Three parks adjoined the river; perhaps the caller planned to use choppers. That would take the heavy street traffic out of the equation and allow a quick exit. But the chopper option didn't make sense; they would be too visible. This would make river access a more likely reason for the choice of meeting place. As he would soon find out, it was none of those options.

CHAPTER
9

M IKE GRIPPED A nondescript briefcase as he headed for the elevator. The first three floors of the Hall contain classrooms and
offices, while three sublevels enclose the research labs. Housing the labs
underground serves two purposes: it provides additional security benefits
and protects sensitive experiments and equipment from cosmic radiation.
The lowest level offers the most significant shielding from cosmic noise
and is occupied by the physics division. The engineering divisions occupy
the two levels directly below the ground floor.

As he entered the elevator and descended, he hastily reviewed his plan.
His heart was racing, and he was shaking, probably a combination of
fear-fueled adrenaline and guilt for stealing top-secret tech. Getting in
wouldn't be a problem; no one would question his presence; he just had
to ensure he wasn't caught leaving with the tech.

The lab would be practically deserted this late on a Friday afternoon,
but due to its highly classified nature, there would be at least one guard
outside the door. Only one was necessary as everyone who entered and
left the room was scanned to make sure nothing was removed, nothing
that could be sold to the highest bidder. Leaving with the bots, that part
of his plan was the trickiest. The scanner was very sensitive; it had to be.
The contents of even a thumb drive could shift the balance of power in
the Middle East or give Russia or China a considerable advantage over the
U.S.

He tensed as he exited the elevator at sublevel 2 and walked toward the
lab. The building had a concentric security system, and the security levels got tighter as he approached the inner sanctum where the high-value
work was done. Although he entered this level almost daily and knew the
guards well, protocols were strictly followed. IDs were checked, and no
electronic devices were allowed to be taken into the lab.

The guard inspected his badge and then looked up to verify that the face in front of him matched the one on the badge. Heeding Jason's warning, Mike had emptied his pockets before he left his office. When an electronic scanner was passed over him, he was clean. Satisfied that everything was in order, the guard saluted him and said, "Good afternoon, Sir."

With an internal sigh of relief, Mike touched his badge to a panel beside the door and heard the familiar swoosh of pressurized air leaving the lab's antechamber as it slid open. He turned back and nodded to the guard. His mouth was so dry he could barely speak, but he managed to say, "I won't be long," as he stepped through the door.

Once inside, he surveyed the room to make sure he was alone. The only sounds were those of soft humming emitted by the computer bank. As he walked further into the room, his footfalls were muted by the anti-static epoxy flooring used to protect sensitive electronics from harmful static electricity. In the event of an aberrant charge, the flooring would dissipate it safely to the ground.

In the center of the room, a circular array of computers emitted the only light. Above each computer hung a large monitor, which mirrored the smaller monitor below. It looked like a Lazy Susan that might be found on a dinner table, although this one didn't move. Engineers accessing the lab's powerful internal server viewed their work on the smaller monitors while security personnel monitored the larger screens above. This configuration enhanced security as no one could access the dedicated server without a security member overseeing them. Additionally, the computers could not be wirelessly linked to printers or off-site devices, preventing sensitive information from leaving the lab.

He continued to scan the room as he quickly walked toward a plexiglass-enclosed lab and swiped his badge. Fear for his family's safety outweighed his guilty conscience as he stepped swiftly inside his lab. He moved the robotic arm into position over the long silicone-clad workbench, then switched on the large magnifying glass that allowed him to visualize the bots.

His fingers were too large to work on them directly; he used micro tools attached to the arm. He reached under the workbench and pulled open one of the drawers where he kept beetle bots in various stages of development. He picked out several bots equipped with enough nanotech for basic movements. He was so emersed in his work that he didn't hear someone enter the lab. The sound of a voice caused his heart to stop, and he almost jumped.

"Mike, what are you doing here on the Friday before a holiday weekend? I thought you were taking your family to the Cape?" It was Commander Garrett Jackson, another professor and researcher who usually worked on sublevel 1 in the macro-robotics unit.

With the help of his "resistance to interrogation training," Mike calmly replied, "Yes, I am, but Nicole got delayed at the hospital, so I'm killing time before she and the girls pick me up. I had a few ideas that I wanted to try out." He could not think of any reason why Garrett would be on sublevel 2, "I don't usually see you in here; are you working on something new?"

Although Garrett's clearance could get him into the lab, he could not access any locked doors. He replied, "No, I saw you get in the elevator and I wanted to hit you up about one of my projects. I took the stairs to try and catch you before you left the building, but the elevator kept descending, I thought you might be down here."

Mike was suspicious but didn't let it show. He smiled and asked, "How can I help you with your project?"

Garrett replied, "Oh we don't need to get into the specifics right now, I can see you're busy. I just wanted to know if you had some extra time next week to discuss it."

Mike replied, "Sure, be happy to. Let me check my schedule and I'll get back to you with my availability. Can we discuss it over lunch, or is it too sensitive for public consumption?"

Garrett seemed to think a minute, "It might be. It would probably be best to speak in private, either your office or mine."

Mike said, "No problem, I'll send you an email on Tuesday morning."

Garrett took this as a form of dismissal, "I'll let you get back to work then." He grinned and added, "Don't get so caught up with your work that you forget about Nicole."

Mike smiled back, "Thanks, I won't. I don't plan to be here very long." With that, Garrett walked away. Mike anxiously waited until he was out of sight and then poked his head out the lab door to ensure Garrett was gone.

He immediately sensed that something was wrong. Garrett had never approached him about a project before nor followed him into the lab.

And that last comment about Nicole, "Was he reminding me that she was in danger?" He pushed these thoughts aside. He didn't have time to contemplate whether Garrett was involved with the kidnappers, but he'd better watch his back.

He returned to the workbench and continued his task. He had little time, and Garret's interruption put him behind schedule. He had to modify the bots just enough to pass for the BB12 prototypes. Unless someone decided to check them under a glass, it should work. He removed the outer shells using the robotic arm and placed tiny electrodes on the bodies. He then added a few sensors to their legs and drilled a small hole in the shell. He quickly glanced at his watch and then stopped to survey his handiwork.

He removed one of the bots from underneath the glass. At first glance, these bots looked so much like the BB12s he felt sure they could pass as one and the same. He put the modified bots into his briefcase, then secured his tools and the robotic arm. As he closed the door to his lab, he checked to ensure everything was in its place. He didn't want anyone to enter the lab this weekend and know he had been there.

He took the modified bots to the other end of the room, to a sizeable floor-to-ceiling cage secured with an electronic lock. Opening this cage required a higher security level than the one needed to simply enter the lab. He quickly opened the gate to where the highest-value prototypes were stored and walked toward one of the individual cells. Again, a badge was required to open the cell door. Every time he swiped his badge, an electronic record was made of his entry. If all went well and he survived his personal mission, he would have to develop a good cover story to explain his movements.

Once inside the cell, he placed his briefcase on top of the cabinet that housed the BB12s. He removed one from a drawer, retrieved one of his modified bots, and compared the two. "Not bad." On the surface, you couldn't tell the difference. But with any luck, no one would even look at these until he could return them. He quickly substituted the modified bots with the prototypes, closed the cell doors, and exited the lab.

Outside the lab door, he faced the same guard who was on duty when he entered. He knew the drill; he did it often enough. He put the briefcase down and allowed himself to be scanned by the guard. He then lifted the briefcase to make the guard's scan easier, trying not to hold his breath.

The guard stopped in mid-motion and focused on one area of the briefcase. Mike felt sweat running down his back, but he kept his expression neutral. He couldn't allow himself to be detained. His family was counting on him, and the clock was ticking. It had taken over a half hour to get the prototype. After what seemed like minutes, the guard lowered the scanning wand, saluted Mike, and said, "Have a good evening, sir."

He headed to the elevator without further comment. "Thank God," he thought, the briefcase had done its job. He had designed it on a dare during his Ph.D. program after another student complained about being unable to take his projects out of the lab to work on at home.

Mike took this as a challenge and began working on the problem. After much research and several attempts, he developed a briefcase with a lead-lined compartment on one of its sides. He used a newly developed reflective material to line the inside of the case and around the leaded compartment. The lead made objects invisible to a scanner, while the reflective material disguised the leaded compartment. Mike kept the briefcase in his locker as a reminder that security wasn't foolproof. But he had no idea if it would fool current scanning technologies. If it hadn't, he would have been detained by now.

He returned to his office and locked the door behind him. He opened a metal locker that held his utility uniform and a set of civilian clothes. He grabbed an empty duffle bag and placed the case containing the BB12s inside. He then opened a second cabinet that held his tactical gear. He grabbed some lower-level drones for reconnaissance, BB goggles, and other specialized tactical gear. The tech would prove more valuable than extra weapons, so he chose them carefully. He put his M4A1 assault rifle in the duffle and two Sig Sauers, extra ammo, and a couple of knives for close combat. He donned his civies, pocketed the burner phone, grabbed his gear, and left his office.

As he exited the first-floor elevator, he noticed the guard surveying his clothing and then his gear. The guard's gaze lingered on the rifle silhouette in his duffle. Casually Mike said, "It's a long weekend. I plan to put in some time on the range."

The guard replied, "Yes sir," and saluted.

Mike had to check his gait to keep from running as he exited the building and headed toward his vehicle. At his Cherokee, he paused, then took out a scanner and checked the vehicle for tracking devices. Having found none, he headed for Gate 3. He was so preoccupied with fear for his family he didn't notice Commander Garret watching him from the opposite end of the parking lot.

He still had one quick stop to make. He prayed that whoever had taken his family didn't just kill Jason and grab the package. He sardonically thought, "If they plan to take Jason out, they better not get too close, or it's game over." As he drove through the gate, he looked at his burner phone; it had been counting down since Jason left his office. It now showed five minutes. Jason should be at the meeting place very soon.

CHAPTER
10

THE BRIEFING ROOM occupies a building founded in the 1800s at the intersection of King and Union Streets. Retaining its historical charm, the current iteration preserves the exterior's authentic nature, adorned with period fixtures and signage bearing old-English lettering. Jason surveyed the building, appearing to appreciate its historic details while inadvertently scanning the river for signs of a vessel. He thought, "Just because you don't see anything now doesn't mean it won't show up while you're inside."

The entrance was bustling with patrons, and he knew he wouldn't get in without a reservation. The caller must be well connected if he had secured one at the last minute. He pulled the brass handle of the large wooden door and casually walked into the restaurant's antechamber. It looked nearly the same as when he brought Sara here; his chest tightened again at the thought of her.

The anteroom was a sizable space with ample room for patrons awaiting their tables. Upholstered couches and leather chairs were separated by dark maple tables that lined the walls, while leaded-glass doors separated the waiting area from the bar and dining room. On the left side of the doors, he saw a podium where the maître d stood. The man wore a starched silver vest over a crisp white shirt; Jason muttered, "I really feel underdressed now."

The maître d' was looking down, checking reservations as Jason strode toward the podium. As Jason stopped before him, he looked up, disapproval written clearly on his face. In a high-pitched voice, he said, "Workmen must enter through the back door." Jason corrected his misassumption and the man changed his tune but not his expression, "Welcome to our establishment, sir. May I have the name on the reservation?"

Jason paused in thought, the man's eyes boring into him. A moment later, he replied, "My friend made the reservation, and I'm not sure what name he used; try Mike Miller."

The maître d checked his reservation book and, with an I-knew-it expression, said, "I'm sorry, sir, I don't see that name."

With a sense of foreboding, Jason thought a minute and said, "How about Jason Falcone?"

The man looked at the book again and said, "Ah yes, sir, I have a booth for you. Your friend has not arrived yet." At this revelation, Jason's jaw tightened and his body tensed. The maître d' hesitated momentarily, then continued, "Would you care to wait here or be seated at your booth?"

Jason knew the man wanted to get him seated and out of sight of incoming patrons. With a sardonic smile, Jason replied, "Seated, please. My friend might be running a little late." He thought, "Well, at least one question has been answered; the caller knows exactly who I am. I wonder what else he knows about me?"

The maître d signaled the hostess, a pretty brunette whose black dress left nothing to the imagination. Her high heels clicked on the floor as she escorted Jason to his booth. As he followed her, he took in his surroundings. The room was impressive, just as he remembered. The first time he dined here, he waited at the massive oak bar on the left side of the room. It had an inlaid glass counter and an antique mirror running along the wall behind it. Crystal chandeliers and polished brass spigots reflected off the glass. He remembered thinking someone must spend their entire day cleaning the mirror and polishing the brass.

Most of the clientele at the bar tonight were typical DC types, young guns trying to make a name for themselves. None of them seemed to be watching him. He also noted no sign of the "old guard," who likely started their holiday weekend early.

He continued to survey the room. There were no children in the restaurant; if there were going to be trouble, he was thankful for that. At the end of the room a long hall led to the emergency exit. He remembered that restrooms and meeting rooms were on the right side of the hall, while the kitchen was to the left. A pleated fabric screen currently blocked the hall from view of the diners.

He mentally took note of all possible exits from the building. In addition to the front door and the rear exit, there would be at least one employee entrance off the kitchen. There must also be a loading door for supplies and shipments. He hadn't seen basement windows on the front of the building, but that didn't mean there wasn't one.

The hostess seated him in a tall booth at the back of the room. The leather scent emanating from the upholstered seats and the soft music from the mezzanine above reminded him of Sara. They had sat in one of the booths, sipped wine, and talked for hours as if they were the only two in the room. His remembrance raised an alarming question: "Did the caller know that he brought Sara here? If so, how did he know it?" More importantly, "Did the caller choose this place to get me off-guard?"

The hostess interrupted these thoughts by asking if he would like a drink while he waited for his friend. He ordered a glass of Triennes Rosé, Sara's favorite wine, then placed the package conspicuously on the table. The hostess, whose name badge read Ashley, flashed him a brilliant smile that showcased her deep dimples. After complimenting his wine choice, she proceeded to take his drink order to the bar. His eyes followed her, "Was she supposed to be a distraction?" if so, it was good.

As he waited, he continued to analyze the situation. If the caller had cross-checked Sara's known contacts with Mike Miller's, it would have taken less than five minutes to come up with his name. To be safe, he had to assume the caller knew some of his unique abilities. The immediate question was, "How does the caller plan to get the package?"

He wasn't under the delusion that the caller would just let him walk away, but he doubted anyone would confront him here. He decided his opponent's best plan would be to remove both him and the package from the restaurant. He tried to anticipate how they would accomplish this, but it didn't matter; he would let it happen.

His next question was, "Would anyone be calling with Nicole's coordinates before he was dealt with?" His answer was a probable yes; they would certainly want to keep Mike Miller far enough from Jason to be of any help. A more critical question then loomed, "Would the coordinates be valid?"

His cell vibrated, seemingly in response to his questions. He answered and heard the caller's eerie digital voice, "Well, Mr. Falcone, you *do* know how to follow directions." The caller continued, "A waiter will be approaching your table to inspect the package. Please slide it to the edge. He will not remove it, but I want some assurance that the package won't self-destruct as soon as I text you the coordinates you want so badly."

He slid the package to the table's edge and prepared to act if anyone attempted to remove it. As the waiter approached, he scanned him for any sign of a weapon but could detect nothing. The man, who was obviously impersonating a waiter, placed his body between the package and anyone who might be watching them. He first did a visual inspection, then picked it up as if weighing the contents. Next, he pulled a scanner, disguised as a candle igniter, out of his pocket and ran it over the package. Satisfied, he placed a menu on the table and walked away.

Jason was taken aback. Although the scanner was not a weapon, he should have detected it. Then he remembered that the waiter had kept a silver tray in front of his pocket as he approached the table. The tray must have lead lining under the silver plating. He silently cursed, "I better up my game if I'm going to help Mike."

His phone vibrated again; this time, a set of coordinates came onto the screen. There was no identification to indicate the source of the text. He immediately forwarded it to Mike, who simply replied with a thumbs-up emoji. Mike was on his way. With dread, he thought, "Were the coordinates legit?" and if they were, "Would Mike make it in time?"

CHAPTER
11

MIKE PLUGGED THE coordinates into his GPS. His hunch was correct; Nicole and the girls were about thirty miles away in a heavily wooded area of West Virginia. His heart was racing; he'd been in a cold sweat since he learned they had been kidnapped. As a field commander, he had been involved in many high-stakes missions, but this was the highest. He initiated pursed-lip breathing to control his heart rate; he couldn't lose it now.

His GPS directed him to turn off the two-lane highway onto a gravel road. The road was narrow and lined with tall brush. He pulled off to the side and parked under their cover. From this location, he was about five miles from the target. He turned off the Cherokee and stepped out into the cool night air. He could hear nothing but frogs and crickets. Animals hunting prey made no sounds. "Am I somebody's prey?" he wondered.

He removed ten light-helo drones from his duffle and programmed them to provide a three-hundred-sixty-degree sweep from his ground zero location to the target. It was nearly dark; he programmed the drones' moving target indicators and thermal scanners. Once the drones neared the mark, they'd release the beetle bots, and he'd get tighter surveillance of the area.

As he watched the monitor, he saw no human presence within the search parameters. Due to the size of the search grid, it took about thirty minutes for the first drone to reach the target. Looking through the remote camera, he saw a small cabin surrounded by overgrown brush. Heavy tree cover meant it would be difficult to spot from the air; good thing he hadn't taken that route.

As each drone reached the target, he reprogrammed the cabin to be ground zero. The helo-drones then deployed the beetle bots. Some flew into trees, others scurried on the ground, and others surrounded the cabin. He then programmed all but one helo-drone to fly a five-mile course, three-hundred-sixty degrees from the back side of the cabin. If Nicole and the girls were in there, he wanted plenty of time to get them safely out and back to the highway before anyone could stop them.

After receiving the coordinates from Jason, Mike called the Base and asked a favor from one of his close colleagues. He had a rescue chopper placed on stand-by; it could reach his location in fifteen minutes, just enough time to get from the cabin back to the highway.

Once he was sure there was no one between him and the target, he slowly drove down the rough gravel road, stopping about a hundred feet from the cabin, as close as he dared get. He had no idea what condition Nicole or the girls would be in. If he had to carry them to the SUV, he would need to make at least two trips, and he didn't want to waste precious time. He programmed his current location to be the rendezvous spot for the helos and the bots, then donned his BB goggles and cautiously stepped out of the vehicle.

Mike concentrated on the cabin while waiting for the other drones to complete their new surveillance grid. He had the remaining drone slowly sweep above the cabin facing its thermal camera downward. He hoped to see silhouettes of Nicole and the girls, but no luck. "Were they in there?" He dared not ask the other question, "Were they alive?"

The bots were completing their perimeter search and now approached the cabin. They began a grid-pattern search of the outer structure, looking for anything indicating a trap, such as a trip wire. So far, the drones and bots had picked up nothing to suggest an ambush.

Three thermal images lit the screen as the bots scurried up the back wall. "Thank God," he almost ran to the cabin but stopped himself; he didn't want to run into a trap. He repeated, "Focus, focus," their safety relied on his ability to remain calm and follow protocol. "Why did the helo drone miss the thermal signal when the bot didn't? What am I missing?" Then he realized the roof must be metal; thermal imaging couldn't see through it. He studied the silhouettes again, they were the right size to belong to his family, and the thermal images indicated they were alive.

He quickly checked the monitor to ensure the outer drones hadn't picked up any sign of an ambush team. Then he watched as one bot crawled along the perimeter of the cabin door. Where a doorknob would have been placed, he saw a hasp with a shiny new padlock through it. The bot released a tiny bit of C4, then scurried away.

Before blowing the lock, he signaled the drones and bots back to the Cherokee. He then programmed a self-destruct sequence in the bots that he would cancel if all went well. He wouldn't leave his tech vulnerable to capture if anything happened to him. He waited a few seconds to see if anyone or anything responded to the noise of the small blast, then he cautiously approached the door.

CHAPTER
12

J ASON WATCHED AS the phony waiter approached with the tray again; this time, it held his glass of wine. As the man placed the glass before him, the contents spilled onto the table. Even with Jason's quick reaction time, he was too late. The waiter blocked Jason from the view of the other patrons, hit him with a paralyzing taser, then injected something into his arm. As he laid Jason down across the bench seat, he muttered out loud that the guest had a seizure. He took the cell phone out of his pocket and mimicked a 911 call.

The waiter adjusted the fabric screen to block the view of Jason's booth. Two paramedics entered the back hall a few minutes later, pushing a gurney. After loading Jason onto it, the waiter ushered them back out, disappearing into the darkness. The entire incident took less than five minutes.

Jason wasn't out for long. His enhanced metabolism cleared the drug from his system much sooner than his captors had anticipated. He kept his vital signs low and made no indication that he was coming to. He wanted to analyze the situation before he let on that he was awakening.

His hands and feet were tied to something, and his mouth was gagged. The gag had a foul taste and was suffocating. He concentrated on breathing slowly through his nose and ignored the gag. He then took a mental inventory of his body, starting from his extremities and working toward his core. He felt no pain and did not seem to be injured.

He was lying on his back in a moving vehicle. When the vehicle slowed or sped up, he felt movement beneath him. The motion was jerky, and he thought he heard wheels squeaking. He must be on a gurney, which meant the vehicle was probably an ambulance.

Two male voices were speaking in hushed tones. They were close, probably less than two feet away; they were saying something about money and a big payday. This was followed by banter about how they would spend it.

Then he heard something about their employer; they referred to him as Señor Black, undoubtedly not his real name. The next part of their conversation caught his attention.

The men were curious about the package and wondered what was in it. It must be valuable because the Señor was adamant that they don't open it. They were arguing about ignoring the order and opening the package. They could take it and dispose of their human cargo if it contained something valuable. But one of them said, "Señor Black is very powerful and will hunt us down and kill us."

As Jason contemplated the implications of their conversation, he heard a swoosh coming from behind his head and felt a rush of cool air. A third voice came from behind him. Someone in the cab must have slid open the window between the compartments and was now talking to the men in the back. He was giving them roughly a fifteen-minute ETA to their destination. He added, "Señor Black wants him awake and unharmed so he can talk with him first." This was followed by a sinister laugh before he continued, "Then we can finish the job and receive the rest of our money. Make sure he's awake before we get there." Another swooshing sound and the draft of air was gone. The voice had come from the direction of the driver's seat, which meant there were probably only three of them.

Jason had anticipated the caller would make a move on him. His only error was thinking it wouldn't happen until he had heard from Mike. He knew the caller wouldn't let him just leave the package on the table and go his merry way. Even though the package had been scanned for tracking devices and explosives, the caller could not know whether it had been tampered with. It was imperative; the package could not be opened until Mike was safe.

He began to question his plan, "Did I miscalculate? Will my actions lead to the death of Mike and his family?" He quickly pushed those thoughts from his mind. As long as only he knew where the actual package was, he could leverage that information for Mike and his family's safety. After all, they were no threat. Mike had never looked inside the inner package and had no idea who the caller was.

On the other hand, Mike had considerable resources and might try to track the caller and seek justice for what Nicole and the girls had endured. He thought, "Damn, too many things could go wrong." As the thought hung in the air, he felt the vehicle slow, and a beefy hand slapped his face.

CHAPTER

13

J ASON FELT THE gag being yanked from his mouth, then one at a time, his hands were untied from the gurney and secured behind his back. His captors shoved him out of the ambulance, and he found himself in a courtyard surrounded by a large building. It appeared to be a mansion or a hall. The air was cooler here; he postulated they must be north of the city, still in Virginia or Maryland. He favored Maryland as the moist air likely meant they were near water. He might not know exactly where they were, but he was sure of one thing; the men had not blindfolded him, so they didn't plan to let him leave alive.

He made some quick calculations. He had been unconscious for about fifteen minutes, and with about another thirty since he came to, it had been about forty-five minutes since he sent Mike the coordinates. Depending on how far Mike had to travel to get to them, he might have already rescued his family, but that was an incredibly optimistic *might*. The more likely scenario is that the caller sent Mike on a wild goose chase and kept Nicole and the girls as leverage.

The ambulance driver took the package and headed toward the structure. The other two men marched him toward an alcove at the base of the building. He was pushed through a doorway, where one of his captors mockingly said, "We're going downstairs, don't trip or try anything funny." The threat fell on deaf ears; had he wanted to escape, he would have done so already.

The stairway was dim; the only light source was a few exposed bulbs hanging from the ceiling. As they descended the stone stairs, the atmosphere became musty and thick with moisture. He saw a wall ahead and thought they were reaching the end of the stairway, but it abruptly turned to the right. When they reached the bottom, the stairs morphed into a long hall with several old wooden doors off each side. The hall reminded him of a scene from the "Shining." Just as he wondered which door led to the grand prize, one of his captors pushed him through the second door on the right.

The windowless room smelled like old wood and dirt. It looked as if no one had been in this room for years. Warped wooden shelves filled with musty old boxes lined all four walls. A computer monitor, table, and metal chair appeared oddly out of place in the middle of the dirt floor. He initially thought he had been taken down here to be tortured for information about the package, but he saw no such devices. However, that didn't mean they wouldn't use one of the other rooms for that purpose.

His captors didn't speak or give any indication of what was coming. He was shoved into the metal chair, the zip tie binding his hands was cut, and his arms and legs were tied to the chair. He put up little resistance; he wanted to see what was coming next. The monitor came to life, and a shadowy figure appeared. A familiar digital voice said, "Welcome Mr. Falcone." Jason didn't respond to the use of his name. The voice continued, "You shouldn't have tampered with the package Mr. Falcone, your failure to follow orders demand that punishment be exacted."

Jason knew that the repeated use of his real name was meant to intimidate him, he diverted with, "What's in the package, what could be worth the lives of innocent children?"

The eerie voice replied, "Death would be a blessing to the woman and her children, there are so many other options." The voice raised angrily as it continued, "You worry about the lives of two innocent children. The content of that package is worth the lives of thousands of innocent children. Don't think for a minute that I will hesitate to kill those little girls if you don't tell me where the real package is."

The image on the monitor faded and was replaced by one that stopped Jason's heart; Nicole, Millie, and Lydia huddled together on a dirty wooden floor. He couldn't tell where they were or if they were alone. Nicole was comforting the girls, speaking softly and stroking their hair. Lydia was sucking her thumb and didn't respond to her mother. He thought, "She must be in shock." Millie was crying and kept telling Nicole how scared she was. Thankfully they didn't look harmed. They were the only family that he would ever have. He tried hard not to lose his cool. He had to work the problem and find a way out of this.

He heard the caller's voice; the tone was flat. "As you can see, they are alive and well for now, but that could change at any minute. It's up to you Mr. Falcone."

He tried to look away and evaluate his options, but the image on the screen kept him transfixed. At that moment, he could think of nothing but the terror Nicole and her daughters were feeling. He mentally shook it off; this was not helping the situation or his friends. He knew that as long as they were alive, he still had time.

Jason's flat expression belied his emotions as his steely blue eyes coldly stared into the monitor. He focused on distracting the caller, hoping to give Mike more time to find his family.

The voice, menacing again, said, "Do I need to hurt one of them to prove my resolve. Maybe the younger one, Lydia; she looks so small and fragile."

Instead of taking the bait, Jason said, "Why are you hiding in the dark like a rat? And that voice, *really*."

This time there was a distinct edge to the voice; did he hit a nerve? "I have a moral purpose; your insults mean nothing to me. I believe you gave up *your* moral purpose to protect your own interests. I intend to right a horrific wrong, one that took the lives of millions, while you're concerned with the lives of a few."

The man behind the voice had placed himself out of Jason's reach but wasn't far away. The driver had entered the building with the package. After overhearing the conversation in the back of the ambulance, he didn't think the caller would risk having anyone else open it.

While his captors had been mesmerized by the eerie voice, he had been sizing them up. They were medium-sized with bronze skin and sported short military-style haircuts. They were muscular and looked like they could handle themselves in a fight. They each had a cell phone, pistol, and a knife. He saw nothing to indicate that they were communicating with the man on the monitor.

He scanned the room for the presence of surveillance equipment. The room's corners were dim, but that didn't hinder him. He took a couple of cleansing breaths and muttered, "Kairos," meaning, do the right thing at the right time. He began pulling at his restraints and rocking the metal chair. The first response came from the closer of the two men when he walked over and punched him in the abdomen.

Taking a punch in the gut was worth getting one of his captors into close proximity. With his enhanced muscle strength and reflexes, Jason broke the restraints on his lower legs, stood, did a one-eighty, and pierced the man's abdomen with two of the metal legs. The man screamed as his hands moved to stop the blood pouring from the wounds.

Initially, the second man stared in shock and horror; how could anyone break those restraints and move so fast? He then pulled a knife from the sheath on his belt and moved toward Jason, who took advantage of the momentary pause to free his hands from the chair. He ripped his shirt off, wrapped it around his left arm, and took a fighting stance.

The second man lunged, leading with the knife, but Jason raised his left arm to block the attack. He spun and knocked the man out with a round-house kick to the jaw. The man fell, his neck bent in an odd direction. While running back up the stairs, he tied his ripped shirt around his waist saying, "You never know, might need it again."

CHAPTER
14

WHEN JASON REACHED ground level, he engaged his night vision and surveyed the courtyard. Under the moonless sky, he saw two additional vehicles. One was a black sedan, and the other was a black Suburban with military plates. This took him aback and caused him to rethink the situation. Did the military set this whole thing up just to draw him in? This opened up new possibilities, but he didn't have time to consider them now.

The ambulance hadn't moved; he sprinted towards it, his long legs crossing the distance in seconds. Using the vehicle for cover, he surveyed the distance between himself and the structure's back entrance. He bolted forward and reached it without incident, stopping outside the large wooden door.

It creaked as he opened it, and he swore to himself, but no one seemed to have heard. Having assured himself that the back hall was empty, he quickly scanned the rooms on the lower floor. It didn't appear anyone had lived here for a while. The upholstered furniture was draped in ghostly white, while the wooden tables were layered in dust. He took the stairs leading upward, two at a time, ending in a great hall with doors opening on either side. "Great," he thought, "the Shining again."

Distant voices emanated from a room at the end of the hall, and he cautiously moved toward them. He recognized one as the voice of the ambulance driver, the third captor. The other voice was raised in anger; it was male and had a slight German accent.

In his haste to discover who was behind this nightmare, he brushed against a vase on a tall table. It hit the ground with a loud shattering sound, and immediately the voices stopped. Quickly, he took the shirt from around his waist, hung it on the table, then took cover in the opposite doorway. He pressed against it and waited.

A pistol barrel led his way as the driver cautiously walked down the dim hall. When he glimpsed Jason's shirt, he fired, the sound echoing down the narrow hallway. The man moved toward the shirt and paused momentarily while trying to make sense of what he saw. It was a moment too long.

Jason sprung from behind and wrapped his forearm around the driver's throat. The man fired wildly but soon succumbed to the choke hold. Jason grabbed a cord from a nearby lamp and secured the man's hands and feet before turning his attention to the room at the end of the hall.

When he reached it, the room was empty. "Mr. Black," he shouted, "You coward. Why don't you pick on grown men instead of women and children." He heard the sound of squealing tires and rushed to the window just in time to see a black sedan speed out of the courtyard. Any thought of giving chase was interrupted by familiar voices.

As he closed the distance from the window to the desk, he heard Mike. A computer monitor displayed nearly the same scene as before, a close-up of Nicole and the girls. But now they were standing, hugging each other, and Mike told them they were safe. What came next dropped him to the floor. He heard an explosion, and the view on the screen became a fireball.

He was immobilized with fear. He instinctively grabbed his cell phone to call Mike, but it was gone. His captors probably gave it to Mr. Black, although it would have done him no good. He slowly got to his feet, looked down at the desk and saw the opened package. The only other thing out of place was a book lying on the floor across the room. Jason felt a sick sense of satisfaction; whoever Mr. Black was, he must have been pretty ticked when he discovered the package contained the Manual of Midshipmen Conduct.

He searched the desk, looking for information about Mr. Black. He found his own cell phone in the top drawer and immediately punched Mike's number; no answer, damn! He finished rifling the desk but found nothing useful. He looked toward the door, "I'm going to have a little talk with that driver."

His stone-cold eyes left no doubt of his resolve as he glared down at the man. Brandishing the driver's gun, he coldly said, "You have one chance to tell me who Mr. Black is before I take out your right kneecap."

The terrified man was sweating bullets and started to plead with him. Jason fired a warning shot into the floor, just beside the man's right knee. The shot motivated the terrified man to speak, "I only know him as Señor

Black; I don't know his real name. He never told us. We were hired over the internet and only saw him in person tonight. He was very private, only I was to see him." The man was shaking now; "please Señor, I don't know anything else."

Jason replied, "You may know more than you think. What is this place, this mansion?"

The driver's voice shook, "I have never been here before. The address was given to us only after we had taken you from the restaurant."

Changing the subject, Jason asked, "How old is Mr. Black and what does he look like?"

The man eagerly replied, "He is tall and thin with a little gray in his hair. He looks about fifty, maybe fifty-five years old and wears nice clothes. And he speaks very well; we didn't understand some of the fancy words he used."

Jason pressed further. "Anything else about him?"

The man paused and looked upward as if retrieving a lost memory, "Yes, he was wearing an unusual pendant, it looked very expensive. It was a gold cross with a black jeweled rose in the center."

Jason mentally stored that information away, then changed the subject again, "Did he say anything about the package, why it was important, or what he expected to find?"

The man adamantly replied, "No Señor, he made me leave the room when he opened it, he even closed the door and locked it, but whatever was in the package made him very angry."

Jason was frustrated, there was nothing more he could learn here, and he was desperate to find out if the fiery scene on the computer was real or a sick ploy by the caller. He started to leave but turned back as he remembered something. "What is that Suburban doing here, the one with the military plates?"

The man tried to avoid his stare, but Jason shot a round into the floor next to the man's other knee. "Please, Señor, I don't want to say, I am ashamed."

Growing irritated and suspicious, Jason replied, "Ashamed of what, exactly."

The man dropped his eyes to avoid Jason's steely gaze. He replied, "Ashamed of kidnapping the woman and her children."

The man was near tears now, but Jason got even closer to him and hissed, "Where are they?"

The terrified man gave Jason directions to the cabin. The next bullet hit him right between the eyes.

CHAPTER
15

As Karl sped away from the mansion, he shook so hard he could barely keep the car steady. He usually led a very cerebral and meditative lifestyle in the Order, and these emotions were new to him. He was a man of science, not a man of evil. The bodies were adding up, along with his guilt. He tried to tell himself to let go of their plan, but he was compelled to see it through.

So far, his efforts to retrieve the package led nowhere. He felt a bit of remorse about killing Mike Miller and his family; after all, it was supposed to be a means to justify the end. But now there was no end, no book! He thought of finding Jason Falcone again and making him talk, to tell him where it was, but his recent experience with the man led him to believe that pursuing that avenue would be dangerous and futile. Again, he thought, "How had that girl found it?" It was only a fate of circumstance that it was found the first time.

Many years ago, two members of the Order had found the book while working at a dig on Crete. They had been part of a conservation team working at Phaistos, the site of one of the Bronze Age Minoan palaces. The original palace had been destroyed by earthquakes, and at least two subsequent palaces had been built on top of it. They surmised that since Phaistos had been built atop a ridge, the older ruins might be accessible from one of the many caves that dotted the island. They spent several seasons searching, finding a few relics here and there, but most caves were dead-ends.

During one of their explorations, one of the men dropped his flashlight, and it rolled to the back of the cave, or so they thought. When they retrieved the flashlight, they realized the rear wall was not what it seemed. It was an optical illusion; a narrow passage was behind the wall. There were many openings in the passage, and they explored each one. It took over a week to find the right one.

As the story went, they discovered an ancient text inside a large pithos jar, a book that held the power to change the world. It was brought back to America, to the Order, where it was extensively studied. But eventually, the book's power frightened one of the men, and he returned the book to its original location, never returning to America or sharing the cave's location. The other man kept the cave's secret for many years and died without revealing its location.

Karl and the members of his Order were desperate to find the cave and hence the book. Written inside was a list, a list that was critical to their plans. Plans that would realign history and restore Germany to its former glory.

At the thought of Germany, he turned to his past and how early experiences in that country affected his worldview. His grandparents had been scholars in pre-Nazi Germany, but after Hitler came to power, they and many of their colleagues were persecuted. His grandmother and parents fled Germany for America, where they made a modest living teaching in German schools. Once war was declared, the schools were closed due to anti-German sentiment.

His family's fall from financial grace meant that his parents could only provide the basics for their three children. But the basics didn't include paying for the type of education Karl needed. His IQ was staggering, so high that he had been offered membership in Mensa at age ten. His parents sought scholarships at American schools but were denied due to their German heritage. They had no choice but to look to their homeland for opportunities for their gifted son. They would never understand how their decision would impact Karl.

The following year, he received a scholarship at a prestigious boarding school in Germany. His family knew the kind of pain the separation would cause, but with the proper education, he could rise above his family's misfortunes. His grandmother reluctantly agreed, and he was sent to live in Germany.

He would only see his parents once again on his sixteenth birthday, when he returned to the U.S. to attend the Massachusetts Institute of Technology. His grandmother was gone by then, and his parents were disappointed that he hadn't stayed in Germany to attend the University in Munich. But they had no idea of his disdain for post-war Germany. Six months later, his parents, brother, and sister were killed in a car crash. The family he had desperately longed to reunite with during his extended exile in Germany was gone.

After receiving news of his family's death, he lost himself in his studies. He distinguished himself at MIT and was eventually admitted to their accelerated doctoral program in theoretical physics. During his first postgraduate year, he attended a seminar, "Science and Religion: Are they one and the same?" He had never been religious, but losing his parents and siblings made him wonder if an afterlife was possible. The guest lecturer, Dr. Andrew Riggins, was a highly regarded scientist; he decided to attend. That decision changed the course of his life.

CHAPTER
16

J ASON'S HEART WAS pounding as he ran into the courtyard towards the Suburban. He was in luck; the keys were still in it. But before touching anything in the vehicle, he donned the latex gloves he had taken from the ambulance. It was one thing for the state police to run his prints, but the military was another matter. As he sped out of the courtyard, he pulled up Mike's coordinates on his cell phone. They matched the location of the cabin where Nicole had been taken.

Thirty miles southwest of the mansion, he pulled over to see if there were anything of value in the vehicle that could be used if he was met with force at the cabin. In the rear compartment, he found two pistols and three Navy uniforms with MP brassards on their sleeves. "They must have used these to fool Nicole into believing whatever lies they told her." He checked the uniforms for size, then placed one of the jackets on.

Squawking from the vehicle's police scanner caught his attention. Someone was responding to a fire near the coordinates he had given Mike. A lump began to form in his throat as he got back behind the wheel and pressed the accelerator to the floor. Approaching the turn-off, he saw the glow of fire in the distance. The lump in his throat became thicker, making it hard to breathe.

The sight of a police presence triggered his ever-present sense of paranoia. Deputies stood in front of two patrol cars that blocked the road. One of them noted the Suburban's military plates and motioned him to roll down his window. As the odor of smoke crept up his nostrils, a burly deputy with a thick Boston accent approached him, "Good evening, sir. Does the Navy have anything to do with this fire?"

Jason replied, "We have no idea how it started, but a lot of the land out here is ours and we're trying to figure out if it's within our jurisdiction."

The officer accepted the explanation and said, "I wouldn't doubt it. We think the point of origin was a private cabin, but the fire is so intense the crew can't get close. Even if it didn't start on federal land, it's burning on it now."

In a matter-of-fact tone that belied his torment, Jason continued, "Do you know what caused the fire?"

The officer responded, "Not sure, the fire guys will check that out but I did hear something about an explosion, maybe it was a drug lab or something like that."

Jason replied, "Ok, I'll get a copy of the fire chief's report to add to my own. Were there any casualties that you know of?"

The officer replied, "We're not sure about bodies at this point but the Fire Chief said there's a burned-out Jeep Cherokee near the cabin, so there might be at least one victim inside. Until we know for sure, no one gets close."

Jason barely mumbled, "Thank you, officer." He drove off with no destination in mind. Time stood still for him; there was no hurry.

A tumultuous storm of emotions raged within him, a turbulent clash of raging fury and profound sorrow. He punched Mike's number repeatedly, each time with the same result. His shoulders slumped under the weight of conflicting emotions. He pulled off the road, exited the SUV, and began screaming. The piercing screams gave way to a subdued, mournful moan resonating through the funereal darkness. He pictured Mike's face and thought about their deep friendship and everything they had been through together.

During a mission in Iraq, Jason was set to meet with a group of rebels to buy information regarding the location of a terrorist leader, Ahmed Jaheem. Jaheem was responsible for the slaughter of thousands of Iraqis as well as multiple attacks on American soldiers. He was the mastermind behind the firebombing near Bagdad, which burned American soldiers alive while they slept. These actions put him at the top of America's most wanted terrorist list.

The meet was set to go down at the marketplace in a small village near Mosul. Undercover CIA had the place scoped for days. Mike didn't want Jason going in alone, so he and several additional Seals accompanied him. The rebels had insisted on setting the meeting place, and Mike wasn't happy about it. Mike thought it was a trap, and the Seals should insist on choosing the meeting place. Jason disagreed, saying he didn't want to spook the rebels.

Jaheem's men had already spotted the CIA agents and had placed explosives around the meeting perimeter. They weren't worried that the explosives would take out the CIA agents and innocent Iraqis. Their goal was to take Jason and the Seals, hostage, then torture and publicly execute them.

Jason tried to walk casually through the market, waiting for Jaheem to show himself. The place was bustling; vendors were selling figs, apples, and pears, and the air was filled with the aroma of herbs and spices. The atmosphere resonated with a cacophony of noise, which worked to his advantage. He doubted anyone could hear him above the din if he had to activate his coms.

He knocked an apple from one of the stands at a pre-arranged time. The stand's owner became irate and started yelling something in Arabic. Jason quickly paid him for the damaged fruit, then dropped down on one knee to pick it up. This was supposed to be the signal that everything was going as planned. The apple had rolled under the stand, and a chill went down his spine as he reached to grab it. There were ignition wires leading in both directions. He tried identifying the origin, but too many people and objects blocked his view. Mike was right; it was a trap.

He activated his coms to warn the others, then all hell broke loose. Shots rang out from behind the market. The Seals returned fire, providing cover for him, but he found himself in a mob of Iraqis trying to escape the marketplace. He tried to push his way through the crowd but was knocked to the ground by a man carrying two children, one in each arm.

As he tried to get back up, he was trampled by fleeing civilians, some hauling goats and chickens. His head was knocked from side to side by terrified Iraqis. As he lay there, his head bleeding and near unconsciousness, he felt strong hands pulling him off the ground. He opened his eyes and looked into the determined face of Mike Miller.

Jason muttered, "No, you need to get away from here fast."

Mike hoisted him over his shoulder and, with his six-foot-two-inch frame, pushed his way through the mob. They barely made it to safety when the marketplace exploded. The op was a bust, but an enduring friendship was born that day. Mike had saved his life, a debt he vowed to repay, and now he never could.

Besides losing Mike, Jason was overcome by the additional loss of Nicole and the girls. He tried to shake off the image of them on the monitor, but failed. Although he hadn't spent much time with them lately, he loved them like family. After leaving the Navy, he worried that if he stayed close to them, they might be harmed if anyone ever came looking for him. Turns out the only thing he was wrong about was the identity of the bad guys.

Thoughts of Mike and his family jolted him back to the present. Seething with fury, a thirst for vengeance consumed him. He had to find the man behind the voice and extract justice for Mike and his family. He would start by locating Sara and find out what was so important about that book, and more importantly, who would kill to get it.

CHAPTER
17

Sara's head was pounding when she finally came to. It took a few seconds to remember what happened. Ugh, her mouth had a bitter taste, "What had been in the cloth?" She no longer had her night vision goggles and felt panic rising within her, "Where are they?" Her eyes tried to adjust to the inky darkness without the goggles, but it was useless. It seemed to press in from all around her, making it difficult to breathe. Her eyes strained to adjust, but there was no relief, only a horrific absence of light that lingered in every corner, lurking and waiting. The backpack containing her flashlight was still on her back, but she was too afraid to retrieve it.

Her body began to involuntarily shake. She thought, "This is surreal, who would do this to me? Are they still here?" Terror flowed from her core, oozing outward and wrapping around her like a cold blanket. But she forced herself to be very still as she listened for sounds of another human presence. But there was nothing; it was deathly quiet.

Deathly, yes, that's an appropriate description of the situation. "Were they trying to kill me?" She decided to lie there for a while to see if they would return to ensure she was dead. "What will they do when they find I'm still alive?" Her mind was reeling. "How did they find me? Did they follow me from the camp, or were they in the cave, waiting for me?" The fact that someone had a cloth soaked in some sort of chemical, probably chloroform, meant they had planned this. That would mean they knew about the book and the device too. She began recounting the events that brought her to this cave, trying to find an answer.

An earthquake on Santorini last year unearthed previously undiscovered Minoan artifacts at the dig in Akrotiri. They were inscribed with Linear A, an early written Minoan language. She was asked to consult because she was one of only a few philologists worldwide who could translate it

For the first few weeks she had transcribed names, accounting numbers, and records of crop harvests. But as she ventured farther into the newly exposed ruins, she found narrative writing on one of the walls. This was highly unusual as the Minoans didn't write narratively. The writing referred to the Book of Knowledge, which was hidden in an underground chamber beneath the palace at Phaistos.

She didn't get too excited because she knew the palace had been buried thousands of years ago. She was more excited about finding the narrative writing. Then one of the team members found part of a clay tablet hidden amongst the ruins. Her interest grew as she quietly read the inscription. The tablet spoke of a second entrance to the chamber where the Book of Knowledge was supposedly hidden.

As she snapped an image of the tablet with her cell phone, she hastily advised the team she would need more time to decipher it. She still didn't understand why she had kept silent about it; it was just a feeling. She told herself she didn't want to excite the team without checking it out first. If there was no way to get to the book, it wouldn't make any difference if she told them about it now or in a few days.

She stayed up late that night making a map from the directions on the tablet. The following day, she informed the dig supervisor that she didn't feel well. Waiting until the others were gone, she took a boat to Crete, followed her rough map, and eventually found the cave entrance. It wasn't easy. There had been many missed turns and false entries. It was near dark when she saw it. It was barely visible, and she almost missed it.

The entrance was small, but she managed to climb through it. Following the map, she found the passage leading to the chamber under Phaistos. The room was magnificent. Several walls had survived the quake, and their colorful frescos looked as vibrant as the day they were created. The images were similar to those on display at Crete. Some depicted women with long dark hair, bare breasts, and beautiful jewelry. While others illustrated large sailing vessels loaded with goods. Conspicuously missing were images of bull jumping, which partially defined the Minoan civilization.

She poked around in the rubble and eventually found the book in a pithos jar, just as described on the tablet. The book's cover was made of animal skin and had four words inscribed above the drawing of a red rose, "The Book of Knowledge." When she opened it, something fell out. A cursory look told her it was a map, maybe another map to this location.

It was late, and she decided to remove the book from its centuries-old hiding place. She would take it back to her room, where she had the proper equipment to inspect it. For now, she would have to rely on the specialized container in her backpack to keep it safe. Like a grave robber, she felt guilty as she and the book left the cave. She didn't understand her hesitation to tell anyone about it, but something about the dig made her uncomfortable. The dig sponsors were on the island but appeared uninterested in the work. She felt they were watching her; it was creepy and highly unusual.

After leaving the cave, she got the eerie sensation that someone *was* watching her. Walking back to her rented SUV, she thought she heard footfalls on the path behind her, but her flashlight beam did not detect anyone. At first, she thought it was her guilty conscience, but the feeling persisted. While driving back to the boat dock, she occasionally saw headlights a kilometer or two behind her. With increasing discomfort, she thought, "Is someone following me?" but she returned to Santorini without incident.

She was shaking as she closed and locked the door of her room, "Was it fear, guilt, or excitement?" She held her backpack close, as if protecting a young child. Then she carefully removed the book from its protective container and laid it on an oil-free surface. She donned special gloves and a loop, then opened it. It was written on paper derived from plants, but she couldn't readily identify them. The front and back covers were made of preserved animal hides, and some type of resin had been used to bind the page edges together. It was unusually durable and was unlike any other ancient text she had seen before. But it was the contents that shocked and confused her.

The book described an advanced civilization that inhabited Crete and its surrounding islands five thousand years ago. She recognized this as the Minoan civilization, whose society archeologists believe might be the basis for the mythic Atlantis. The author's description of the culture also matched what modern archeologists have discovered about them; ancient people who engineered hot and cold running water, sewer systems, and earthquake-resistant buildings. A people who utilized advanced agricultural practices and traded with distant lands.

The author, Michael, said he inadvertently traveled from 2080 to the Bronze Age. When he realized he couldn't return to his own time, he bestowed knowledge from the future to the island people and created an advanced society. He described himself as a scholar who wanted to improve the ancient people's lives and, in doing so, his life as well.

His intention was to guide them, not rule them. He refused to be treated like a god or a king. When the people insisted on building a grand palace in his honor, he directed them to create a cultural center to benefit everyone. The center would be a place where knowledge could be shared freely among all people, even among those who traveled to the island from distant places. Its design allowed for the expansion of space, accommodating large gatherings by opening up rooms, or creating more intimate settings by closing off sections.

To keep an accurate calendar of his days in 3500 BC, he designed a room with an alabaster seat on the north wall facing four windows. The workers were directed to position this seat in a specific location to ensure the sun would hit directly on the back of the chair during the winter solstice. That sign would mark the beginning of a new calendar year. On the wall behind either side of the seat were two griffins facing one another. Michael wrote that he combined the lion, used as a symbol by England, and the eagle, used as a symbol of the United States, to remind him of the two places he called home.

Sara remembered being stunned when she read those passages. She had visited this structure; she had seen the alabaster seat. Michael was describing the palace of Knossos on Crete.

Michael claimed to be a physicist and Rosicrucian. He described the Rosicrucian Order as a fellowship of scientists who felt that true enlightenment could only be achieved by combining the scientific and mystical arts. He said science had already resolved many fundamental physics questions, such as aligning string theory with Einstein's relativity theory and the relationship between string theory and dark matter. But quantum physics, specifically quantum entanglement, was responsible for his presence in the past.

Sara knew from her science courses that quantum physics involves the properties and behaviors of the very building blocks of nature; quantum particles. Scientists don't actually see them; they only see evidence that they exist. Through experimentation, physicists discovered that when two particles, such as a pair of photons or electrons, become entangled, they remain connected even when separated by vast distances. Alert Einstein labeled this as "spooky action at a distance." But she did not know anything about using that connection for time travel.

But Michael did, and he experimented to see if this was the answer to time travel, but alone, it was not. He explained that for entanglement to be used for time travel, you first had to create a pathway by folding the fabric of space; he did this by making waves. These waves were likened to something Sara thought sounded like wormholes.

He drew a diagram in the book that looked like a wavelength. He then drew a line through the waves near the trough. If the waves were similar in depth, the line would run through them evenly. He postulated that if time and space were made of a fabric of strings and those strings were undulating, like waves, a wormhole could walk you through their base from one entangled particle to the other.

Sara wondered how one would go about causing the type of waves needed for efficient time travel. Physicists had already speculated that the universe is made up of dark matter, the matter that fills the voids between the strings of space-time fabric. Maybe the dark matter reacted to something near it, creating the waves. She knew that swells in a wave pool could be controlled; apparently, Michael had found a way to do this with dark matter.

Michael said that there was another criterion that had to be met before time travel could be achieved. To enter the waves and move through time and space, you had to find holes in the fabric, holes which he called portals. He traveled the world developing a list of locations where these portals existed.

He then developed a device that could do two things: first, accurately predict where in time two entangled particles would be located; second, create high waves in the fabric of space to get a shorter wave line between the particles. The shorter the line, the faster you travel back through time. There was one limitation, you couldn't travel farther ahead than recorded history, as time and space were too closely related. Space was constantly expanding, so you couldn't jump ahead of it; you could only stay behind it, like following the wake behind a ship.

Michael decided that his first human experiment must be on himself. After adjusting the device to go back in time five years, he turned it on, only to find he had actually traveled five thousand years. He had miscalculated the time difference between the two particles and found himself in a cave which he eventually dated to thirty-five hundred BCE.

He also discovered that not all things would travel backward in time. You could only take objects that were either present or capable of being produced in the past, such as cotton. He deduced this because he had been wearing a cotton shirt and flannel pants when he left his current time and traveled backward. When he landed in the Bronze Age, his shirt was missing its plastic buttons, and his flannel pants were missing the zipper. He was surprised to note that although the zipper didn't make it, his rose pendant had. He surmised that the pendant was made of precious metals that must have been present in ancient times, while the material used to make the zipper was a modern alloy.

The clothes were a minor inconvenience, but the device was critical to his ability to return home; however, it did not make the journey with him. It was made from a metal alloy that hadn't been discovered yet. It must still be in the future, leaving him unable to return to his own time. After hiding his clothes, he decided to make the best of it. He found pieces of wood outside the cave door and fashioned them into a cross. He then took the rose pendant from around his neck and affixed it to the cross with its chain. He walked to the nearest village and, due to his *magic*, which was basic science, was heralded as a God by the islanders.

Time travel for Michael would be a one-way trip; he would never be able to share his discovery with the world. He wrote the book several years later, hoping future generations might benefit from his discovery. But he was worried that someone nefarious might find the book and learn about the device. He did not want the book and the device to be found together as it would be too easy for the unenlightened to accidentally initiate the device. He made a map with directions for finding the device and placed it in the book.

He knew theoretically where the device was located as it should be right where he landed in thirty-five hundred BCE. He had the palace at Phaistos constructed above it, then built a series of underground chambers where he hid the book. At the exact location where he calculated the device would eventually be found, he built a chamber decorated with frescos of roses, then closed it off with a hidden door. The book was written in Latin, but it would take a scholar who could translate the islander's rudimentary language to decipher the map and find the Rose Room. He had faith that a member of his fellowship would find the detailed notes and equations he had included in the book, retrieve the device, and bring him home.

After reading the book, Sara thought, "If this is a hoax, it's pretty elaborate." Someone went to a lot of trouble to hide the book and supposedly the device. She didn't have enough time to sort it out, so she sent the book to a friend in America for safekeeping until she could do more research. But she kept the map, which is how she wound up here, in the same chamber as she found the book. Given her current situation, she thought, "If Michael's book was nonsense, why would someone be looking for it, and more importantly, why would someone want to kill me for it."

CHAPTER
18

Meeting Andrew Riggins was a pivotal moment in Karl's life. After the lecture, he introduced himself to Andrew, and they became fast friends. He learned that Andrew was a member of the Rosicrucian Order. He was intrigued by this, and after a while, Andrew introduced him to the Fellowship, a worldwide brotherhood that studies and practices the metaphysical laws governing the universe.

He found a home in the Order, a home he had longed for during his formative years in Germany. He was surrounded by a family of scholars who shared a common goal; one that sought truth and enlightenment. With Andrew's mentoring, he rose through the ranks, gaining respect and power within the organization.

He never married, as the Brotherhood emphasizes attaining enlightenment over marriage and family. But over time, he began to think of Andrew as a surrogate father. He deeply respected and admired him, aspiring to mirror his remarkable qualities.

Conversely, Andrew thought of Karl as the son he would never have. He knew Karl had been emotionally damaged by his exile to Germany. His family felt they were doing their best for him, but Andrew knew better. Karl's wounds might have healed if he had been given a chance to reconnect with his family, but their untimely deaths precluded it.

One winter, Andrew became ill. Karl expressed his concern, but Andrew kept his personal matters private. Karl saw him become increasingly frail and worried that he might be dying. Karl's entire family was gone, and he couldn't face the possibility of losing Andrew too. Andrew was his rock, his stabilizing force, the one person he trusted.

The Fellowship believed that each member walked their own path and that others in the Order should not interfere. But Karl's worry caused him to confront Andrew. Andrew's facial expression belied his response. He didn't confide the nature of his illness but said he was working on new treatments and told Karl not to worry. But Karl did worry, and his concern grew as Andrew's illness took its toll. By spring, Andrew was rail thin, extremely weak, and confined to bed. Karl was beside himself and spent hours in prayer, trying to prevent the inevitable.

One evening Andrew called Karl to his bedside to confide in him. Karl didn't want to go; he feared Andrew was succumbing to his illness. Members of the Fellowship do not fear death; they believe it is merely the path to another realm of existence. Karl did not fear for Andrew's soul, but for his own.

Andrew began by reiterating that members of the Order practiced metaphysical travel. Karl knew this; he practiced it as well. However, it was Andrew's confession that shocked him. Initially, he thought the disease had caused Andrew to lose his mind, but out of respect, Karl sat down and listened to a story that was so fantastical that, at first, he didn't believe it. Andrew claimed that physical time travel was possible. Many years ago, he and Brother Josef found an ancient book in a cave on Crete. He closed his eyes and recounted the story and the book's content.

When the story concluded, he added, "Josef and I couldn't translate the map's directions, but we used Michael's equations to replicate the device. Amongst the book's diagrams and schematics, we found a list of what Michael called portals, or entrances to the wormholes. We located one in South America and successfully sent simple objects back in time, at first a few minutes, then a few days. We eventually started sending small animals, but they never survived the trip. We weren't sure why this occurred, but we did design an experiment to find out *when* it occurred. Results indicated that they survived the initial trip backward but did not survive the return. We postulated that time travel is a one-way trip."

Andrew was becoming restless and struggled to get comfortable before continuing. "One day I arrived at the lab and found the book and the map were gone. I confronted Josef, who said he had returned them to their original hiding places. He felt we had mined all the data, and the book was too dangerous to be left at the temple compound. I realized later that he made a copy for himself."

Andrew coughed before going on, "I knew Josef's family had been persecuted by Hitler. It must have been horrific because he could barely speak of it. As we experimented with time travel, he talked about the possibility of returning to pre-World War II and killing Hitler before he became so powerful that no one could touch him. At first, I thought he was just posing a theoretical case for preventing the Holocaust, but as time passed, I realized he actually thought it was possible."

In a hushed, conspiratorial tone, Andrew explained how Josef planned to do it. He ended the story by saying he and Josef drifted apart, and a few years later, he learned Josef had left for Europe to continue his work on the origins of the Black Plague. He never saw him again.

Andrew then confessed his reason for sharing the story. He worried Josef might proceed with his evil plan. He besieged Karl to find the device and return to the past to prevent Josef from implementing his agenda. As he began to divulge the book's location, a fit of coughing overtook him. Blood oozed from his mouth, and he was gone within minutes.

As the days following Andrew's death passed, Karl recalled Andrew's confession and wondered if the story was just the ramblings of an old man near death. If it were true, he wanted to find the book, not to honor Andrew's last request but for another, more important purpose.

CHAPTER
19

S ARA CONTINUED TO lie there quietly, and after what she thought was at least an hour, she tried to find her night-vision goggles. She groped around the floor but couldn't find them; they must have been knocked away when she fell. She began making concentric circles, carefully searching the cave floor with her hands, inching out a little farther with each completed pass. She was eventually rewarded for her efforts and found the goggles a couple of feet from where she collapsed. She put them on and oriented herself. She saw a white rag lying on the chamber floor but nothing else.

She retraced her steps to the cave entrance, making as little noise as possible. Every few feet, she stopped and listened, but nothing, no sign of life except her breathing. She braced her eyes as she approached the cave entrance, preparing to be blinded by the sun, but there was no light. There was now a pile of debris where the opening had stood just hours before. Her heart beat wildly, and her breath caught in her throat. That's why she was alone. Whoever drugged her had blocked the entrance and left her to die.

She opened her backpack and removed the small spade she carried on digs. She had to shovel herself out before her goggles died. She had a small flashlight, but holding it in one hand while shoveling with the other would slow her down. She started digging, but dirt from above kept falling and negating her work. She tried climbing to the top of the debris pile using rocks for footholds but kept sliding down. She was terrified of dying down here; she couldn't give up.

The digging made her not only thirsty but hungry. She stopped and took stock of her backpack contents. The map was still there. They must not have known she had it with her; she put it aside for later. She had a bottle of water and a couple of granola bars, "How long will that last me?"

She took a sip of water and a bite from one of the bars; she would need to ration them.

After hours of digging, she was getting nowhere. She thought, "Maybe there's another entrance, or even a pool of water that had seeped into the cave." Once there had been an entrance to the book's chamber from above, from the old palace. She hadn't explored the room carefully. Maybe there was part of the old entrance still accessible. She began working her way back to the chamber where she had been drugged. Along the way, she listened for any sign of water seeping into the cave.

Before long, she was back in the chamber. During the return trip, she found nothing, no sign of another entrance or water. Desperately, she examined the walls more closely and found the opening to another room, "Maybe it will lead to an exit." As she slowly entered, something on the walls caught her attention. She removed her goggles and surveyed the room with her flashlight; then, she saw the drawings.

She moved closer to inspect them. The first was a man walking out of a cave holding a cross with a rose in the middle of it. The next was the man standing atop a hill, looking down at people from an early civilization; they were using a wheel powered by Kri Kri goats to crush fruit. She moved to the next drawing. The man was sitting at a wooden table, looking at the rudimentary blueprints of a cargo ship. This was followed by another image of the vessel being loaded with goods. The final drawing was of the same man; this time, he held the book in one hand and a cross in the other. "These *must* be drawings of Michael; they are visual depictions of the writings in the book."

She still thought that the book was a hoax, written in Latin to add to its credibility. But if these drawings are authentic and appear to be, the author was describing events that actually happened. She looked at the drawings again, trying to imagine other possibilities. These couldn't be part of a hoax, "Could the man in the drawings be responsible for bringing advanced knowledge to an ancient civilization; to creating the mythical Atlantis?"

"I must be crazy." The book just couldn't be genuine, but the fact that someone left her here to die was indisputable. There must be something here that they didn't want anyone to find. She had risked her life trying to find the hidden device mentioned in Michael's book and wasn't even sure it was there. Even if there were a device, it wouldn't exist yet, or would it? It might have appeared when its alloy was discovered.

She pulled out the map again. She had been trying to translate the last line. Linear A was developed as a means of accounting, not as a means of narrative communication. The map attempted to describe something, utilizing a language created for a different purpose. After further study, she came up with something like, "The rose shows the way."

She decided to spend a couple of hours exploring the chamber. She had to find another way out, but if something led her to the hidden room, she would check it out. But that's all the time she would allow. If she came up empty, she would return to the entrance and continue digging. She again fought to quell the panic swelling inside her; she would find a way out of here, she had to.

As her eyes darted around, she noted the walls opposite the drawings were covered in dirt and debris. She took a brush from her pack and began removing the dirt. A drawing began to appear; a flowering bougainvillea tree. She moved over a few feet and cleared another patch of wall. She was at the edge of another drawing; she moved over a bit more, continuing to brush the dirt off the wall. This time she saw a fig tree. She noticed a pattern; the next drawing was of a eucalyptus tree.

She moved around the chamber, clearing dirt and debris from the wall until she uncovered a beautiful red rose. "The rose leads the way, this had to be it!" Her panic turned to excitement as she ran her fingers over the area. She found the margins of a large stone and used her fingers to trace them. She then took her spade and dug into the depressions she had created with her fingers.

After working on this for several minutes, she felt the stone move. With effort, she got her spade deep enough into the recess to pull the stone forward. As it crashed, she saw a hole and cautiously crawled through it.

She was in a well-preserved room, one that hadn't suffered the damage the other rooms had. Its walls were covered with colorful drawings, and its floors were made of beautiful frescos. In the center of the floor was a large fresco of red roses encircling a wooden cross. On the crosspiece, she saw a wooden box with a rose carved into the lid. Her heart was pounding fast. She opened it. Her shoulders drooped as excitement quickly turned to disappointment.

The box did not contain a device. It contained another book. But that didn't make sense. Had the person who drugged her gotten to it first? She didn't think so. The stone didn't look like it had been disturbed for many years; besides, he wouldn't have left anything behind. She looked down at the small leather journal, now in her hands. It had a black rose stamped into the front cover. She opened the journal; the first page simply read, "For the Fellowship," she turned the page.

I have taken the device. I plan to use it to save our brethren from the Holocaust that swept Germany. I know I am breaking my oath to do no harm, but I am compelled to do so by a sense of greater duty. If I am successful, I will save thousands of our brothers in the Order and prevent the genocide of millions of European Jews and Jewish sympathizers. I do not ask for forgiveness but pray for your understanding.

She felt her knees buckle as she slid down, her back scraping against the wall. All this, and the device wasn't even here. She would probably die alone in this dark hole and she hadn't even found it.

She thought about the man in the cave drawings with advanced knowledge. Those drawings certainly looked like authentic Bronze Age cave art. Maybe her intellect had failed her, but the more she found, the more she believed the book. Now she had another mystery: "Who took the device, and what was the *harm* the author was referring to?" She anxiously turned the page:

I have left the device at the Mont; my fate will be the same as those who may be harmed by my actions. That is my penance. Do not try to follow me; you will have no idea when I will arrive in the past. I plan to live there for quite some time before I execute my plan. I will only get one opportunity and want to ensure that's all I need.

I have developed a weaponized virus based on the $H1N1$ virus that caused the Spanish flu. All those who survive it will have immunity to the original 1917 flu that will spread over the entire planet. That is how I have justified my use of the weaponized version. I have left the formula, not only for the virus but the means to make a vaccine as well. You will find them in this journal. I do this on the off-chance that the virus cannot be contained in 1914. I plan to see that Hitler is infected and dies before he can become the monster, we all know he became. I would have preferred to kill him directly to save the innocents, but we know from historical accounts this is not possible.

She continued reading:

Brother Andrew and I found the book that Michael made when he was stranded in 3500 BC. Michael was a genius, his grasp of theoretical physics and quantum mechanics was difficult to emulate, but we did our best. A few years into our time-travel project, I realized that we could use Michael's work to adjust the historical timeline, an adjustment that would save thousands of German Rosicrucians. But Andrew was against doing anything that would alter the course of history, even if it would save some of our most enlightened leaders. Despite any arguments I made to the contrary, he remained adamant in that belief.

I had no choice but to quietly recruit a small group of brothers who believed as I did, brothers who had lost countless family members at the hands of Hitler. The physicists among them helped me with the quantum aspects of the project. The group will also provide a cover story for my absence and prevent Andrew from following me or trying to foil our plans. We call our group the Black Rose.

Sara was stunned. Despite his arguments, there could be no justification for altering history and killing millions. With a sense of dread, she kept reading:

I am primarily educated as a physician, although I have also trained in virology, which made developing the virus an easier task. What was more difficult was making sure it could make the time journey unaltered. Michael had theorized that only those things that could be produced at the specific date you traveled to could make the journey. So as a backup, I took a piece of the viral DNA and the tools available in 1914 to replicate the virus.

Sara paused and thought, "Is the writer's plan plausible?" After the 2020 pandemic, she was sure that viruses could be weaponized, but that wasn't the issue. The real leap of faith is time travel itself. Sara felt nauseous; she didn't believe what she just read. If whoever wrote this journal delivered a weaponized virus in 1914, millions of people now alive might never have been born. "Wait a minute, maybe he already carried out his plan, and those that were born after the first world war were born to parents who had survived the virus?" But no, that can't be true; history recorded the Spanish flu in 1917, not a separate flu in 1914. The virus hadn't been released yet.

She thought of several possibilities: first, the journal was a hoax; second, the virus hadn't been released yet; third, the journal's author hadn't survived the time travel; fourth, he had failed at his mission. There could also be other possibilities; maybe the virus didn't survive the journey through time. The writer may have wound up in a different year than the one he planned to travel to. If you believed the book, that's what happened to Michael.

Sara anxiously flipped through the rest of the pages. They were filled with equations and formulas, nothing that could help her. The journal's author did not identify himself, but there was no mistaking that he was a member of the Rosicrucian Order, sometimes referred to as the Fellowship of the Rose.

She had found nothing in the hidden room that could help her get out of the cave. Defeatedly, she retraced her steps. Examining the cave walls as she made her way back to the collapsed opening, she found no other passageways that might lead out. She had to face the reality that she would die here, along with any hopes of stopping the person who wrote the journal.

She began to cry. Tears mixing with dust caused muddy rivulets to fall off her cheeks onto the cave floor. With a sense of overwhelming regret, she slid to the ground. "I'm only twenty-eight, I don't want to die. I still have so much I want to do; work, marriage, babies. Why did I ever get involved with that book?" She had only one hope now, "Jason," she thought.

CHAPTER
20

J ASON ABANDONED THE Suburban on a side road and ran five miles to the Annapolis Seaplane Base, where his Cessna Grand Caravan EX was moored. He took the chance that no one would be waiting for him as there was no digital footprint linking himself or Mike to the plane. He purchased it after he and Sara split, so she couldn't be connected to it either. It was one of the largest non-military seaplanes on the market. They had aptly named it the Tern, after the waterbird with the longest flight distance.

Jason's love of scuba diving motivated the purchase. The Land Rover was well-equipped to reach dive sites off the Central American coast, but eventually, those sites became too popular. The Tern gave him access to isolated islands, feeding his need to be off-grid. More importantly, a seaplane was not easy to track.

Mike had access to the plane as well. He liked to take Nicole to the Keys for date weekends while her mother watched the girls. At this thought, Jason reeled as he relived seeing the explosion on the computer screen. A tempest of wrath brewed within him. He would find Mr. Black, whoever he was, and make him pay. He hoped the package's contents would help him do just that.

While in Mike's office, he diverted the caller's attention while Mike removed the inner package, replaced it with a navy manual, and resealed the outer one. Then Mike nodded at a photo of the Blue Angels hanging on his wall, a signal that Mike was planning to hide the inner package in their locker at the seaplane base. If, by some miracle, Mike was alive, he would be here, waiting for Jason to show.

Fortunately, the private seaport used fingerprint technology for entry as Jason and Mike kept the keys to the Tern in their locker. He wasn't there to fly; he had to find out what was in the package, but he could always take the plane if he needed a quick getaway.

He took cover behind some buildings and watched for any sign that he had been followed. After an hour, he had neither seen or heard anything suspicious on the ground or in the air. He broke cover and casually walked to the gate's entry pad. If anyone *was* waiting for him, now would be the perfect time for them to strike. He pressed his finger on the pad, opened the gate, and walked in without incident.

Two pilots were in the lounge watching a baseball game on TV. They barely looked up when he walked into the room. He then heard something that caused him to stop in his tracks. A news report broke into the game:

This is Bryan Morris with breaking news. Four bodies have just been found in the burned remnants of a cabin in rural West Virginia. The police are looking for a man in his early thirties with cropped blond hair and blue eyes. Weight approximately 190 pounds, height at least 6 feet. He was wearing a military police uniform. Anyone with information about this individual should call 555-289-3466. Do not approach the individual, as he may be armed and dangerous.

As the pilots turned to look toward Jason, he ducked into the alcoves where the lockers stood. Opening their locker door, he grabbed a ball cap off the inner hook and placed it on his head. He found the package just where Mike had left it. Grief nearly overwhelmed him when he realized that Mike hadn't returned to rendezvous with him. He had been hoping Mike would be here, grinning and asking what had kept him so long.

He grabbed the package, his flight jacket, waterproof backpack, and the keys to the Tern. After hearing the breaking news, he decided to hide out on the plane for a while. Depending on what he found in the package, he might need to use it. He exited through the back door, walked across the dock to hanger B, deactivated the alarm, unlocked the door, and climbed aboard the plane. His augmented hearing and vision had not detected anyone who might be following him. Once aboard, he was out of view.

The plane's cabin had been custom designed to his specifications. A fully stocked kitchenette was at the rear of the cabin, next to a small bathroom. Seats in the middle section were parallel to the outer wall and could be converted into beds. There were four leather bucket seats, two behind the cockpit area and two in front of the kitchen area. The largest space, behind the cabin, was reserved for cargo. Currently, it contains diving and camping gear, but it could carry a lot more. Theoretically, he could stay in here for days without anyone the wiser.

He entered the windowless cargo area through the dark cabin and found the camping gear. He sat on a camp stool and surveyed the package atop a makeshift table. He reread the note taped to the inner wrapping:

Mike, I'm so sorry to put you in this position. I had to send this to someone who could not be connected to me. I need you to get this to Jason, preferably with no one knowing. But I can't be sure that someone won't find out who this package is addressed to. Watch your back; I have no idea what these people will do to retrieve it. Please don't open it! Jason has no family to worry about and is better equipped to handle the danger. Thank you so much, and again, I'm sorry to get you involved.

He reread the note again, this time looking for any sign of a hidden message but saw nothing. Then he carefully peeled the note from the wrapping paper, nothing beneath it. Next, he examined the wrapping itself. It looked to be standard brown shipping paper. As he carefully unwrapped the package, he hoped to see a note from Sara that would help explain everything.

But the package contained only one item; a book that appeared to be ancient. The front and back covers were made of some type of animal skin, and the paper inside looked very fragile. On the first page, there was a rose and cross symbol; this caught his attention as Mr. Black was said to be wearing a pendant with a rose and cross.

He turned to the next page and tried to read it, but it was written in Latin, and he could only translate a few words. He kept turning pages to see if he recognized anything else, but he couldn't translate enough words to make sense of the content. There were some drawings at the back of the book, so he studied them.

There were drawings of a coastal village, with people from an ancient civilization doing various daily activities. The author drew buildings and other structures in great detail. There were schematic drawings as well, possibly representing some type of equipment.

He had picked up quite a bit of archeological knowledge from Sara, so he tried to methodically examine the book how she would. He looked at the front cover, took out his phone, and pulled up his translation app. There were only four words above the drawing of a red rose. The translation came up as, The Book of Knowledge.

To find out why Mike and his family had died, he had to have the book translated. There was no one left he could trust but Sara. "Was she in hiding, was she kidnapped, was she alive?" He had so many questions. It was imperative that he find her; she was the nexus of this ugly chain of events. Mike said that she was on Santorini. He hit favorites on his phone and touched her number, but for the umpteenth time today, he got her voicemail; he didn't leave a message.

When the book failed to yield any answers, he picked up the wrapping and inspected it again, turning it over and over under the light. Then he saw something. He could make out tiny numbers on one of the edges. "That a girl," he thought. He punched the coordinates into an app that directed him to a remote location on Crete. He quickly moved to the cockpit and started the engines.

CHAPTER
21

THE BOOK WAS vital to Karl's plans. Despite what he might have told Andrew, he had no intention of preventing Josef from releasing the virus. Andrew had been unaware of the depth of his hatred of Hitler, a hatred that was born during the painful separation from his family. During his dreadful years at the boarding school, he became obsessed with the notion that Hitler's maniacal regime was responsible for his family's situation, hence his expatriation.

He remembered his grandmother recounting stories to him and his siblings about life in Germany under the Nazi regime. His grandparents taught at the University of Munich, where his parents met. Theirs was a family of scholars, his grandfather was a physicist, and his grandmother was a historian.

Early in the war, his grandparents noticed Jewish professors were quietly disappearing. Initially, they were told the academicians had left to work for the Nazis, but his grandparents didn't believe it. They heard rumors the Nazis were rounding up German citizens of Jewish descent and taking them to work camps.

Grandmother said the environment at the University was one of secrecy and fear. Hitler's internal security organization, the Schutzstaffel, known as the SS, began interviewing faculty members about their work and loyalty to the Fuhrer, looking for anyone who might want to defect to the West. Faculty and students were being watched; it was a taut atmosphere.

Within weeks engineering professors and mathematicians began disappearing. High-ranking Nazi officials were seen at universities recruiting them to work on secret weapons programs for the Fuhrer. When one of his grandfather's close colleagues, Dr. Fredrick Schlossberg disappeared, his grandparents suspected he had either been coerced or, even worse, taken by force. When Fredrick's family vanished soon after, his grandparents stealthily prepared to flee Germany with their only child, Peter, Karl's father.

When his parents were killed in the automobile accident, Karl buried his grief, his grandmother's stories of Germany, and all the nights he cried to himself sleep at the boarding school. He had been the youngest student at the school, but he was treated like an adult. There were no loving hands to bandage his knees when he fell or place a reassuring hand on his shoulder when he was scared. To survive, he hardened himself against childish emotions that made him more vulnerable.

Andrew's recitation of Josef's plan caused those repressed memories to violently surface. But Andrew was no longer here to provide a calming influence as those negative emotions roiled within him. However, he soon realized Andrew had provided the means to erase his family's exile to America, his subsequent expulsion to Germany, and ultimately, his family's death.

A few weeks after Andrew died, he was working in the lab when he was approached by one of the elder members, who handed him a note and a key. The message was from Andrew. Karl was to sort through his belongings and take what he wanted. The rest would be destroyed. He spent the next few months going through outdated journals and notes of procedures and inventions that were now obsolete. One night he came upon a box with the word "Crete" on it. Anxiously he opened it and found instructions for building the time travel device that Andrew wanted him to build.

Karl's mind snapped back to the present. Andrew had been gone for over ten years, and he was still searching for the book. Neither Andrew nor Joseph had written down the portals' locations. With the help of Michael's diagrams and equations, he tried to find them on his own, but so far, he hadn't been successful. Without the book, he might never find them.

He had long since discovered that Josef had vanished shortly after arriving in Europe and now believed that Josef had used the device to carry out his plan. Eventually, Karl infiltrated the small group of brothers who had kept Josef's secret and convinced them that he supported their mission. Sharing Andrew's notes with them went a long way in that regard. He swore to them that he would do everything possible to ensure Josef succeeded. He did not tell them that his motivation was to erase the

Nazi regime and return his family to pre-war Germany, to end his torment, and live his life in peace.

He desperately needed Josef's plan to succeed. It was the only measure of hope he'd had since Andrew died. But he was conflicted; he knew he was contravening Andrew's wishes. While he admired Andrew for his kindness and ability to forgive others, Andrew grew up in a loving family that had not endured the persecution and degradation that his family had. Karl was sure that if Andrew had lived, he could have convinced him that Josef was right.

Although Karl had never met Josef, he felt a kinship with him. Josef had the strength and vision to conceive a uniquely bold plan, and he hoped wherever, or more precisely, whenever, Josef was, he had the will to carry it out. But the plan was now in jeopardy. After all his years of searching, *that* archeologist had discovered the book, and it was up to him to get it back. His best chance of doing that was to find her. Fortunately, he knew just where she was.

CHAPTER
22

J ASON FLEW THE Tern up the coast to Nova Scotia and docked at the
Port of Halifax. He secured the plane, grabbed his backpack, threaded
through a crowd of whale watchers, and hailed a cab to the airport. A light
rain was beginning to fall, and the sidewalks were crowded with people
who had hastily pulled out their umbrellas. He scanned their faces, looking for anyone who might be looking for him, but saw no one suspicious.

As his cab stopped in front of the terminal, he paid the driver, jumped
out, and hurried to the ticket kiosk. He lucked out and got the last seat
on a flight departing for Athens via Montreal. With a couple of hours to
wait, he decided to grab breakfast. He purchased a newspaper from a vendor, then walked the concourse looking for an empty table in the back of
one of the restaurants.

The terminal was bustling with travelers rushing to one gate or
another. As he walked, he scanned the crowd, looking for anyone who
didn't fit in. A well-dressed man in his thirties leaned against the wall,
watching passengers as they scurried toward their departure gates. The
man looked oddly out of place; he had no carry-on or luggage of any
kind. Jason thought, "He might be under-cover security, but they usually
blend in better than this guy." As he walked past the man, he purposefully
looked straight at him. The man smiled briefly but gave no sign of recognition or discomfort. A woman exited the nearby restroom, the man
strode toward her, and they both walked away. He internally scoffed at
himself; the crowds in the terminal were triggering his paranoia.

He found a rear table with an unfettered view of the concourse and
ordered a double expresso and a Greek omelet. Pretending to read the
paper, he surreptitiously watched the entrance. As he thought about the
book stowed in his backpack, he remembered a line from the third Indi-
ana Jones movie. Sean Connery had just been rescued by his son, Harrison
Ford, and Connery said, "I mailed you the book so they wouldn't find it."

Jason pondered this for a few minutes. "Should I find a locker and leave the book here?" But in the end, there was nothing else he could do. The book was safer with him.

He jumped at the sound of silverware banging on a nearby table. Fighting his instinct to find cover, he quickly scanned the area and saw a mother trying to entertain two small children while waiting for their order. He sympathetically smiled at her, and she gave him a look that said, "I'm sorry for all the noise."

After breakfast, he wandered the concourse looking for a T-shirt that would scream tourist. After purchasing a shirt with a huge maple leaf on the front and a Canadian flag on the back, he boarded the plane. During the flight, he booted up his laptop, reserved a seaplane off the Greek mainland, and then paid a hefty price to have it outfitted with a small Zodiac. He could swim from the plane to the island, but Sara couldn't.

He checked Sara's coordinates against the map and located an isolated beach a little over ten kilometers from the target. He couldn't get a vehicle on the plane or in the Zodiac, but he could get a collapsible Moped on board. Mopeds were commonplace in the tourist areas; he found a vendor near the airport and reserved one. He would utilize it to get to a village on Crete where he could rent a vehicle with four-wheel drive. His next move will depend on what he'll find at the coordinates. He prayed he would find Sara alive.

By the end of the next day, he had operationalized his plan and was in the village of Kokkinos Pirgos looking for a vehicle to rent. Every fiber in his body shouted for him to hurry, but he didn't want to appear to be anything but a leisurely tourist. His Moped slowly drove past the long beach where a rainbow of sun umbrellas shaded tanned bodies of all shapes and sizes.

His first stop was a white-washed shop adorned with colorful window boxes, where he bought a ballcap and sunglasses. His purchases would protect him from the sun and shield his face from prying eyes. As he drove past shops and taverns, the aroma of Greek cuisine filled his nostrils, and he realized that he hadn't eaten since the night before.

The rental lot was hard to miss. It was decorated with colorful flags and signage in at least four languages. The place was pretty deserted, and it looked as if most of the four-wheel drives had already been rented. It was after midday, a little late in the day, to be renting a vehicle, so he told the rental agent, Yiannis, that he wanted an early start the following day. Noticing Jason's T-shirt, Yiannis tried to engage him in conversation about Canada. Jason threw him a few bones, left his Moped with him, and drove off in one of the last jeeps on the lot.

To ensure he wasn't being followed, he stopped at some local ruins before heading to the target coordinates. It was nerve-rackingly slow, and he was desperate to find Sara. Near dark and satisfied that he wasn't being tailed, he turned off his headlights and proceeded to the coordinates.

The GPS readings led him into the foothills, ten kilometers below the ruins at Phaistos. The terrain was rocky, with sparse foliage and steep gorges. He left the road and drove as far as possible across the rocky terrain. When thick vegetation made it impossible to go further, he left the jeep in the brush and began his trek to the target.

His GPS app led him to the edge of a narrow gorge. Without signs of a trail to the bottom, he slid down, dust flying everywhere. Reaching the bottom, he wound through the gorge, scaring off a few snakes and small animals. He augmented his hearing, hoping to hear some sign of life, but all he heard was the screeching of birds flying overhead.

Rounding a bend, he stopped. He faced a wall of dirt and rock that appeared to result from a recent landslide. Crete is a volcanically active island, so a landslide wasn't unusual, but this one just happened to be at the exact coordinates written on the wrapping paper. He inspected the ground near his feet. It was dusty, and he could see two other footprints beside his. One small and one large, both ending abruptly at the debris. The smaller of the two could belong to Sara. With a sense of extreme urgency, he asked himself, "Is she trapped somewhere in that pile?"

Running back to the jeep, he discovered a narrow trail that hadn't been visible from above; he would use it to carry Sara out of there. After grabbing the emergency shovel and extra water bottles, he returned to the debris pile, climbed to the top, and started frantically digging.

He dug all night and it was nearly dawn when the shovel broke through to a void. Digging even faster he eventually had a hole wide enough to crawl through. Peering down through the opening, a body, Sara's body, came into view. His chest tightened; he couldn't tell if she were alive or dead. Fearing a cave-in, he resisted the urge to push himself through the hole. After digging for what felt like an eternity, the opening was stable enough to withstand his weight.

Grabbing the shovel and backpack, he carefully climbed through. Heart pounding, he rushed to Sara's side feeling for her carotid artery, praying to find a pulse. It was faint, but she was alive! Gently shaking her, he cried, "Sara, Sara, can you hear me? It's Jason." He stroked her face, but nothing. He tried again and again, eventually, she moaned. Lifting her head, he poured a tiny amount of water into her mouth. It seemed like minutes went by before she swallowed it. He performed a primary survey, checking for any severe injuries. Finding none, he grabbed their gear, lifted her over his shoulder, and cautiously climbed out of the cave.

When they were safely away from the opening, he gently placed her down in the shade. Reluctantly leaving her, he scouted ahead to ensure it was safe to return to the jeep. Seeing or hearing nothing, he carried Sara to the vehicle and strapped her tightly in. She was moaning more now, but her eyes remained closed. Before they sped off, he gave her more water.

They had driven only a kilometer before he saw an SUV coming up behind them; he pushed the jeep to go faster. They were now fishtailing on the dirt roads. "Damn," he wished he had the Toyota. The SUV was gaining on them. He hoped all the dust blowing up behind them would provide some cover. Sara's head swung from side to side, but he could do nothing for her now.

Suddenly the other vehicle was alongside; a gun barrel in its open window pointed directly at them. He could not get Sara down; he had to keep the SUV behind them. A sharp curve loomed ahead and he turned tightly into it, forcing the other vehicle behind them. With tensed muscles and a vice-like grip on the steering wheel, the race continued for several kilometers, following the contours of the ridge-line.

A long arch-supported canyon bridge was directly ahead of them. He figured the men chasing them would use the straightaway to pull beside them again. A question came to his mind, "Why aren't they firing?" There had been plenty of opportunities to shoot through the back of the jeep or even shoot out the tires. A flat tire would cause them to roll at the speed they were traveling.

Then it hit him, "They want this to appear to be an accident." Once on the bridge, they would force him over the side, their jeep would hit the bottom of the gorge and burst into flames. The fire would obliterate any evidence of Sara's ordeal but also destroy the book. They must not know he had it.

As the road straightened, Jason slowed, and the other vehicle came up beside him. Tires squealed as he hit the brakes, the smoke of burning rubber encompassing them. As the SUV sped past, Jason gunned it. Metal screamed against metal as he rammed them from behind. The force of the impact sent Sara's head forward barely missing the dash. The other driver desperately tried to regain control, but Jason had quickly reversed and how hit them broadside with as much speed as he could muster. The SUV began rolling, picking up momentum as it bounced off the bridge abutment and careened over the side. The glow of fire cast a red reflection on the canyon wall as he and Sara crossed to the other side of the bridge.

CHAPTER
23

J ASON WANTED TO reach the seaplane as quickly as possible, but he took back roads to evade detection. Their radiator was blowing steam and he was unsure how long the vehicle would last. He had stopped several times to add water, but it was useless. Sara needed immediate medical treatment, but Crete wasn't safe. He had acquired medical supplies on the mainland, and with his battlefield medic training, he could at least start an IV and get some fluids into her. He briefly wondered if anyone would be waiting for them at the seaplane, he would have to worry about that when they arrived.

The vehicle was rattling and belching smoke as they reached the beach where he had stashed the Zodiac. It was empty, and there was no sign that they were under surveillance. He gave Sara a few more sips of water, then placed her in the boat and sped off. The smooth azure water was a stark contrast to the rough jeep ride. Sara was moaning again and talking nonsense. Once in the plane, he laid her head on a pillow, started an IV, revved the engine, and left the coast of Crete.

Reviewing his options, he chose what he hoped was the safest. They flew back to the airport where he had rented the seaplane. Sara remained hidden while he procured a small jet. When no one was watching, he transferred her into it, and they lifted off, heading for Germany.

A hospital in Greece had never been an option; Mr. Black would be expecting that. His best bet was to get her to Landstuhl, where she would be secure. He got another liter of fluid into her during the flight, but she still wasn't making sense. He hoped the delay in treatment wouldn't cost her life, but with people trying to kill her, his choices were limited.

The closest military base to Landstuhl was Ramstein. He had to convince the tower chief of his association with the military, and hopefully, they would let him land. The thought of returning to Landstuhl triggered his anxiety, and he immediately questioned his decision to go back. He remembered the months he spent there, his pain, and the shock of discovering what they had done to him.

His primary physician was Dr. Bryant, a brilliant trauma surgeon. As he began to regain strength and recover from his injuries, he noticed things that didn't make sense. During his physical therapy sessions, he was always alone with the therapists. He had seen other recovering soldiers working in groups, but not him. He couldn't be sure, but he thought he was recovering faster than the others and had much greater strength and agility. He also noticed that sometimes his vision and hearing were more acute than he had remembered.

He will never forget the day he confronted Dr. Bryant with his concerns. The doc's response was etched into his memory and would remain forever acute. They were outside the hospital in the garden area; he could still smell the flowers. It was late spring, and the days were getting warm. He could hear the buzzing of bees in the garden and remembered thinking how odd that he could hear them over the noise of aircraft overhead.

At first, Dr. Bryant just looked at him. Jason saw the struggle in his eyes. The doc spoke in a low tone, almost haltingly, as if unsure where to begin. "My boy, I'm not sure you realize the extent of your battlefield injuries. If not for new technological advances in surgery, you would have been left both blind and deaf. As If that wasn't bad enough, your burn scars would have made it almost impossible to move your body normally, and you would have faced years of reconstructive surgery."

Jason paled, and he started to say something, but the doc raised his hand.

"The surgical trauma team and your superiors met to discuss your case. Two main factors informed our decision to enhance your body: first, you have no close family, and second, your military record was outstanding. Additionally, you have an unshakable moral aptitude, you demonstrate outstanding critical thinking under fire, you are an excellent role model and your men would follow you anywhere," he stopped and winked, "and above all, you are loyal and humble."

He started to protest, but the doc continued, "Despite your debilitating injuries, your brain function was intact. This made you the perfect candidate for our enhanced soldier program."

Jason replied, "Never heard of it."

"And you probably never will; it's quite confidential. I may even get into trouble just telling you this, but I believe you deserve to know now rather than later. And I also believe it will hasten your recovery. You won't spend time and energy questioning everything."

Jason's face was incredulous as he asked, "But how? How did you fix me and more importantly, what did you do to me?"

"Ah my boy, that's the real question. It's very technical. Let me give you the basics, you'll learn more as you progress. To mitigate the damage to your retina from the blast we placed a neuronal implant from your ocular nerve to your brain. You don't actually see with your retina; you basically see through a computer. This allowed us to enhance your vision with a computer program. You have night vision, thermal vision, telescopic vision, and a type of x-ray vision that allows you to see metal objects, like weapons, that might be hidden."

Jason had an oh-no moment and said, "Sounds like a military upgrade to me."

"You're right of course, this tech doesn't exist in civilian hospitals and even if it did, it would be too costly for practical use. Your enhanced hearing was done essentially the same way. You had significant inner ear damage due to the blast. You would have needed high powered hearing aids, if you could have heard at all."

The doc continued, "Now these enhancements are pretty straight-forward. Similar neuronal implants are being placed in patients who were born blind or deaf. Even quadriplegics can use neuronal interfaces to allow them to write or speak, we've just taken it much farther."

Jason asked, "What about my burns? I have scars but they're not nearly as bad as some burns that I've seen. You said I would have problems with movement, but I move just fine, in fact better than fine. That's one of the first things I noticed."

"That's a little more complicated and uses cutting-edge technology developed at DARPA. First, we had to use cells from your unburned skin to essentially grow more skin. It isn't artificial; it's actually yours. This decreases the likelihood of rejection and certainly helps with cosmesis. Then we took DARPA's "Smart Skin" and wove it just under your new skin, attaching it to your subcutaneous tissue; it's called an artificial skin interface."

Jason thought, "This sounds like science fiction," but asked, "What the hell is Smart Skin?"

The doctor answered, "An artificial product that is constructed of millions of flexible sensors. They're made of nanorods that are encased in an artificial polymer. The sensors provide a feedback loop to your brain. Pressure sensors are triggered when you touch something or vice versa, pain sensors are triggered when the polymer is damaged, etc."

Jason replied, "My skin feels a little different but I just chalked it up to burn damage and scars from the skin grafts. I figured they were autografts; I had no idea that I had all that tech underneath."

He started to say more, but the doc stopped him, "I've said enough for now. I think you have a basic understanding of how and why your body has changed. I'm sure our superiors would have waited and chosen a better time to tell you these things, but I'm just a doctor, more interested in science than politics."

The doc stood, "I want to make another point before I return to work. Your body is still yours, no matter what we've done to it. You have control of how and when you use your enhancements. Don't feel sorry for yourself, be grateful that you're not dead or living in silence and darkness, unable to do the most mundane tasks. That would have been the real tragedy here. Think about what you've learned, and if you need to talk to someone, I'm here for you."

Jason was suddenly thrust back to the present when the landing beacons at Ramstein came into view.

CHAPTER
24

K ARL FOUND HIMSELF restlessly pacing within the confines of his room. Amidst a crucial meeting with his covert group, an unexpected call from Eric shattered his focus. Eric informed him that the team they sent to Crete was presumed dead after their vehicle careened off a canyon bridge. Definitive identifications would have to wait until dental records could be obtained, but Karl knew that would never happen.

"How many mercenaries do I have to lose?" He growled, "It has to be Falcone; that man is a menace." At least none of the hired men could be connected to him; Eric had ensured that.

After the fiasco at the mansion, he didn't want to dispose of any more bodies, and Falcone's escape meant they could no longer meet there. He didn't have time to look for another clandestine location, so they were meeting in his lab for now. Although his lab was private, meeting anywhere within the temple complex was dangerous, exacerbating his mounting stress.

An annoying twitch had developed in his left eye, and he had lost his temper more than once. Fearing the Fellowship would take notice and censure him; he began self-isolating and spoke only with members of their covert sect. He excused his erratic behavior by telling himself, "I'm working too hard, I just need to get more sleep." But it wasn't the work; it was the nightmares that kept him from sleeping. The latest had centered around the unknown fate of his grandfather.

Ernst, Karl's grandfather, had been a physics professor and likely candidate for forced recruitment to the Nazi weapons program. This situation alone was untenable; however, the certainty that their son, Peter, would be forced to enlist in the Wehrmacht spurred his grandparents into a perilous flight from their homeland.

His grandmother, Anna, recalled Ernst's quivering words as he told them of his plan, "We have been presented with a way out—a chance to escape this nightmarish existence. But we must proceed with utmost caution. Our lives, our freedom, hang in the balance."

Before sharing the details of their escape, he made them promise they would never reveal the existence of the underground network that provided their forged papers and transportation. In addition, he made them promise that if any of them were captured or detained, the others would continue with the exodus.

Karl's grandmother cried when she told this as well as other stories of their homeland. This was particularly so when she recounted their last night together in Germany. Ernst, Anna, and Peter had remained at the University long after the faculty and students had gone home. They would be leaving that night, and their first hurdle was exiting the school unseen. The University's basement was connected to an old tunnel system used to unload goods from the river in years past. It was archaic, but the tunnels were still open. They were to follow a map of the old route to the river, where a boat awaited them.

As they were about to leave, voices echoed down the hall; it was the SS calling out for Ernst. Anna and Peter had already disappeared out the rear entrance, but Ernst was trapped. They waited for him in the tunnels, but he never appeared. Anna wanted to return for Ernst, but her promise to him propelled her steadfastly onward.

She and Peter hid on the boat as it traveled west on the Isar River. They eventually crossed the Swiss border at Deisenhofer in the back of a delivery truck. From there, they traveled by rail to Zurich, where the underground had booked them on a flight to America. After the war, Anna made numerous inquiries about Ernst, but he had disappeared into thin air.

When Karl was old enough to leave the boarding school on short excursions, he also inquired about his grandfather. Once, he was able to get away long enough to travel to the University of Munich to see if anyone remembered him, but all he found was a dead end.

Karl's left eye twitched violently as his thoughts returned to Eric's call. The backup team had entered the cave and saw no sign of the girl. She either dug herself out, or Falcone had rescued her; he favored the latter. Her activities in the cave had led them to a previously undiscovered room adorned with roses. When his men entered, all they found was an empty box. Despite their attempts to stop her, she found it when no one else had.

His hopes and dreams of reuniting his family were in danger of shat-tering. That woman now had both the book and the device. With Falcone protecting her, she was a real threat to his plans. They had to be stopped at all costs. Thanks to Eric's technological genius, he knew exactly where they were headed.

CHAPTER
25

W HEN THEY WERE close enough to initiate radio traffic, Jason identified himself and stated he had an injured American citizen on board. In hopes it would speed things up, he added, "Dr. Bryant at Landstuhl is expecting us; he will verify our credentials once we land." He knew he was taking a risk landing at the Base, but if they used a public airstrip, he would be detained by security. It was imperative that he stay with Sara.

Their plane was met by an ambulance and guard detail. They were both searched, and their IDs were checked. The guards then followed the ambulance to the emergency room, where they were met by Dr. Bryant. He was an older man, around sixty, with thinning gray hair and wire-rimmed glasses. He looked more like a professor than a renowned trauma surgeon. His wife had also been a physician, a neuroendocrinologist. In a strange bit of irony, she died of a brain tumor over a year ago.

He gave Dr. Bryant a brief report on Sara's condition and the emergency treatment he had rendered. After the doctor completed a cursory examination, Jason took his arm and looked him in the eye, "Doc, you're the only person I trust to take care of her. There are some pretty bad people trying to kill her, we need anonymity, and we need to keep contact with your staff at a minimum."

Dr. Bryant nodded knowingly, "Let's get her into a private bed and start running some diagnostics."

The doctor dismissed the military guard, and he and Jason accompanied Sara to a private room in the intensive care unit. Her heart rate and blood pressure were dangerously low. Dr. Bryant inserted a central intravenous line in her neck, following which an RN came in to draw labs and hang more fluids. When the nurse had completed her tasks, Dr. Bryant introduced her to Jason, "This is Elsa. She will be your primary nurse for the next several days." He rechecked Sara's BP before continuing, "I have worked with her for many years, she is highly skilled and knows how to maintain confidentiality."

He then turned to Jason, "Elsa, this is an old friend of mine. He is here to protect this patient from people who want to harm her." He placed a protective hand on Sara and continued, "He will likely scrutinize every procedure and every person who comes into this room. It will not be personal; he is just doing his job and I know he will let you do yours."

Elsa nodded. She had cared for many VIPs before and knew the drill. Jason nodded as well.

The doctor turned back to Elsa, "Please arrange a cot for him to sleep on as I know he will not leave her side."

He adjusted his glasses and spoke to Jason again, "Elsa will get her settled and I will be back as soon as I get her lab results. I see no sign of neurological damage; I think we are dealing with dehydration causing both vascular collapse and acute kidney injury. She should start responding to the fluids soon."

The doctor left the room, and with Jason's help, Elsa began removing the rest of Sara's clothing and washing away the dirt. Jason was relieved to see her wounds were superficial. They were just finishing when Dr. Bryant returned, "The lab results indicate acute renal injury and rhabdomyolysis, a condition caused by prolonged pressure on skeletal muscle cells. The pressure kills the cells and the byproducts of this process build up in the blood stream eventually clogging the kidney tubules. This presents a twofold injury to the kidneys, the first being the dehydration itself."

He looked at Sara's vital sign monitor and continued, "I want to wait six hours to see if her kidneys start responding. If they don't, we might need to initiate dialysis to remove the waste products from her blood." Dr. Bryant saw the fear in Jason's eyes and softened his tone, "But I doubt that will be necessary. Let's just wait and see."

Sara's eyes fluttered, then slowly opened. Elsa dimmed the light as Sara fought to focus. Jason bent next to her and said, "Sara, its Jason. You're safe, you're in a hospital." He squeezed her hand, and his voice started to break. He continued, "You're being treated by the same doctor who treated me after my injuries."

In a weak raspy voice, she replied, "Jason, thank God, you found me."

She tried to say more, but the doctor interjected, "Miss ah Sara, your kidneys have been severely injured by dehydration and damaged muscle cells. We're giving you large amounts of IV fluids to see if we can jump-start your kidneys. We'll recheck your labs in about six hours; that will give us an idea if we're headed in the right direction."

She nodded, then he asked about her other injuries, "You have an abrasion on the side of your head and deep scratches on your arms and hands, but otherwise we don't see any other sign of injury. To your knowledge, is this a correct assessment?"

Sara nodded and said, "Yes, the head injury occurred when someone placed a rag over my face and I passed out. But the scratches came from trying to dig my way out of the cave."

Tears formed in her eyes as her voice broke. He said, "That's enough explanation for now; you need rest. I'll be back to check on you later."

Sara immediately fell back asleep. Jason was emotionally exhausted and had been awake for almost forty-eight hours. He must have looked like it because Elsa told him to lie down on the cot and try to get some sleep. Sara's vitals were improving, and they could do nothing more than wait. She promised to watch the door and not let anyone enter while he slept. He did as she instructed and fell asleep almost immediately.

Six hours later, Dr. Bryant returned; Sara was asleep. He informed Jason that Sara's kidney function was improving and they would not need to perform dialysis. She would still need continued fluids and monitoring for another day or two, but she would be fine.

He sat down on the cot next to Jason and, with a concerned look, said, "My boy, I heard you left the military. Are you still having problems adapting to the changes in your body?"

Besides Mike and Sara, the doc was probably the only person on earth he could talk openly with about his enhancements. He replied, "Look, doc, I appreciate everything you did for me. It was not your decision to save my life; that order came from higher up. But my life is really not my own anymore, so in reality, my life wasn't saved; it was taken from me." He paused for effect, then continued, "After my recovery, I went on dozens of missions and probably saved a lot of people, but I was empty inside. I had to blackmail the military into letting me leave, then worry that a rival faction might want my tech to basically reverse engineer me. That fear has led me to live off the grid, always watching my back, never knowing who to trust. That's why Sara and I broke up; I didn't want someone to use her to get to me."

Dr. Bryant looked at the still-sleeping Sara and asked, "Is that what happened here?"

Jason shook his head, "I really don't know why anyone would want to hurt Sara, but they do. After I pulled her out of a cave on Crete, we were pursued and only got away through a little luck."

The doctor shook his head, "I know what you're capable of, Jason. I think luck had very little to do with it. Think about it, would you have been able to save her without your enhancements?" He patted Jason's leg, "Think about it, my boy; maybe you're not as cursed as you believe you are." He got up and said, "I'll check-in with you in the morning. If there are any problems tonight, the nurse will call me. Her name is Yva, and she is as good as Elsa. Good night."

Dr. Bryant walked wearily out as Yva walked in. The doctor nodded at her while she replaced the almost depleted IV bag with a new one. Then she checked Sara's catheter; her urine output was slowly increasing. He laid back down, feeling certain now that Sara would recover. Bringing her here had been the right move, but where would they go next, "I'll think about that tomorrow."

The following morning, Sara was alert and anxious to talk to him, "Jason, I need to tell you about the package I sent."

He gave her a furtive look and hushedly said, "That will need to wait until we're out of here and somewhere secure."

He turned as Elsa rolled in Sara's breakfast tray along with a caregiver tray for him. He looked up to thank her and noticed she appeared nervous. Instinctively his hand dropped to his knife sheath, and he looked toward the door, half expecting someone to come bursting in.

Elsa covered for him by quickly glancing at the door herself, "It's OK, no more lab draws for now, she's doing much better this morning," then turned and walked out. Jason was now on full alert, "Was someone watching them?"

Sara continued to improve, and they made forced small talk to pass the time. Just before the end of her shift, Elsa brought in their dinner trays. Before leaving the room, she looked at him and nodded slightly at his tray. Suspecting Elsa was sending a message, he blocked the view from the doorway before lifting the lid. There was a note taped to the top of a relatively thick envelope. It simply read, "They know you are here."

CHAPTER

26

KARL USED THE voice digitizer when communicating with the mercenaries, providing only the information necessary to complete their mission. He kept all knowledge of his plans to himself. No one outside his small group would ever learn about the book or their efforts to protect Josef's mission.

The briefing was nearing its close. Karl said, "They are untouchable in their current location, but they'll soon be on the move. Wait for the encrypted message, once you receive it, you'll need to move fast." He added, "I want them eliminated at all costs, retrieve the packages if you can, but your first priority is the man and women."

He started to signal the end of the call, then stopped. "As you are aware, this man, Falcone, is an ex-Navy Seal with special abilities. Do not underestimate him; he has already taken out three mercenary teams. If you don't want to be the fourth, you must stay several steps ahead of him. The tracker has been initiated, and you have the codes. There will be no further direct contact. Do not fail."

He sighed deeply as he terminated the call, then stifled a yawn; he hadn't slept in days and hoped fatigue was not affecting his ability to remain objective. He had never meant to hurt anyone, but circumstances had changed everything. So many people had died already, and now he planned to eliminate two more. He assured himself they would be the last. It was a small price to pay to reunite his family and rewrite his own history.

CHAPTER
27

J ASON QUICKLY REPLACED the plate cover. He would wait until dark to open the envelope. The doc came around at nine that evening. After examining Sara, he smiled and turned to Jason, "She is doing well, she's a very lucky girl."

The doc winked at her, "We are going to discontinue the catheter and the IV fluids tonight and see how you're doing in the morning. If your labs still look good, I will discharge you."

The doctor's expression then became somber. He looked back and forth between them, "I will be in the OR all day tomorrow. If I do not see you before you leave, take care, and Jason, think about our conversation yesterday."

He placed his hand on Jason's shoulder and quietly said, "Your life *is* yours Jason, it's up to you to decide how you want to live it." He shook Jason's hand and warmly said, "It was good to see you again my boy. Please send an email every now and then to let me know how you're doing."

Jason smiled, "I will, and not just because I owe you big time. Hopefully I'll get a chance to repay you some day." The doctor looked back at him with an expression Jason couldn't read.

Before Dr. Bryant left the room, he walked back to Sara. With a faltering voice, she shook his hand and said, "Thank you, there really are no words to express my gratitude."

Smiling at her, he replied, "You are very welcome my dear." He pointed at Jason and said, "Take care of this one, will you," then he walked out of the room.

Jason anxiously awaited while Yva discontinued the tubes and lines that had saved Sara's life. He had to look inside the envelope that was now under a pillow on his cot. Something was wrong; he didn't believe the doc's story. He was trying to let Jason know that they needed to leave before morning.

When the lights were finally out, he got his first chance to look at the envelope. A type-written note read, "The car is parked in the employee lot, first level, number seventeen. The key card will get you into the parking garage and out the security gate."

He surveyed the rest of the contents. In addition to the keys and key card, there was a map of the hospital with arrows showing their current location and the location of the parking garage. He also saw two passports, one for David Johnson and another for his wife, Elizabeth. The photos on the fictitious passports matched the ones on their real passports. He also found enough Euros to get them home. He thought, "Someone has put a lot of effort into planning our escape. Getting forged passports of this quality must have taken some time." Jason thought it had to be Dr. Bryant, "Whoever did this must have started planning the day we arrived."

Sara was awake, and she could hear keys and papers being shuffled. She started to ask him what was up, then Yva entered the dark room and placed some linens on a chair next to her bed. Then Yva walked out without saying a word.

Jason approached Sara and whispered, "They know we're here." At this news, she instantly froze, and her heart began racing. If she had still been connected to the monitor, it would have alarmed. He continued, "I know you've been through hell, but I need you to stay calm. If we're going to get out of here, we need to act casual, we need to act like we belong here, and we know where we're going."

He looked over at the linens Yva left. He found two pairs of scrubs and shoe covers between the folded sheets. He turned back to Sara and said, "I've been watching the activities in the hall. It looks like most of the staff work eight-hour shifts, so there will be a shift change at eleven pm. We'll make our move then." She nodded. He returned to the cot and spent the intervening time memorizing the facility map and their route out of the city.

By shift change, they had donned the scrubs and shoe covers that concealed their dirty boots. With their backpacks on, it looked as if they were going off-shift. They had been isolated in a private room that only Elsa, Yva, and Dr. Bryant had entered. Neither the staff nor security would recognize them.

Jason looked into the dim hall and motioned for Sara to follow him.

As they neared the exit, they walked by an empty nursing station. Jason had just been thinking, "So far, so good," when a voice called behind them. Jason gave a reassuring glance at Sara, then casually turned. A tall, muscular nurse was looking suspiciously at them. He said, "Excuse me, can I help you with something?"

Jason replied, "Yes, we heard Dr. Bryant might be around here, we wanted to give him an update on one of his patients."

The nurse, whose stance had been guarded, now relaxed. He replied, "He left here a few hours ago, haven't seen him since, sorry."

Jason quipped, "No problem, it's not an emergency; we'll speak with him in the morning." He then turned, and Sara followed him out the door.

They tried to walk casually toward the parking garage, but it was not easy. Beads of sweat had formed on Jason's brow, and Sara visibly shook. They found the car, a white Volkswagen sedan, and drove out of the garage, using the key card to raise the arm at the exit gate. Jason turned north on 62, then took the ramp for A-4.

Sara finally felt like she could speak without anyone overhearing. She asked, "Where are we going?"

To which he whispered, "The Swiss border, hopefully we can get a flight to Montreal from Zurich."

Jason was scanning the car's mirrors, looking for anyone following them. The fact he saw no one didn't mean they were in the clear.

Sara had been bursting with information about the book. She blurted, "I have so much to tell you, do you think it's safe to talk now?"

He shook his head and quietly said, "I haven't had a chance to check the vehicle for bugs, for all I know someone could be either listening or tracking us right now."

She turned her head to look out the rear window and said, "Do you think we're being followed?"

He replied, "I don't think they'd risk that, besides the doc chose the most common vehicle in Germany, so it would be hard to tail us." He continued, "Look in the glovebox and see if there's anything useful in it, like a note or map."

Sara pulled out a few papers and said, "The rental agreement has your fictitious name on it. If we get pulled over, everything should check out."

He glanced sideways at her, "This has all gone a little too smooth for me. We can't be sure if it was Dr. Bryant who helped us escape, we might just be driving into a trap."

CHAPTER

28

THEY USED THE forged passports to cross into Switzerland, then their own to enter Canada. Anyone following them from Germany would have difficulty tracking them to the Tern, and even if they did, he could lose them over water.

After landing in Montreal, they took a commuter jet to Halifax, where they boarded the Tern. Jason looked at Sara and said, "Buckle up for take-off. I want to get as far away from the port as possible before dark."

Sara did as he asked, but she couldn't help herself. Now that they were alone, she just had to know, "Jason, before we go any further, please tell me the book is safe."

He nodded and said, "It's in my backpack."

She was aghast, "You mean you brought it with you."

He looked sideways at her and somberly said, "You have no idea what that book has cost me, there was no way I was going to let it out of my sight. As soon as I'm sure we're safe, you are going to tell me what this is all about."

She replied, "OK, but it's a very long story and I'm not sure you're going to believe it."

Jason countered, "After what I've been through, I'm ready to believe just about anything."

Sara chuckled and said, "I have a feeling that I will need to remind you of that."

Less than an hour later, he landed the Tern off Devils Island at the mouth of Halifax Bay. He returned to the cabin, gave Sara a quick tour, and said, "I'm going to drop anchor and set the alarm."

She replied, "It's been a long day, I'm going to freshen up then open a can of something, I'm starved and I bet you are too." He nodded and stepped out onto one of the floats.

When he returned to the cabin, Sara had soup and crackers ready. She looked up, said, "I found a bottle of wine, too," and pointed to two paper cups. She had pulled her long blond hair up into a ponytail and without make-up to cover the freckles across her nose, looked like a teenager. He felt the familiar longing, but he had no idea how she would respond if he kissed her now. Someone was trying to kill her, and that took precedence over everything.

They ate quickly, then Jason looked intently at her and said, "Now, please tell me what this is all about; what's so important that you were almost killed?"

She replied, "OK, I will tell you the whole story, but you must promise to suspend your disbelief until you've heard everything." He nodded his agreement, and she began. "I need to give you some general background about two things that will initially seem completely unrelated."

He nodded, and Sara continued, "I'm sure you've heard of the ancient civilization of Atlantis. Most scholars believe that Plato based his story of Atlantis on a prehistoric civilization known only to ancient Greeks, one that Plato used to communicate his philosophical views."

Jason said, "Yes, I've read about Plato's views and his possible motivations for writing the Atlantis story. But the story is just that, a story, a myth."

"I know, everyone believes that Atlantis is a myth. Some archeologists believe that Plato could have been writing about the Minoans, a civilization that flourished on the islands of Crete and Thera, during the Bronze Age. The island of Thera, modern day Santorini, was nearly destroyed by a volcano causing most of it to sink below the sea, just like Atlantis."

He didn't say anything. He wanted her to get on with the story; he just nodded.

She took a sip of wine and continued, "Atlantis was said to be the home of a virtuous society, one more interested in the pursuit of science than war. They engineered sewer systems and hot and cold running water, engineering feats that wouldn't be seen again until the Roman era, 1500 years later!"

Jason said, "OK, so what?"

Now I want to discuss something you might find a little confusing, so bear with me. "Have you heard of the Rosicrucian Order?" He shook his head, so she went on, "They are a fellowship of scholars: philosophers, physicians, historians, astronomers, and scientists who strive to understand the true origins of God and the universe."

He replied, "O...K," and she continued.

"What's essential in explaining the book is the Fellowship believe the Order originated in Atlantis and was exported to Egypt."

Jason began to object to this discussion.

She paused and put her hand up, "Plato wrote that the Atlanteans traveled extensively throughout the Mediterranean, establishing trade with other countries, the most significant being Egypt. Legend has it Thutmose III was an Atlantean and brought sacred knowledge to Egypt. Under his rule, priests were sent to Atlantis to learn the mysteries and bring the knowledge back to Egypt. Eventually, every temple had a School of Mysteries where the guardians of wisdom practiced. Since these schools were associated with temples, the priests guarded the knowledge and used it to keep power."

He interjected, "What mysteries?"

Sara cocked her head, "That's a good question. Think of the mysteries as an attempt to answer the basic questions of existence: Who am I? Where do I come from? What is my purpose? These questions have been referred to as the mysteries of life. Incidentally, these are the same questions the Rosicrucians attempt to answer."

He made a yeah-right expression and said, "OK, go on."

"After the fall of Atlantis, the Egyptian priests became the sole guardians of knowledge, or the mysteries. In reality, the ancient physicians, alchemists, and astronomers were practicing science, not mysticism. I mention the connection with Egypt because that's how the Rosicrucians believe their knowledge was preserved. The science was basically imported from Atlantis, but the question remains, where did the Atlanteans get *their* scientific knowledge?"

Jason took this opportunity to wryly answer the question, "I don't know, do you?"

Her emerald eyes cast a downward glance, evoking a sense of reluctance. "Alright, now I'll get to the book." She still felt guilty about taking it and only gave him a quick run-down of the message on the clay tablet. "Since I thought this was some sort of hoax, I didn't tell anyone about it. I decided to find the book first, if there really was one. I followed the clues on both the tablet and drawings and found a narrow passage deep in the cave system where the drawings indicated the book was hidden."

She then described how she found the book and why she mailed it to Mike. She apologized for getting Mike involved, but Jason said nothing. His jaw tightened, but he didn't want to discuss it now.

She finished with, "Jason, the book has a rose and cross on the first page." She paused for effect, "The rose and cross are symbols used by the Rosicrucians just as the term, sacred knowledge is."

Jason looked at her as if to say, so what? But instead, he said, "You already told me that the origins of the Rosicrucian Order date back to Atlantis, and then you connected the story of Atlantis to the Minoans who lived on Crete. This doesn't sound very radical to me, so what's the big deal?"

She replied, "Let's consider for a moment that the book dates back to the Bronze Age. It was written in Latin, but Latin wouldn't become a written language until centuries later, just like Minoan plumbing wouldn't be seen again until the Roman age. Now here's where I need you to keep an open mind. What if someone from the future traveled back in time and taught the Minoans how to engineer farming implements, earthquake-resistant buildings, and plumbing, accomplishments we have archeological evidence for. We also have evidence that the Minoans were capable of distant sea travel on sophisticated sailing vessels, which is how they could have traveled to Egypt. Again, engineering feats that were remarkable for the Bronze Age."

He looked at her like she had just grown two heads, "You're asking me to believe in time travel?"

She sighed, "Just wait, there's still more to the story."

He got up, walked over to his backpack, and retrieved the book's container. After opening it, he placed it on the table before them and said, "It certainly looks ancient, but even historians have been fooled before." He used a napkin to carefully open the front cover. On the first page, he again saw the rose and cross symbol.

Sara pointed at it, "The Rosicrucian cross. As a religious symbol the cross was first used during the Babylonian empire, some three thousand years after the Minoan civilization disappeared."

He countered, "That still doesn't prove that time travel was involved."

She replied, "No it doesn't, but since you don't read Latin, let me summarize the book for you."

Sara told him about the author, Michael, and how his description of the Minoan civilization closely matched the archeological evidence. She also told him about Michael's rationale for choosing griffins to adorn the wall behind an alabaster chair, which was thought to be some sort of throne.

"Jason, think about it, the United States wasn't formed until 1776 AD. If Michael was a member of a previously unknown civilization who just happened to wind up on Crete, how would he know about the U.S.?"

Jason again countered, "Maybe the book was intentionally made to look old. You said yourself that archeologists had already discovered many of the things that Michael described, maybe he was only writing down what he read, and perhaps he placed the book in the cave after 1776 AD? Sara, there are logical alternatives to believing it was time travel."

She nodded and explained about the quantum entanglement theory and the portals, "Michael described a device that he used to inadvertently travel back to the Bronze Age. He filled the back of this book with schematic drawings of the device in case they couldn't find his. That is one reason he drew the map, to hopefully lead members of the Order to his device. That is precisely what I was doing when they drugged me and trapped me in that cave, trying to find the device."

Jason shifted in his seat. His eyes met hers as he tentatively asked, "So did you find it?"

She shook her head, and Jason got an I-told-you-so look on his face. Before he could speak, she said, "I didn't, but someone else did, and they left a journal in its place. But, if you flatly believe that none of Michaels' story is true, you won't believe the journal either." She grabbed her own backpack and pulled out a leather-bound journal. He noted the black rose stamped into the cover. "The Rosicrucian who took the device does not identify himself, but after reading this journal, a wave of fear coursed through my entire body."

The next thing Jason heard was the faint sound of a boat motor.

CHAPTER
29

"HOW THE HELL did they find us," Jason asked himself as he raised the anchor. He yelled back into the cabin, "We must have trackers on us, that's the only thing that makes sense. Check everything you have on, your clothes, everything in the backpack, even your shoes. Then check my backpack. But do it while you're buckled in, this might get a little bumpy."

As he revved the engines and the floats lifted off the water, Sara heard gunshots ring out as bullets pinged off the side of the plane. She frantically took off her boots and checked them first, but nothing. Then she felt her clothing, nothing. Next, she dumped out her backpack and inspected the contents. The only thing that hadn't been in it before was a letter from Dr. Bryant. She didn't have time to read it now.

She yelled toward the cockpit, "I can't find anything."

Jason yelled back, "Check the buckles and fasteners on the backpacks, look for anything that appears newer than the rest."

She complied but found nothing. He then realized, "You idiot." They knew about my scanning abilities because they used the tray to shield the scanner at the restaurant; the tracker must be hidden in something that would make it undetectable. Over the din of the engines, he yelled at her, "Don't worry about it, just hold on tight; this will be rough."

The plane lurched from side to side as he tried to outmaneuver the vessel shooting at them from below. Seaplanes had a limited altitude, and apparently, their pursuers knew it. His only hope was to get over land; he banked southwest. He would lose them over the peninsula, then head for one of the barrier islands. Unfortunately, he wasn't fast enough. Gunfire raked the side of the plane again. He banked and pushed the plane as hard as it would go. Gradually he began pulling away.

He yelled to Sara, "Are you OK? I think we're out of range now," but she didn't answer. He couldn't take his eyes off the controls, so he kept calling her name, to no avail. He forced himself to stay in the cockpit. He had to get to the other side of the peninsula, over water, so he could land.

The plane began to stutter. He checked the fuel gauge and saw the needle was in the red. One of the bullets must have hit the fuel tank. He had to land ASAP, "Where's the damn water?" The plane was now shaking violently. He could barely keep it level; one of the ailerons must have been hit too. In the distance, he saw a deserted bay off one of the barrier islands. With muscles straining, he forced the plane to turn toward it.

Damage to the aileron was causing the plane to roll. If the wing tip hit the water, they would flip, and the plane would break apart. Beads of sweat ran down his back as he fought with the controls. The water was coming up fast. In a desperate attempt to keep the plane from ditching, he powered down, retracted the flaps, and worked to keep the plane level as it hit the water.

The fuel alarm was screaming loudly as the Tern roughly hit the sea. He thought, "God, I hope we're not breaking apart in the water." He checked the gauges to make sure they weren't sinking; a structural assessment of the plane would have to wait. He didn't smell smoke and prayed they weren't on fire.

He rushed to Sara. She was lying on her side. The paleness of her skin contrasted with the dark blood underneath her. She had been hit in the back of her chest, and he knew it was bad. He tried to position her so he could assess the wound and try to stem the flow of blood, but she protested, "No, no."

She briefly opened her eyes, and falteringly said, "Promise me you'll read the journal, you have to stop them. The book is real, that's why they want it so bad." She closed her eyes again and, in a barely perceptible voice, said, "I love you." He felt her body go limp. He checked her pulse; she was gone.

He held her tightly to his chest, trying to infuse his life force into hers. Then he wept. A mournful groan escaped his body, then he held her quietly. As he blankly stared out the window at a beautiful sunset, his eyes reflected regret and pain.

He awoke to rays of sunlight streaming into the cabin. He was still holding Sara. She was cold now; he knew it was time to let go. As he laid her across the seat, her neck extended backward, and he noticed something, something under the skin, near the site where her central line had been. He ran his fingers over the area and was now certain. Sara didn't have a tracker on her; she had one in her, and it had been implanted at Landstuhl. It had to be the doc, but why? He was stowing the contents of both backpacks into his waterproof pack when he saw the letter.

Jason, I'm so sorry, my boy, but they have my daughter. Somehow, they knew you were coming to Landstuhl. To save her, I had to implant the tracker in Sara. They warned me they would know if I didn't comply. I did everything I could to help you escape, hoping that only you, with your enhancements and skill, could stop them. I pray you are safe. Please don't return; it will only make matters worse. I beg you to forgive me.

He cleared the lump of regret that had formed in his throat. He had drawn the doc into this but could not help him now. This letter proved that his adversary would go to any length to get the book. He had no intention of obliging him. He grabbed his gear, kissed Sara on the forehead, and set the demolition charges.

Jason stood on the shore of Capers Island and watched the Tern sink below the water line. The sun was rising on the horizon, and gentle waves kissed the shore. This was surreal; how could this pristine beach be witness to Sara's burial at sea? He'd experienced the normal teenage crushes, but she was the only woman he had loved. Despite the odds against it, he had hoped they would find each other again. Now that hope died with her.

He felt weighed down, as if he was being buried alive. Everyone he ever cared about was gone. Despite his self-imposed isolation, he had never felt so alone, even when his parents died. He clung to his promise to stop the people responsible for all this death.

CHAPTER
30

T HE PLANE WAS now completely submerged. He turned and started his trek toward the opposite side of the island. He swam to the mainland and convinced a tour bus driver to give him a ride into Charleston. The bus was full of people who were laughing and enjoying the sites. He blocked out the sounds as he planned his next move.

When he landed at Dulles, it was pouring rain. He used the fake passport to rent a car, which he left at a kiosk fifty miles from his cabin. Rain soaked him as he walked the rest of the way home, completely forlorn. With all his skill and enhancements, he had not saved the people he loved. In his solitude, he replayed the events of the past week. Sara's story was so far-fetched it was ridiculous. He had finally seen the book, and there was nothing of value in it, no rare jewels sewn into the hides, no treasure map, nothing that should have cost five lives. Then he thought, "Wait a minute, there was a map. Could the nonsense about a device be a cover for something more valuable?"

He forced his mind to work the problem; it was better than the alternative. He was angry, but more than that, he was resolved. He owed Mike, Nicole, the girls, and Sara, an explanation. The only way he would get one would be to find the people responsible. He had to solve the mystery of the book to do that.

He surreptitiously approached the cabin from the tree line. It looked exactly as he had left it. He avoided the pressure pads that would trigger the alarm as he walked toward the front door. Nothing looked as if it had been activated; no footprints in the dirt, nothing.

He keyed in some numbers on a hidden touchpad, then pressed his palm against it. After an electronic click, the door swung open. He closed it and hurried to his bedroom to access the security computer. After seeing no flags on the digital footage, he ran through it manually and saw nothing abnormal. He was relieved that no one had found a connection between him and this property. He was secure; exhaustion took hold of him. He lay on the bed and almost immediately fell into a fitful sleep.

He had nightmares about trying to find something that eluded him, something that was hidden in shadows. After ten hours, he awoke in a cold sweat. He stripped and showered, standing under the hot water for twenty minutes before toweling off. He shaved off a week's worth of stubble, then inspected his face in the mirror. His face hadn't changed, but he was a different person. His eyes reflected a dual persona; someone filled with rage yet completely hollow. He had to channel that rage into something productive or he would lose himself to it.

His stomach growled; he hadn't eaten much in the past week. He made a cheese and spinach omelet and, with his stomach no longer protesting, poured a second cup of coffee, walked over to his desk, booted up the computer, and logged onto the internet using an encrypted server.

He searched Rosicrucians, then narrowed it down to Orders on the East Coast. He scrolled down the names, none familiar, then the addresses of East Coast temples. He compared them to the address of the mansion where he had been held captive. It was less than five miles from one of the temples. The estate was registered to BR Enterprises, but he could find no information about who or what BR stood for, "Could the B stand for Mr. Black?"

He went to the barn and accessed the hidden entrance to the lab below. After placing his backpack on the stainless-steel worktable, he donned gloves. He heard Sara say, "The oils on your skin will ruin the documents."

Carefully, he removed the book and the leather journal and placed them on the table. He decided to inspect the book first. He wished he could carbon date it or analyze the ink, but he didn't have the equipment or the expertise. It had been in Sara's possession; she read it and believed it was thousands of years old, so he would have to go with that. He had another problem; he couldn't read Latin. He opened a translator app, but it was so slow that it would take months to read. The few pages he translated confirmed what Sara had already told him.

He turned his attention to the journal. It was written in English, so he had no trouble reading it, at least not until he got to the pages full of chemical equations. He thought, "What kind of a sick mind would consider releasing a weaponized virus on a naïve population? It could kill more Rosicrucians than Hitler did." He knew that some intellectuals were eccentric, but this guy was insane. At least he had a name for the people who killed his friends; BR stood for the Black Rose.

He analyzed the plan described in the journal. The author said he would live in the past for many years and mentioned 1914. If he was after Hitler, that date made sense. Hitler would have been on the Western Front in 1914.

He went back to the book again. He couldn't read Latin, but he could read schematics. He decided to concentrate on the last section of the book. He spent the next few days uploading the schematics into an engineering program on his computer. He expected the program to put up error messages as he progressed through the schematics, but it didn't. He was so intrigued he barely ate or slept.

Three days after returning home, he saw a computer rendering of the device for the first time. The schematics translated into something that looked like a smartwatch made of an unusual metal. The atomic numbers on the schematics matched those of a beryllium-copper alloy. The alloy, one of the most resonant metals in the world, would be perfect if the designer wanted to initiate or propagate a wavelength.

If the book was genuine, it made sense that the device wouldn't have traveled back in time with Michael. Copper had been discovered as early as 4000 BC, but beryllium wasn't discovered until 1797. However, the man who wrote the journal *could* have taken it back to 1914, but instead, it was purposefully left at the Mont. He looked at the schematic again. If he found the correct Mont, he would at least know what the device looked like. He knew then; he had already decided to find it.

His first task was identifying where the journal's author had made the time trip. He opened the book and looked at the list of portal locations that Michael had found. Only a dozen or so were associated with Mont, French for mountain. He googled a map of France. Michael had drawn landmarks next to most of the locations on the list. Next to the Mont, he had drawn a structure. He located Mont Blanc and Mont Cenis in the French Alps, but neither had a building associated with them. He saw another Mont close to the French coast of Normandy.

He zoomed in and saw Mont-Saint-Michel, an ancient abbey on a rock island. "That has to be it." The abbey dated back to the turn of the eighth century and had enough underground crypts to hide the device. He then googled a blueprint of the abbey and compared it to the landmark in the book. There were definite similarities. "Only one way to find out." He would head to France and, "who knows, maybe to 1914."

CHAPTER
31

K ARL'S FACE WAS beet red and bloated with rage. He was furious that
Falcone had escaped again. It took several minutes to calm himself.
At least the woman had been dealt with. Her body was found when his
divers located the sunken plane. He was sure that she had given Jason the
book and the map. Falcone had to die; things had gotten out of hand, but
their plan must succeed.

He felt guilty about Dr. Bryant and his daughter. Their bodies were
found at the bottom of a ravine two days ago. The Landespolizei deemed
it an accident. Apparently, their car had veered off the road during a rain-
storm. After ordering their deaths, Karl had told himself, "It was Jason's
fault they had to die. They would still be alive if he hadn't gone to the doctor for help."

He had to devise a contingency plan on the off-chance that Josef left a
trail, something the archeologist found in the caves, something indicating
what he planned to do. Karl could think of no other reason why Falcone
disappeared after they killed the woman. No matter how slim, he was left
with the possibility that Falcone figured out how to travel to 1914 and
stop their plans.

The Black Rose was using its collective intelligence to find at least one
of the portals. Brother David was meditating, feeling for alterations or
defects in the black matter that pervades the universe. He was near to
achieving the objective, and Karl knew it was only a matter of time before
one of the portals was located.

The other Black Rose members were divided into two groups; the
first was studying maps of France for possible locations to intercept Falcone. The second group sought clues about where Josef went after leaving
the U.S. Karl's job was to devise a plan to stop Falcone. He had the
book; he might lead them to the portal if they could find him. Unfortunately, despite Eric's digital prowess, he could not locate Falcone. As Karl

contemplated his next move, his phone buzzed. He answered but could hardly get a word in before Brother Vincent excitedly blurted, "We have an idea where Josef might have gone."

Josef had been seen in Normandy shortly before he disappeared. This was an interesting development. Karl had barely ended the call from Vincent when Eric informed him that Falcone had popped up on the radar; he just booked a flight to France. Brother David held the last piece of the puzzle when he reported an unusual energy surge near the old abbey on Mont-Saint-Michel, off the Normandy coast. Karl was ecstatic, "All the pieces have finally come together."

Karl dispatched men to watch the abbey. Falcone had proved to be a contentious adversary; he would need a contingency plan if they failed to stop him there. Although it would be a one-way trip, someone had to be waiting for Falcone when he arrived in 1914, someone who could blend in unnoticed. A debate arose as to who should make the journey. Most members of their group spoke fluent French, but Brother Charles Robertson, a stout bald man in his early sixties, won out due to his physical attributes. If Falcone noticed him, he would never consider Charles a threat.

Charles's objectives were twofold: the first was to stop Jason, and the second was to find Josef and ensure he was still capable and willing to release the weaponized virus. Charles would concoct a sob story to complete his first objective, making Jason the villain. He would then hire henchmen to take him out. Times were tough for the working class in 1914, and Karl felt sure the right men could be hired for the job. If anyone tried to track their activities back to Charles, he would simply disappear.

Finding Brother Josef would be a more difficult task. The Black Rose knew he would need to position himself near the Western Front if he wanted to infect Hitler. Josef was a physician, but a hundred physicians would be treating the wounded; they needed more information. The only photos of Josef were of a young man. Karl had taken them to a specialist who digitally aged him. He gave copies of the renderings to Charles with the hope that Josef hadn't changed too much, especially about releasing the virus.

Charles's mission had a lot of unknowns, and he couldn't contact the Black Rose if something went wrong. He would arrive in 1914, about three months before Germany declared war on France. They had no idea where Josef was, so Charles would need to wait near the Front for him to show himself. Three months should give him enough time to prepare. On the other hand, Jason could arrive in France any time before the start of the war. They hoped Charles would already be in place when and if Falcone made it to 1914.

Karl's thoughts turned to Jason and the book again. "That meddling female," he thought, "I wish she were still alive; I would get the book from her and make her tell us everything." He then realized something, in 1914, Falcone would be utterly alone with no better idea of how to find Josef than they did. There was also a chance that some of his enhancements wouldn't work; the odds would be even. "Stop worrying," he told himself, "Falcone will soon be irrelevant."

CHAPTER
32

J ASON'S MIND WAS made-up. If he found a device at the Mont, he would trust Sara's belief in the book. She had asked him to stop the Black Rose with her dying breath. If the device worked, he would do just that. It would be a one-way trip, but he didn't care; he had no one to return to.

The most challenging part of his mission would be to find the journal's author. He decided to track Hitler instead, hoping that by doing so, he would cross tracks with the Black Rose. He would take him or them out before the virus could be released. Hitler would be on the Western Front, along the Franco-Belgian border. He would head there and hope he wasn't too late.

His nose was itching, and he tried to resist the urge to scratch it again. Over the past two weeks, he had grown a fledgling mustache, as was the fashion in 1914. The itch was annoying, but he hoped the facial hair would help him blend in.

During the flight to Paris, he reviewed his plans. In 1914, the Mont was undergoing a significant restoration; plenty of workmen were around the abbey. Once he found the device and made the trip backward, he would disguise himself as one of them. With luck, no one would look close enough to realize he was an imposter.

Pontorson was the closest town to the abbey. Once, there he would change into a vintage suit and a pair of leather boots that laced to the knees. Zippers weren't used in clothing until 1925, and the last thing he wanted was a clothing mishap that would get him noticed. From Pontorson, he would take the train north to Paris and purchase clothing and gear more appropriate for his mission.

First, he had to get safely in and then out of the abbey. It was likely that the Black Rose would be watching for him; he couldn't approach it directly. Instead, he'd take the train from Paris to Granville, 54 km north of the Mont. From there, he would swim to the island's northwest side, where a sheer rock wall protects the abbey. That would be the least likely location on the island to be guarded.

He vacillated between thinking he had gone crazy to believing Sara and the book. He wasn't sure of anything he was doing, let alone what you should take when traveling through time. For all he knew, he'd wind up like Arnold Schwarzenegger's character in "The Terminator," naked as a newborn baby. "I guess I'll deal with that when and if it happens."

He had nothing or no one to lose. For one of the few times in his life, he decided to just go with it. He wasn't sure what would be waiting for him on the other side of the portal or if he would even survive it.

PART TWO
FRANCE, 1914

CHAPTER
33

RATS WERE SQUEALING in the distance as Jason woke on the cold, hard ground. His breathing quickened, and as he jumped up, he felt the space swim around him. His ears were ringing, adding to the din of the rats, "Did I make it?" he thought. The last thing he remembered was locating the device within a rock crevice inside one of the underground crypts.

He employed his night vision and surveyed the musty catacomb. The stone walls and archways were structurally the same, but he noticed piles of debris that weren't there before. "Welcome to 1914," he muttered, quickly changing his clothes. He packed his rucksack, stowed everything else into the waterproof backpack, and grabbed the device. The Black Rose might know where the device had been hidden; he would need a different place to hide it.

It would have been pitch black without his night vision. If anyone had followed him, they would have to wait until he got upstairs before they struck. It had taken him most of the night to make the swim, get into the abbey catacombs, and find the right crevice. If time travel were nearly instantaneous, it should be breaking dawn outside.

He hid the device and his gear and found spiral stone stairs on the southeast wall. The stone felt cold and rough under his hand as he quietly crept upward. Reaching the top, he faced another wall, turned to the right, and saw a large door. He calculated it was about ten feet high, four feet wide, and at least six inches thick, with hinges and a doorknob made of iron. To his chagrin, there was a hefty lock under the knob. He was about to pick it but decided to try the knob first; luckily, it moved. Cautiously he opened it, trying to be as quiet as possible, then silently cursed as the creaking of old hinges echoed throughout the stillness of the abbey.

Stepping through the doorway, he squinted, momentarily blinded by the dim, muted light that filtered in. He adjusted his vision before he proceeded further. The hall opened up, revealing a vast room filled with imposing pillars that towered above him, the Big Pillars Crypt. Scaffolding, neatly stacked around the room's edges, stood in testament to the ongoing restoration work within the abbey.

After years of England and France vying for the island, France won out. The Mont had become a source of national pride and reverence; the government decided to renovate the buildings, starting with the abbey. The goal was to upgrade the electrical, plumbing, and heating without seriously changing the historical structure of the Mont.

Reorienting himself, he found another stairway leading upward and emerged into a large windowed hall framed with stone arches. Pre-dawn light was visible through stained glass windows. "This must be the Wall of Light." As he entered the room, tall humanoid shapes caused him to duck into the stairway. He listened for a few minutes, and after hearing no movement, he took a second look. The tall shapes were actually sculptures, appearing like silent sentinels standing watch in the room.

Carefully maneuvering around statues and scaffolding, he finally reached the windows where he surveyed the scene below. His gaze traced the path of the levy road as it extended towards the shoreline. He had arrived precisely on schedule; the receding tide revealed the marshy ground between the Mont and the levy road.

He kept working toward the east, where the main entrance stood. It was too risky to leave that way, but if the abbey were under surveillance, that is where the guards would likely be. As he stepped into the entry vestibule, he saw two large doors, eight by twelve feet each. On either side were floor-to-ceiling windows that looked onto the terraced entrance.

He surreptitiously glanced out and saw two men sitting near a small kerosene heater. He wasn't sure if they were waiting for him to show or protecting the abbey from unwanted visitors. Any doubt that he was in 1914 evaporated when he saw their attire; he would fit in nicely.

One of the men stood up and pointed at the window, "Hey Andre, did you see something move in there?"

The other guard responded, "What do you think, you saw a ghost? There's nobody in there. We been here all night, no one could have gotten in there without us seeing."

The other guard motioned for Andre to be quiet. He approached the large front door and tried to open it; it didn't budge.

Jason watched as the man returned to a makeshift table and picked up a ring of ancient keys. Under his breath, he muttered, "Time to go;" he had no backstory for being in the abbey at dawn. A key ground in the massive old lock, and as he ducked down a rear hallway, the front door screeched open. He saw a prayer room to his right; entered it and flattened himself behind the door, stowing his pack under a pew. He slowed his breathing; even a whisper would reveal his position in this tomb-like space.

As the guard entered the vestibule, the clanging of keys and heavy footfalls announced his presence. Seconds ticked by. Despite the chill of the abbey, beads of sweat formed on his brow. The footsteps drew nearer; the guard was in the rear hall, pausing before each doorway. Jason's heart raced, but he kept his breathing still.

The guard was now at the door of the prayer room. Jason held his breath and silently reached for his knife. Was this guy an innocent guard or was he sent here by the Black Rose? Either way, he would need to act.

Suddenly, a voice pierced the silence. The other guard called out, "Nicolas, what are you doing? The workmen will be here soon. If you're caught in the abbey, there will be hell to pay."

Jason heard the guard in the doorway slowly turn and walk back to the entry, "OK, I'm coming, don't get your socks in a knot."

He had to move fast. His French was very rusty, but he thought the other guard said something about men coming. He was probably talking about the work crews. Sounds like they'll be arriving soon, and he wanted to be long gone by then.

He silently left the prayer room and continued along the north wall. Arched windows framed an abandoned rose garden. Looking beyond it, he saw the empty cloister. The rising mist crept through its double pillars giving the place an eerie look of abandonment. The monks would be awake by now if they had remained on the Mont. Moving cautiously forward, he made his way to the back of the abbey, where the Mont's natural defenses precluded the need for guards.

He reached the end of the seemingly endless passageway and navigated through several small rooms before locating the back door. "So far, so good," he hadn't got lost. With so many narrow hallways, staircases, towers, and heavy wooden doors, he couldn't have made it this far if the abbey's floor plan hadn't been available online.

"Uh oh, I might have spoken too soon," as he stood before a massive back door with an equally impressive lock. As he fished out his toolkit, he saw a set of keys hanging on an iron hook. There were at least a dozen ancient keys; he started with the largest, "No luck." He tried the next largest; the door unlocked with a loud thud. Hopefully, his assumption about natural defenses was correct, or the sound would announce his presence to anyone out there.

As he slowly cracked it open, the door creaked loudly in protest, but he saw no one outside. Carefully he opened it wide enough to pass through, then crouched low behind a short stone wall surrounding the rear terrace. Not seeing or hearing anyone, he navigated the uneven stone stairs and took the path toward Saint Aubert Chapel near sea level. From there, he turned southwest and followed a rampart to Tour Gabriel, one of the bastions of the fortified wall. The mist was thicker back here, and he hoped no one would spot him.

As he stealthily moved toward the front of the island, the sound of voices drifted through the mist. He quickly scanned the path, looking for cover. There was a low stone wall to his left and a sheer cliff to his right. Dropping over the stone wall, he pressed his body as close to it as possible.

The voices drew closer. Most of his French was limited to simple phrases and words, helpful only if you're looking for directions or ordering food. He couldn't understand what they were saying, but their voices were more argumentative than guarded. One of them said something like hanté, which he thought meant haunted. He internally chucked; the guard must have thought he saw a ghostly apparition in the window rather than a transplant from the future.

They were on the island's west side now, and the light was a bit dimmer. This would work to his advantage if he had to go on the offense. Just then, a rock slipped beneath his foot and loudly fell toward the sea below. The guards stopped suddenly, and he heard their concerned voices above him. He silently pulled his knife from its sheath and waited, prepared to strike. It seemed now as if they were arguing about what to do.

He couldn't press any further into the wall and would clearly be seen if they looked over the edge. He picked up a rock and pitched it ten feet sideways. The guards looked down, but not straight down; their eyes followed the sound. They exchanged more argumentative words and walked past him, not bothering to look at his position.

As they receded into the mist, he glanced upward and verified they were the same two guards he had seen on the front terrace. Other than these two men, he had not encountered a soul. He hoped his good luck would continue until he got across the bay. He had planned this mission for the lowest tides, giving him a better chance of crossing the sandy marsh unseen in the thick mist.

Once the guards were out of sight, he saw his opportunity. He ran toward the front of the abbey, down the cobblestone streets, then sped for the front gate and made for the road. Damp sand kicked up behind every footfall, making running more difficult. It took at least ten minutes to reach the road. "I hope they didn't see me," he cursed. If the guards followed the path, he would be out of their view for at least a half hour. But if they had turned around, he would be immediately visible from their elevated position.

The windblown sand stung his face, he couldn't have heard shouting even if they called out for him. He started his long trek across the bay, keeping low beside the levy road. There was no cover, and the mist was thinning. He would be visible to anyone driving or walking along it. He wanted to climb up to the road and start running, but he couldn't risk it. If he were seen by the approaching workmen, they would suspect him of doing something unlawful.

A few minutes later, he heard the sound of wagon wheels. In the distance, he could just make out a line of three horse-drawn wagons heading his way. There was nowhere to hide. Before they got close enough to see him clearly, he climbed up the side of the levy onto the road and started walking toward the abbey. He had to think quick, he could pretend to be a worker, but as soon as he spoke, they would realize he was lying.

CHAPTER
34

A S THE WAGONS approached Jason from behind, he turned and waved to them. He half-hoped they would just roll right by, but no such luck. The horses pulled to a stop next to him, and he looked up at the man driving the wagon. He was burly with thick eyebrows that matched his bushy mustache.

He said, "Bonjour Monsieur."

Jason knew enough French to respond in kind, then quickly followed this with, "parles-tu-anglaise?" The expression on the man's face quickly changed from friendly to surprised, then suspicious. Jason pointed to himself and said, "American journalist for the New York Times newspaper."

The man turned his head toward the men in the back of the wagon and said, "Pierre."

A robust man with a sturdy build stood, climbed down the rear of the wagon, and walked toward Jason. He said, "I speak some English; what are you doing here?" Jason breathed a sigh of relief and then launched into his back story.

He introduced himself as John Smith and told Pierre he was a journalist sent to France to report on the International Expedition and the French Grand Prix. He also wanted to report on the Tour de France if he had time. Pierre translated this for the men in the wagon, one of whom appeared to be the foreman.

By now, the two other wagons had caught up to them. Several men climbed down to listen to the translated conversation. The foreman said something to Pierre, who turned to Jason and translated, "You are a long way from Lyon. What are you doing at Mont-Saint-Michel?"

Jason replied, "On the voyage over I heard about the wonderful work being done at the Mont. I thought our readers would be interested and would want to visit when the work is completed."

Pierre smiled, then translated for the foreman. Everyone was smiling now, and Jason could tell Pierre was a well-respected and trusted crew member. The foreman began a long conversation with Pierre. When it ended, Pierre turned to Jason and said, "We will take you to the Mont and show you our work so that you can report it." As if an afterthought, Pierre added, "Where are you staying?"

Jason replied, "I am staying in Pontorson for a couple of days."

Pierre said, "After you've seen everything, we will take you back to Pontorson. Did you walk all the way out here?"

Jason replied, "Not all the way, I rode partway with a farmer."

Pierre nodded his head and then motioned toward the wagon. Jason climbed inside as the men moved to make room for him. The foreman said, "Bienvenue Monsieur," and shook Jason's hand.

A couple of men in the other wagons spoke some English, but since Pierre was the most fluent, he became Jason's designated tour guide. Jason's earlier experience with the abbey had been limited due to the dim light and his need to escape it without being seen. As they approached, he looked at it appreciatively. The sun had broken through the mist, and its rays glistened off the abbey's spire onto the arched windows. It was almost too bright to look at directly.

Even from this distance, the Mont was impressive. It was tiered like a wedding cake, with houses and shops rising up the Mont toward the abbey. The architectural style was a mixture of Romanesque and Gothic. The medieval wall at the base extended halfway around the island, with bastions at every bend of the curve. The lowest buildings in the village were partially hidden behind them.

The abbey itself was immense, occupying the entirety of the island that rose above the village. Trees and foliage sparsely dotted the Mont, and he knew from experience that most of the trees were on the island's far side. As they veered east, he saw the opening he had run through earlier. He looked through it and saw a single narrow cobblestone street weaving between stone and half-timbered buildings.

The wagons stopped, and the men disembarked. Pierre took Jason's arm and began reciting the history of the Mont, most of which Jason already knew. Pierre began, "In the 700's St. Aubert, the bishop of Avranches, had a vision in which he saw the Archangel Michael, who urged him to build a small chapel on the island. So, le Mont is dedicated to the Archangel St. Michael." Pierre squinted as he pointed upward, "From down here, you can barely see the sculpture of the Archangel sitting atop the spire."

Pierre continued as they followed the narrow street, "Around two hundred years later, the Benedictine monks took control of the Mont and made it a place of pilgrimage and commerce. Pilgrims used to come to the Mont to pray to the Archangel. This was dangerous due to the extreme tides, and some pilgrims would drown or get stuck in quicksand."

Jason had been awake for over twenty-four hours; he stifled a yawn as Pierre continued, "During the Hundred Years War, and other wars as well, the Mont was besieged and sustained damage. Parts have been destroyed and rebuilt, which accounts for the mixture of building styles. It makes our work here more difficult as the walls do not meet up accurately, and many angles and small rooms go nowhere."

Pierre paused to catch his breath, "However, the abbey is very sturdy. It is built primarily of granite and limestone. The original church was built over three crypts that extend deep into the rock bed and as other buildings were added, underground chapels and crypts support them as well."

They continued weaving through the village, climbing in elevation as they went. "The English tried very hard to take the Mont from us," a smiling Pierre declared, "but the French are strong, and we prevailed. During the revolution, the monks left, and the abbey became a prison. But about fifty years ago, we began renovations," now they were standing at the front entrance, "and here we are today," Pierre waved his arms at the front of the church.

Pierre toured Jason through the abbey for the next few hours, pointing out the various rooms and architectural features. Now that the sun shone brightly through the tall windows, Jason could see the intricately carved sculptures that lined the stone walls.

They wandered through the refectory, the cloister, and the nave while Pierre continued his verbal history of the abbey. The refectory's intricately designed tile floors complemented walls adorned with inlaid pillars that stretched upwards to form graceful arches. The entire ceiling, with its bronze-like color, arched elegantly overhead. Wooden benches were positioned along the walls, spanning the whole length of the room. It was indeed a magnificent place. He unexpectedly thought, "I would love to bring Sara here," but then he remembered the mission, and his mood became solemn. He had to stay focused on the present, or was it the past?

Pierre noticed the change in Jason's demeanor and said, "I know; this is a very reverent place."

Jason continued documenting their journey through the monastery's various levels, creating written diagrams along the way. He explained to Pierre that making diagrams would help him write his story. He wasn't much of an artist, but Pierre seemed impressed.

It was nearly lunch when their tour of the abbey concluded. They had walked down into the crypts and catacombs, even passed the niche where the device was hidden, and Jason got a much better view of the layout. He was sure he could easily find his way back.

Out of reverence for the abbey, the workers did not take their meals inside it. Instead, they established a dining room in the nearby village in what must have been an old tavern. Jason wasn't surprised by the interior design, "This must have been built during the English rule of the Mont," he thought. Dominating the room's focal point stood a long pine table flanked by benches on either side. Light emanated from a gas lamp suspended above, casting a warm glow upon the table's surface.

The tantalizing scent of food and the invigorating aroma of coffee wafted toward him. His eyes sought the source, and his gaze fell upon two pots resting atop a large enamel stove. The enticing smells caused his empty stomach to growl voraciously, but he hadn't brought food with him, and if he did, it would have been packaged in the wrong century. Realizing he had nothing to eat, each man in Pierre's work group gave him a small portion of their lunch. He gratefully took the bread, stew, and mug of coffee they proffered.

The conversation faded away during the meal, only to become lively afterward. These men appeared to have known each other for quite some time, and he wished he could understand more of what they were saying. Looking at their faces, he couldn't help but wonder if one of these men was working for the Black Rose. He would have embedded a man with the workers if he were in charge of that evil group.

Pierre and the men were interested in hearing about life in New York. Pierre would ask the questions and then translate the answers for the rest. Fortunately, Jason was prepared, and the men were impressed by his descriptions of turn-of-the-century New York, particularly electricity, transportation, and building projects.

After the lunch break, Pierre said he needed to get to work. He described the various buildings and chapels on the Mont and invited *John* to explore on his own for the next several hours while the men finished work for the day. They agreed to meet at the entrance to the village.

He spent the next couple of hours doing reconnaissance in the village and along the wall, gathering any intel he could use if he survived and returned to the Mont. When he was finished, he located the spot where he was to meet Pierre and lay down on the sand with his head on his rucksack. The sand felt warm on his back, and he fell asleep listening to waves crash against the levy. Had he been awake, he might have noticed one of the workmen closely watching him.

CHAPTER
35

J ASON SAT NEXT to Pierre for the six-kilometer ride to Pontorson. The men were tired after the long workday, and the conversation was minimal. As they neared town, Jason noted that it had narrow dirt streets lined with stone cottages in various hues of gray. It was early evening, and few people were out.

The wagon stopped in front of the Pontorson Hotel, and Jason said goodbye to the men. Again, he wondered, "Who among them might be working for the Black Rose?" Then a second question occurred to him, "How many of these men, good people who had shared their lunch with him, would survive the coming war?" He turned to Pierre, asked for his mailing address, and promised to send him a copy of the story he would write about the Mont. Of course, there would be no story, but soon war would be declared, and no one would question why they hadn't received it.

The hotel was a two-story stone building with several attic dormers facing the street. Gas lights illuminated the alcove where Jason scraped his boots before entering. The hotel's operating hours were posted on the front door, and as he opened it, a bell tinkled, alerting the clerk that someone had entered.

The lobby was warm and inviting, with wood plank floors and a large limestone fireplace. The floor was covered with a well-worn Parisian rug, and the room was illuminated by gas-powered sconces and a large crystal chandelier. Thick velvet drapes were drawn for the night, keeping the cold at bay.

The room's sole occupant, a guest, sat in an upholstered chair reading a newspaper. The bald man was portly, and the buttons of his suit jacket strained against his girth. When he heard the bell announce a visitor, he looked up but didn't acknowledge Jason. He then took a sip of his wine, looked back down, and continued to read his paper. Jason thought, "Maybe he's waiting for someone."

The hotel desk was to his right. Most of the wooden cubicles contained keys, meaning the hotel had plenty of vacant rooms. As he walked toward it, a tall man with a mousy face and thin greasy hair appeared from a back room to greet him. Jason hoped he knew enough French to ask for a room. He must have said it right because the clerk replied, "Très bien, monsieur," and took a key out of one of the cubicles behind him.

He motioned Jason to follow him up the stairs to a room that overlooked the street. The small room was sparsely furnished with a chintz-covered single bed, a nightstand, and a chiffonier that looked like it had seen better days. Despite its sad appearance, it was clean and sufficient for his needs. Jason nodded his approval, then the clerk pointed down the hall and said, "Les toilettes."

He followed the clerk back to the desk, inquiring about a tavern where he could get a late dinner. The clerk mentioned the tavern's name but said it so quickly that Jason couldn't quite understand it. The clerk then walked to the front door, opened it, and pointed down the street. He then inquired about a train schedule, and the man pointed in the opposite direction.

The station was nothing more than a ticket booth with benches nearby for passengers to sit while waiting. There was a handwritten schedule posted in the window. He could barely read the departure time for Rennes, a transportation hub approximately sixty kilometers southeast of Pontorson. From there, he would take a train north to Paris.

He turned and walked in the opposite direction to search for the tavern. The town was small, and he didn't have far to go. In 1914, taverns had no menu, so the house special would hopefully be good tonight. He sat at the bar, where a hearty plate of meat, bread, and cheese was placed before him. He finished the meal with a glass of wine, which was surprisingly good.

Returning to the hotel along gas-lit wooden sidewalks was a surreal experience and reminded him that he was actually in 1914. If anyone had told him he would be here, he would have said they were nuts. But Sara had been right about time travel, and he could almost hear her say, "I told you so."

His mind swiftly shifted gears, moving from retrospection to a heightened state of awareness as he noticed movement in the alley just up ahead. He subconsciously initiated his enhanced fight-or-flight mechanism, then analyzed the situation. It would be unlikely that anyone waiting for him would use a gun due to the noise and attention it would create. Most likely, they would try to jump him with a knife or a blunt instrument. The question was, how many men and how many weapons?

As the wooden sidewalk approached the corner of the alley, he saw a glint of steel in the moonlight. The assailant must have thought the alley's darkness kept him hidden as he stepped toward the sidewalk. Before he could strike, the side of Jason's hand chopped down on the man's forearm. He heard the crack of bone, and the knife hit the sidewalk with a thud. He pivoted around the corner, into the alley, and faced his attacker.

The man was brawny, with a long scar down the right side of his face. He had drawn his right arm to his chest but was not running away. He reached down to pick up a pipe with his left hand, leaving his head unprotected. Jason gave him a swift kick in the face with his boot, and the man went down. Down, but not out.

The man was rolling to his left, trying to get the pipe, when Jason, kneeling down, placed him in a chokehold. With a cold, stern voice, Jason asked, "Who are you working for?" When the man did not respond, Jason repeated the question in French. Still no response.

Jason looked him over carefully. He was one of the workmen from the Mont. He hadn't been riding in Jason's wagon, but he was in the tavern at lunch. Jason wondered, "Is he Black Rose, or is he just trying to steal from an American who might have money?"

Jason wanted to interrogate him but never got the chance. He heard a commotion coming from the back door of the nearest building. Not wanting to be hauled into the local police station, he quickly knocked the man out and left him beside his knife. He had just gotten out of sight when someone from the tavern noticed the man lying on the ground and started yelling for help.

He returned to the hotel without further incident. Stopping at the entrance, he quickly straightened his clothing and entered the lobby. It was empty except for the clerk, who pointed at the clock and then to Jason. The hotel door was usually locked at 9 pm, and it was 9:05. He quickly apologized for returning late and headed to his room. Nothing appeared to be out of place. He touched the money belt around his waist, thankful it had remained secure. He cleaned up using the water pitcher and towel on his nightstand.

As he got into bed, he thought about the attack. He wished he'd had more time to interrogate his assailant or rifle through his pockets. The man certainly didn't fit the description of a highly educated Rosicrucian, but that didn't mean he hadn't been hired by one. He had to assume that at least one member of the Black Rose was close-by, maybe even registered at this hotel.

CHAPTER
36

BREAKFAST WAS LAID out in a small parlor just off the lobby. As he walked into the room, he felt the warmth from the fireplace and noted that the other guests were already seated. He filled his plate with eggs, potatoes, and porridge from the mahogany buffet and joined the three men sitting at a large round table in the center of the room. It was just breaking dawn outside, and the table was illuminated by a crystal chandelier. A customarily reserved Jason Shaw now became the inquisitive journalist, John Smith.

He introduced himself to the other three guests and recited the backstory he gave to Pierre and the abbey workers yesterday. He sat next to the bald man, who barely acknowledged him. To his left was a tall, thin man with unruly hair that refused to be tamed. He looked to be in his thirties and said, "A pleasure to meet you, my name is Paul Dumas."

Directly across from him sat an elderly man who introduced himself as Jules Arnaud. Jason turned to the bald man on his right with an expression that asked, "And who are you?"

The portly man replied with a distinctly English accent, "My name is Roger Carroll; I'm traveling through France on private business for my government." He emphasized the word private, then looked away and took a bite of food, indicating he wasn't interested in a conversation.

Paul Dumas had a thick French accent, and Jason had to listen intently to understand him. He was very animated and said, "I am in Pontorson for the local agricultural fair. My company makes farming implements. Would you be interested in hearing more sir?"

Jason could only translate a few words of what Dumas had just said. "How stupid," he thought, "you were going to try to get information from people you can't understand!" Jason then reminded Dumas that he was a journalist and tried to say, "I live in the city, in New York. I'm sure your machines are wonderful, but I don't have use for them."

With dread, Jason looked across the table at Jules Arnaud and nodded. Arnaud looked about sixty, with a warm smile and friendly nature. Unexpectedly, the older man spoke English quite well, "I see that you are surprised at my ability to speak your language." He proudly said, "I am Belgian; I come from Bruges." Jason had seen pictures of the town; it was a beautiful city in the post-war world. Arnaud continued, "I joined the Légion étrangère at eighteen and have traveled extensively."

Jason knew that the French Foreign Legion recruited volunteers from other countries to fight in lands where they had a national interest. So, Arnaud must speak quite a few languages.

Arnaud smiled broadly and continued, "I am here visiting an old friend and prefer the comfort of the hotel rather than a cramped guest space." He was an affable man whose grey eyes twinkled when he spoke; for some unknown reason, maybe the brotherhood of soldiers, Jason liked him immediately.

He kept Dumas and Arnaud engaged in conversation, but Carroll finished his meal and left the room with a curt nod. Jason had been trained that if you want someone to slip up and give themselves away, get them talking. Apparently, Carroll knew that trick since he worked for the English government. Or did he?

Jason didn't want anyone to know he was leaving town that day. He had purposefully paid for a two-night stay, hoping it might throw off anyone following him. He casually left the dining parlor and was at the rail station at 7 am to catch the 8 o'clock train.

Like most boys, he went through a phase where he was fascinated with trains. When he was seven, his parents took him to the railroad museum in Old Town Sacramento. Now he stood in awe as he regarded the vintage steam engine. He climbed the stairs onto the wooden floorboards and took a few minutes to look around.

The car was bright, with large windows extending from one end of the carriage to the other. Passengers could sit on long horizontal couches or forward on leather-clad wooden bench seats. About half the seats were occupied when he boarded. The conductor, his uniform neatly pressed and adorned with shiny brass buttons, walked down the aisle efficiently and meticulously, checking tickets and collecting fares. Jason nodded at him, displayed his ticket, and paid with the pre-circulated francs he brought from New York.

He opted for a window seat to see the passing sites but soon realized his misassumption. As the train pressed forward, only vast farmland unfolded before his eyes. Occasionally the monotony would be broken by glimpses of distant steeples or farmhouses. With war coming, many men would need to leave their farms and villages to fight. He thought, "What would the countryside look like when it was over?"

He was nearly thrown from his seat when the train screeched to a halt in the middle of a grassy field. A chorus of voices erupted, and as the other passengers righted themselves, he leapt from his seat and out of the train car toward the steam-powered locomotive. As he got closer, he saw debris on the track and under the engine car. The conductor pointed at the tracks and rapidly gave orders to his crew.

Jason's expensive attire and persistence finally got the conductor's attention, and in halting French, Jason asked, "What happened here?"

Thinking Jason was a wealthy American, the conductor replied in English. "There was some kind of metal on the tracks," pointing toward the debris, he continued, "farm equipment I believe." Not wanting to alarm the American, he reassured Jason, "The train was not seriously damaged but it will take some time to repair the tracks. We will be on our way as soon as possible, please don't worry."

Jason didn't immediately return to his seat. He needed time to analyze the situation and could think more clearly outside the noisy railcar. Most farm equipment out here was made primarily of wood. "What farmer would leave expensive metal equipment on the tracks." He saw no sign of anyone who looked like a farmer. No, he didn't believe this was just an accident. Someone deliberately tried to sabotage the train. His mind went back to breakfast at the hotel. One of the guests, Dumas, Paul Dumas, was an equipment salesman. "Could he have done this?"

First, the knife attack, and now this. Someone knew who he was and why he was here. But who? Had he been sitting at the same table as the insane Rosicrucian author? No, whoever wrote the journal, they couldn't be responsible for this. The author would have no way of knowing anyone was after him or had even read his manifesto. "No, someone either followed me here or knew I was coming." That only left the Black Rose, which meant it could have been anyone at the hotel.

CHAPTER
37

THE TRAIN ARRIVED in Rennes shortly after five pm. It was a large town situated at the convergence of two rivers, the Ille and the Vilaine. The streets here were cobbled and much wider than the streets of Pontorson, and for the first time, he saw a few motorized vehicles.

As the train slowed into the station, Jason was one of the first passengers to disembark. He positioned himself behind one of the luggage dollies and watched the rest of the passengers leave the train. He saw that Carroll had been on the train with him. It could be a coincidence, but he was skeptical of coincidences like this. He decided to follow him and see where he was headed.

He tailed him across the bustling platform; the man appeared to be looking for someone, possibly him? After fifteen minutes of wandering through the station, the bald man hailed a cabriolet. The streets were crowded with passengers either coming or going, and the cab didn't make much headway. He decided to follow it on foot for a while. As they got farther from the station, the traffic thinned, and the cab sped up. Jason hailed one himself and continued to follow from a comfortable distance.

They were on the Rue d'Orléans, passing in front of the impressive Palais du Commerce, located on the Place de la République square. The Palace would eventually be U-shaped, but in 1914 only the west wing was complete. The cab driver said it had suffered a fire in 1911, but no damage was visible. He slowed to allow Jason a better view of the structure.

The center pavilion, with its long line of stone-arched doorways, opened to a rear courtyard. The second floor was golden yellow with a double row of long windows facing the square. The roof was hipped with skylights bathing the uppermost level. At the top was a large dome supported by pillars. It was majestic!

His cab sped up and followed Carroll's as it turned onto the Boulevard de Chezy. Carrol stopped at the Hotel Dieu and Tavern, but Jason's cab continued to the next intersection, where he signaled his driver to stop. He looked back to see Carroll entering the hotel. Fortunately, there was a large park between the intersection and the hotel. It provided cover as he cautiously walked back to Carroll through the flowerbeds and greenery.

The gardens became more formal as he approached the hotel's east side. Sculptures and large rose bush mounds were interspersed along the path. He followed ornate wrought iron fencing that lined the way, keeping patrons off the flowerbeds. He passed couples strolling through the garden, but no one paid him any attention. He fit in quite nicely with his mustache and fine clothing.

He followed a pathway that veered off to the right and ended at a terraced dining area off the hotel. He soon located Carroll sitting at a table with another man. The man's back was toward Jason, but he looked tall and thin in his fifties with a bit of gray in his hair. They were off in a corner, as if they wanted to be alone, and seemed intent in conversation. He tried to look at the other man's face but couldn't see it without breaking cover and giving himself away.

He was able to pick up a few broken words spoken in French. From what he could tell, it sounded like a business meeting. He heard something about a bank and money and maybe something about Lyon. He heard nothing to indicate that these men were involved with a plot hatched by the Black Rose. It looked like Carroll was a dead-end.

He hailed a cab back to the station to retrieve his rucksack. The cab driver spoke some English, so he asked if there were other means of getting to Paris besides the train. The driver indicated that rail was the only practical means of transport between Rennes and Paris. A motorized vehicle wouldn't work; the only roads outside the city were meant for horses and wagons. He said to himself, "OK, it'll have to be rail," but not directly to Paris; they would expect that.

The driver dropped him back at the station, where he cautiously approached the baggage check and collected his rucksack. He thought, "This old rucksack stands out against this suit; purchasing nice luggage will definitely be on my Paris shopping list." He stopped and picked up a copy of the train schedule before searching out a hotel.

The following day, he took the train to Normandy, booked passage north to Le Havre, then boarded a train to Paris. He disembarked just before the train entered Paris and hired a horse-drawn wagon to take him into the city. He was definitely taking the long way around, but there was an advantage. The extended travel time allowed him to adapt to the culture, seeing men wearing top hats and women dressed in long, form-fitting skirts and jackets. He devoted considerable time to observing their mannerisms and closely observing their interactions. Their odors he could do without; heavy perfume and cigar smoke, not to mention that many people only bathed once a week. That was a cultural norm he would not adhere to.

CHAPTER
38

KARL HAD ARRIVED in 1914, about a year before war was declared. He wanted ample time to create a backstory that would strategically position him near the Front. He wasn't worried about running into Jason; Falcone had no idea what he looked like.

He had a natural disdain for Paris. It was dirty and chaotic, both of which were states he loathed. He found a suitable hotel in the business district, one which he knew Falcone would never choose. At the appropriate date, he placed an advertisement in the newspaper, one that Charles would be watching for. They had arranged this scheme before Charles left. It was the best way to ensure he could be located if anyone else from the Order made the trip.

They met in a pre-arranged place, the dining room at the Hotel Dieu and Tavern in Rennes. During their meeting, Charles told him that Falcone had survived an attack by one of their henchmen and was on the train headed north. Charles was worried about leaving the train, he didn't want to lose sight of Falcone, but if he hadn't made the meeting with Karl, there would be no way for the Order to contact him again. Karl reassured him, telling him not to worry; Falcone would eventually come to them.

To get Charles out of his way, Karl said, "Look, Charles, you said he was posing as a journalist and going to Lyon to cover the race. Go there and wait to see if he shows up." As Charles nodded in agreement, Karl continued, "If he shows, post an advertisement, but this time it should say, "B. The weather is fine here. Why don't you join me."

Charles replied, "Good idea, I'll check the board for departures to Lyon."

Karl let Charles pay the bill. They rode back to the station together and shook hands before boarding their respective trains, Charles to Lyon and Karl back to Paris.

After meeting with Charles, Karl knew his decision to travel back in time was correct. Karl had long assumed he had some form of obsessive-compulsive disorder as he perseverated about every minor detail. It didn't matter if it was a lab experiment, an article for publication, or the plan to release a weaponized virus in 1914. Charles was a competent member of the Order, and Karl had wanted to believe that everything would proceed as planned. But what if something *did* go wrong; he needed to be here.

An expected bonus came from his time travel experience; the night-mares had ceased, his mind was sharp again, and the annoying twitch was gone. Even if Joseph could not complete his mission, Karl was driven by the unshakable belief that he was destined to succeed and Hitler would die in 1914. His grandparents would never have to flee Germany for America.

Before his time trip, he had reviewed the lab notes Andrew left. He was convinced it was an error that caused the animals to die. He told himself, "They never actually proved a human couldn't use the device more than once." He refused to believe he had come this far and would never be reunited with his family. Seeing his family again and meeting his grandfather had become an obsession.

CHAPTER
39

J ASON ARRIVED IN Paris on May 28, exactly one month before the duke's assassination. During the extended trip, he worked on his French, which had improved significantly. However, unless he stayed in France for years and learned the different dialects and slang words, no one would ever mistake him for a native.

As the hired wagon entered Paris, his senses were assaulted by the diversity of sights and sounds. The sepia photos he studied had morphed into live chromatic videos. The streets were wide and teemed with horse-drawn wagons, bicycles, and motorized vehicles. Colorful advertisements for manufacturing, garment, and entertainment districts were painted on the sides of buildings. People from all walks of life and all manner of dress filled the sidewalks.

He smiled when he saw directions posted for the electric tram and subway lines as the streets of Paris were something to avoid. They smelled of horse manure and were full of potholes, making the wagon a rough mode of transportation. He thought of the James Bond phrase, "Shaken not stirred."

The wagon passed the Arc de Triomphe, built over 75 years ago to honor those who fought and died in the French Revolutionary and Napoleonic wars. The names of all French victories and generals were inscribed on its inner and outer surfaces. After WWI, the tomb of the unknown soldier would lie beneath it. Looking south he saw the Eiffel Tower, somewhat isolated from the city's center. The tower, or Iron Lady, served as the entrance to the 1889 World's Fair. As the tallest structure in Paris, it could be seen from quite a distance.

His first destination was the vibrant retail clothing district situated in the heart of Paris. Wearing his sole vintage suit, he recognized the necessity of broadening his wardrobe. Requesting the driver to wait, he strode towards the esteemed men's clothing store, avoiding the dung and debris on the road.

The door creaked loudly, announcing his presence. The beady-eyed shopkeeper turned and eyed him suspiciously, "He must be wary of foreigners," Jason said under his breath. He chose two new suits, several shirts, an overcoat, and a top hat. As he pulled money out of his pocket to pay for the clothes, the shopkeeper haughtily said, "I do not accept American paper money, sir."

Jason replied, "No problem." The shopkeeper's frostiness thawed considerably as Jason placed a ten-dollar gold coin on the counter.

The rest of his supplies were procured at a large general store at the corner of a busy intersection. His last stop was a portmanteau shop, where he bought a steamer trunk to secure his purchases for the drive to the hotel. The trunk had two sturdy locks that would support his story of a transatlantic journey and keep his gear secure in Paris while he traveled north.

It was mid-afternoon by the time he arrived at the Terminus Nord Hotel. He didn't think he'd been followed and hadn't seen the bald man, Carroll, since Rennes. He strode confidently into the lobby, making eye contact with anyone who appeared to be watching him. He was looking for a face he had already seen or someone who might not fit in. In actuality, he was the one who didn't fit in, but he was trying his best not to stand out.

The large room was remarkably grand. Light from electric chandeliers reflected off leaded glass mirrors that hung from wood-paneled walls. Lush furnishings sat on oriental rugs, and well-dressed clientele filled the room. There were working phones at the hotel desk and runners to send overseas telegrams. He saw an opulent dining room to the left of the lobby, and instantly his stomach growled. He hadn't eaten since early morning, but his stomach would have to wait.

In contrast to his experience in Pontorson, the clerk's understanding of English and his improved French made the check-in process straightforward. But when he informed the clerk, whose name badge read Louis, that he needed to take a room for ninety days, Louis's brows raised slightly, and he was immediately at attention. He had been paid handsomely to alert a tall, refined Englishman if an American journalist checked into the hotel. He excitedly thought, "If this is the one, I can get the rest of the payment."

Louis's wife was a horrible nag, and he wished he could leave her, but that would create a scandal in the family. Although if they knew about his little petite amie, Monique, there would be quite an uproar. He smiled as he remembered how Monique looked in the fancy lingerie purchased with the first installment of money.

Jason changed his cover story. A wealthy American ruse would throw off anyone looking for John Smith, the American journalist. He advised Louis he would be traveling and wanted to use the room as his base. To grease the wheels, Jason said that he would pay for the room upfront. He then took another Gold Eagle out of his pocket and placed it on the desk. As he grabbed the coin, Louis' wide grin revealed tobacco-stained teeth. Then, rubbing the coin in his palm, he nodded excitedly and said, "Merci."

He signed the registrar as Albert Martin, a name that would pass as French, English, or American, and would not stand out if anyone associated with the Black Rose checked the register. He volunteered that he had come over on the SS France, stayed in Le Havre for a few days, and then onto Paris for some financial business. After giving Jason directions to the Bank of France, Louis rang a bell, and two porters came forward to carry his trunk. As Jason strode towards toward the grand staircase, Louis's heart sank; the American wasn't a journalist after all. He would report the wealthy American anyway. Who knows, the Englishman may pay him for being so attentive.

The third floor wasn't as loud as the ground floor, but the downside was waiting for the only hotel elevator to bring up his trunk. He would have to grab his rucksack and leave by the back stairwell if he wanted a quick escape. The porters grunted as they lifted his chest off the elevator, and Jason followed them into his room.

He was met with the pungent odor of stale tobacco smoke, its lingering presence evident in the stains marring the once-brightly colored wallpaper. Glancing at the large four-poster bed, he quipped to himself, "I wonder when the sheets were last washed." When he slept on the ground, he didn't mind the idea of bugs; it came with the territory, but he didn't want them in his bed. He turned to the porters, "Could you ensure my sheets are laundered tomorrow?" They looked at each other with expressions that said, "Is this guy real?" but nodded.

He walked over to a long window and looked out onto the boulevard. Across the street was the rail station, the Gare du Nord, with people and various modes of transportation bustling around in front of it. To the south, beyond the chimneys and coal-sooted rooftops, he had a partially obscured view of the Seine.

He turned toward the porters as they stowed his trunk in the corner. Their name tags read Jean and Marcel. Jean was tall and lanky, with dark combed-back hair and a pocked face, while Marcel was short and stocky with a slight limp. They were very eager to assist a wealthy American, and their eagerness heightened when Jason tipped them a franc each. This was a lot of money, and Jason hoped it would buy a few favors. He advised them that his second trunk had been inadvertently left at the rail station in Le Havre. The railway was sending it down to the Gare du Nord, and it should arrive tomorrow. They nodded understanding, and he thanked them as they left the room.

Standing in a luxurious hotel room in 1914 Paris, he thought of Sara again. The historian in her would have relished seeing Paris like this. He yearned for her; just the thought of her caused physical pain. She was the only woman he'd been with since his injuries, and she helped him work through some of the anger he felt over the changes to his body. The only thing he could do now was honor her last request; to stop the Black Rose from killing thousands of men, women, and children.

He picked up the hotel phone, which was answered almost immediately. He ordered an early dinner and unpacked while he waited for its delivery. While eating at a small dining table near the window, he listened to dissonant sounds rising from the street. Smiling to himself he said, "Well, you made it this far; now what are you going to do?"

Over the next several weeks, he prepared for his trip north to the Belgian border. He purchased a second trunk and filled it with weapons, ammo, and other essentials. He would take his rucksack and the extra trunk with him and leave the rest of his things locked in his room. By now, he had established a cordial relationship with Jean and Marcel and was sure they would keep an eye on his belongings. He learned they were both saving money to start a delivery business and were very animated when they spoke of their hopes and dreams for a better life. With a sense of sadness, he wondered if either would survive the coming war.

A few days later, word of Duke Ferdinand's assassination at the hands of a Serbian spread through Paris. Some upper-class Parisians expressed outrage that a ruling-class member would be targeted, but the hubbub died quickly. President Poincare made a quiet trip to Russia to confirm the long-established Franco-Russian alliance, but otherwise, life generally went on as usual in the City of Lights.

Jason knew that various European alliances were in play at the start of WWI. A series of wars in the late eighteen hundreds had established Germany as Europe's dominant military power. As a result, France and Russia formed an alliance to counter the military strength of Germany and its close ally, Austria-Hungary. Britain, also worried about the Germans, formed an entente, or loose unofficial coalition, with France and Russia. Britain also vowed to honor its commitment to protect neutral Belgium.

A month after the duke's assassination, Austria-Hungary declared war on Serbia, and Germany followed suit. A week later, Germany declared war on France, then began a bloody march through neutral Belgium toward Paris.

Germany's offensive was called the Schlieffen Plan, named after a German military officer. By invading through the north, Germany hoped to get behind the French forces who were securing the Franco-German border to the east. The desired result was to trap the French army between the two German forces. Germany would then demand complete surrender.

As Jason recalled Germany's plans, he was formulating his own. Sara had reminded him that Hitler served as an infantryman on the Western Front during the early part of the war. If the journal's author wanted to infect Hitler, he would need to position himself near the Belgian border, where the French and German armies would be separated by only a few miles. The Black Rose would have made the same assumption. If they sent someone to stop him, all parties would converge at the Front. Once word of Germany's advance arrives in Paris, the railways will close to civilians, and the French army will confiscate all railcars. "I need to get on a train while I still can."

CHAPTER
40

CAPTAIN RAPHAËL LAURENT's lunch had just arrived. Since his wife's death, he cooked his own dinner but splurged at one of the cafes close to the station for lunch. As he was savoring his ratatouille, a waiter approached with a note. His irritation at being disturbed was clearly visible on his beefy face. He brusquely said, "What is this? I don't like to be disturbed during Le déjeuner."

In an apologetic tone, the waiter replied, "Oui Monsieur, but the gentleman insisted it was imperative."

Laurent rudely grabbed the note and read it:

Captain, I'm sorry I could not deliver this message in person, but I must remain anonymous as the current political climate is very tenuous. An American, Albert Martin, has been staying at the Terminus Nord Hotel. He spends much of his time watching troop movements from his hotel window, one that just happens to face the station. He claims to be a wealthy American, but I believe he is a German spy. I just received word that he is leaving Paris, heading north to rendezvous with German troops in Belgium. You must act today to stop him before he delivers French intelligence to the Germans.

Laurent looked longingly at the ratatouille, with its tender chunks of eggplant, succulent tomatoes, and zucchini intertwined with bell peppers and onions. He then forced himself away from the table and returned to his office. He was up for promotion and thought, "Catching a German spy would be the pièce de résistance."

Within thirty minutes, he and two of his men were at the Terminus Nord Hotel. They asked the valet if Monsieur Martin was in his room. The valet shook his head but pointed to a tall man walking toward the hotel. Jean and Marcel witnessed the interaction and tried to warn the generous Monsieur, but they were too late.

CHAPTER
41

AFTER SECURING RAIL passage at the Gare du Nord, Jason was walking back to his hotel when he was accosted by two gendarmerie officers. One of the officers grabbed him by the elbow and began to escort him to an awaiting vehicle. Jason was credulous; he had done nothing to deserve this kind of treatment. He protested, but it was of no use. He would have to play this out and see where it led.

He was taken to a station in the heart of Paris and placed in a dark room devoid of all furnishings except a hard chair. He was left alone without providing the slightest bit of information regarding his detainment. While waiting, he tried to devise a rationale for his arrest, if that's what this was. But he could devise no plausible reason; the Black Rose must somehow be involved.

The officer had taken his identification and papers. If they tried to verify his credentials, they would find a dead-end. He used a false address on his identification and listed no contact information. Thankfully passports wouldn't be required until the next world war. He just had to pray that his forged credentials would be worth the money he paid for them.

An officer entered the room and, without speaking, led him into an interrogation room. He watched as a rotund man with a plump face and bulbous red nose entered the room. He was sweating profusely in his tight uniform and wheezed faintly with each exhalation.

"My name is Captain Raphaël Laurent; we have some questions for you," he paused, looking Jason up and down, then continued, "Monsieur Albert Martin, is it?"

Jason replied arrogantly, "It certainly is. Now why have you detained me; I have broken no laws in your country."

Laurent countered, "Why exactly *are* you in our country Monsieur?"

Jason defiantly looked back at Laurent with a none-of-your-business expression, "I'm here on financial business, business that I don't intend to discuss with you or anyone." He added, "Do I need to speak with an avocat or lawyer before we proceed? My financial business is very private, and I don't intend to be persuaded by the gendarmerie, the police, or anyone else to disclose the details." He paused for effect, as if he just had a revelation, then asked, "Is this a shake-down? Are you detaining me in hopes that I will pay for my release?"

Laurent feigned offense and quickly replied, "No Monsieur, we are not interested in your financial business, or your money. As far as an avocat is concerned, we only have a few more questions and think I think we can consider this matter closed."

Jason irritably said, "Well get on with it then, I don't have a lot of time to spare."

Laurent was intentionally silent for a few minutes, then looked soberly at Jason, "You appear very interested in the troops leaving from the Gare du Nord, can you explain this?"

With a tone of disbelief, Jason retorted, "Your troops are going to fight against the German army, who wouldn't be interested in seeing them leave?"

Laurent ignored this question and coldly asked, "You bought a ticket north, Monsieur; this seems very odd. Many of our citizens are fleeing south, yet you buy a ticket north."

Jason was surprised, but kept his expression neutral. He had purchased the ticket only minutes before he was detained. He replied in an exasperated tone, speaking slowly and deliberately, "I bought a ticket to Le Havre. I want to leave before the Germans enter France. I came across the Channel and docked at Le Havre and I'm taking the same route home. If you let me, I'll show you the ticket."

The captain nodded, and Jason produced a ticket from his breast pocket. As he displayed it to the captain, he said, in a conciliary tone, "Look, I'm an American. I am sympathetic to your cause; I just don't want to get stuck in the middle of it. I will try to drum up financial support for your war with my wealthy friends back home. Now I'd like to go. I need to prepare for my departure."

Looking deflated, the captain gave a nod to his men, who returned Jason's credentials, then escorted him out. Captain Laurent's face turned a beefy red when he realized he'd been tricked, and even worse, he'd left an excellent ratatouille behind. He could still smell the basil and oregano. He'd have *them* for lunch if he ever found out who tricked him.

A grin crossed Jason's face as he grabbed a cabriolet back to the hotel. Buying the ticket to Le Havre was gut instinct; he felt his plans had been proceeding too smoothly. The Black Rose wouldn't want him near the frontlines, but that's precisely where his other ticket would take him. The detainment was inconvenient, but at least he knew one thing, the Black Rose was still following him.

On July 18, without further incident, he boarded the train and headed north to Belgium through Lille. Leaving Paris, he saw large crowds waving flags and men rushing to enlist in the army. Unfortunately, they believed that the war would be over in a matter of weeks. Jason solemnly thought, "They have no idea of the devastation Germany will wreak on this country." Two weeks later, he had a front-row seat when Germany declared war on France.

CHAPTER
42

J ASON ARRIVED IN Lille during the first week of August. The war was less than a week old, but German forces would be at the Franco-Belgian border within a few weeks. He was running out of time.

The town had grown up along the shores of the Deule River and, owing to its natural resources, became the center of the textile and mining industries. Before the industrial revolution, riverboats shipped goods, but now Lille was a rail hub. He noted it was strategically located between the Lys, Escaut, and Scarpe Rivers, making it an ideal advance post between Maubeuge inland and Dunkirk on the sea.

He saw the influence of Dutch design on the town's red brick buildings, and soberly thought, "Brick is good protection from fire, but not German artillery shells." He also took note of the industrial buildings near the center of town. These would likely be retooled for military use in the coming weeks.

Stepping off the train to claim his trunk, he snugged his light-weight jacket tighter, the air was much cooler up here. It would have been a respite from the heat of Paris if not for the choking coal smoke billowing from the factories. He scanned the area, but no cabriolets, motor cars, or trams were in sight. He thought, "I might have to drag this trunk to the hotel," but after a few minutes he hailed a passing horse and wagon. The driver helped him hoist the trunk into the wagon and smiled when Jason tipped him handsomely.

After checking into the Hôtel et Restaurant de la Paix, he put the next step of his plan into action. He reprised his identity as an American journalist, but now he was covering the German advancement. Traveling in France had become effortless, but while he was becoming more comfortable in 1914, he was becoming less confident that he had made the right decision to come here.

During the long train ride from Paris, he replayed the events since his arrival at the Mont and realized he was no closer to finding the journal's author than when he arrived there. He needed more intel. His missions as a Navy Seal were supported by cutting-edge intelligence technology and had been meticulously orchestrated; this mission was a complete departure from those procedures. As his trunk was delivered to his room, he thought, "I feel like I'm operating with blinders on, or even worse, like I'm looking for a needle in a haystack."

He had no idea what the journal's author was calling himself, so he just referred to him as the traveler, and the traveler could be anywhere. He had no physical description to go on and didn't even know how old the man was. However, there were some practical limitations the traveler would have to consider when carrying out a plan devised a century after it would be executed. "Hell, there were practical limitations to just acclimating from one century to another."

He had spent hours upon days in Paris trying to locate doctors who might fit the traveler's profile. "Know your enemy" was a fundamental concept drilled into him at the academy. He began to compile a profile of the traveler from a list of questions he needed to answer. One of those questions centered around time. The journal gave no indication of when the traveler would arrive in the past, so he tried to come up with a likely timeframe. The traveler would have arrived on the Mont just as he had. The abbey had served as a prison under several rulers but closed for good in 1863.

The traveler wouldn't have taken the chance of landing in a prison; he must have arrived after its closure. Consequently, his arrival could have occurred at any time within the last fifty years. But fifty years seemed a long time to wait before deploying the virus. Something might inadvertently occur to either himself or the virus, and his trip would be for nothing.

He focused on narrowing the possible timeline. The traveler was a highly educated physician who had risen within the Rosicrucian order. That would make him anywhere from thirty to fifty years old when he arrived at the Mont. His current age would depend on how long he had been here. It would be unlikely for a man over sixty to make it close enough to the Front to deliver the virus. If the traveler was thirty when he left, he would have been in this era for no more than thirty years.

There was also the question of the virus. The journal said the traveler had brought the virus with him or could assemble it once he was here. Since passage through the portal is a one-way trip, the Black Rose couldn't determine whether or not the virus survived the journey. The best bet was that the traveler also had the ability to make it once he was here. His gut told him that he would be looking for a physician who had access to a lab and was at least fifty years old. He wouldn't necessarily be recognized as an American as he had been here for many years.

That brought up another question. Where had he been living? He was going under the assumption that the traveler was American, but that wasn't a certainty. Maybe he was French, then he thought of something else. The Mont is very close to the English Channel. Was it possible the traveler was American and crossed to England to avoid language and culture barriers? He might have even said he was a physician from America, and the Brits would have welcomed him. He thought, "That makes better sense than staying in Europe as an American physician." He might be entirely off the mark, but his gut added an English physician to the traveler's profile.

This thought experiment brought up another issue. Physicians worked in field hospitals close to, but not directly on the front, where the virus needs to be released, but ambulance drivers did. He decided to add a volunteer ambulance driver to his journalistic cover. It wasn't a lie; all Seals were trained as medics, and he had driven through heavy fire before. Besides, this would allow him to monitor the frontline and check out the field hospitals closest to it. He thought, "Next objective, find an ambulance."

Fortunately, it was still early in the war. The French were sending troops toward the east, to the Franco-German border, not realizing the extent of the German march through Belgium. This oversight meant the French army hadn't commandeered motorized vehicles this far north.

The following day he paid a hefty price for a motorized truck with a stake-side rear bed. He covered the bed with a white canvas and painted a red cross on both sides. It took him a few minutes to decide whether or not the red cross would be recognized in 1914, but he remembered that it was first used as a medical symbol during the Geneva Convention of 1864, so he was good.

Deprived of the luxury of armor plating, he silently expressed gratitude to his uncle for teaching him fabrication skills. Utilizing scrap metal, he diligently reinforced the rig's outer surfaces. "It'll protect me from rife fire, but it will be useless against the German heavy artillery guns." He procured a half-dozen gas cans and added racks for their storage. Looking at the cans, he quipped, "I hope I'll be able to find fuel."

He knew the odds of surviving the frontlines were slim. For the hundredth time since he landed in 1914, he wished he had some tech with him; drones, bots, anything, especially advanced weaponry. He needed something to give him an edge and ensure he would survive long enough to stop the virus attack. Unfortunately, the only tech he had was the tech inside him; he muttered, "That will have to be enough."

As he was making his preparations, the Germans were advancing through Belgium. He heard stories of horrendous war crimes. Priests and civilians were being executed, women and young girls were raped, and churches and monuments were destroyed. Two days later, he saw the first Belgian refugees straggling into Lille. They came by wagon, horse, bicycle, or foot, fleeing with only what they could carry.

The next day, he learned that the British Expeditionary Force had arrived by train in Hazebrouck, approximately forty-five kilometers northwest of Lille. Now that the fighting was closer to the northern French border, ambulances would be needed to transfer the wounded from the battlefield dressing stations to advance field stations.

The field stations were mobile, allowing them to stay just behind the Front. Finding one would be like trying to hit a moving target, "I'll need some serious intel." He packed his gear and headed to the field hospital to report for voluntary service. Being a foreigner, he thought, "I hope I don't get arrested again or shot as a spy."

CHAPTER
43

I T WAS SEPTEMBER 7; Jason and his makeshift ambulance were on the outskirts of Hazebrouck. The battle of the Marne in the northeast was underway, and Paris was threatened. He thought about the porters, Jean and Marcel, and whether they had enlisted or were still at the hotel. Even the mousy-faced hotel clerk, Louis, could be at the battlefront. The face of war was all around him, and he had to keep reminding himself that he was not here to change history but to prevent someone else from changing it.

Hazebrouck had been a small market town before it became a busy railway junction in the 1860s. It was now a crucial military target for the Germans as nearly all British supplies had to pass through. It was also the location of several casualty clearing stations which stabilized wounded soldiers before they were sent to stationary hospitals farther from the Front.

During the drive from Lille, he had not left his truck. He was worried that it would be confiscated by the military or even by civilians fleeing northern France. He slept in the back, with the canvas sides down and his hearing enhanced. The area below the bench seat was accessible from the bed, giving him access to his gear and weapons. He knew he could never fire on Allied soldiers or civilians, but he could scare them off.

As early fall came to northern France, the nights were getting colder. Sleeping bags were hardly efficient, but he lined his with woolen blankets from Paris. Anticipating the difficulty procuring food during the trip, he bought extra bread, cheese, and processed meats before leaving Lille.

Nearing Hazebrouck, he noticed the farms on the city's outskirts hadn't been abandoned yet. Food would become scarce as the German line got closer, so he stopped at a farmer's market to replenish his supplies. The fruit stand offered fresh grapes, cheese, bread, and goat milk. The apple harvest was nearing its peak, and adding apple juice and other apple-derived products was a welcome addition to his meager food selection.

At least a dozen or so farms appeared to be represented at the market. There were no men, only women and young children. The women were wary of the strangers in their town. Scarves covered their hair, and they wore long skirts covered with aprons. A mix of languages was being spoken, primarily French, but also what he thought was Belgian and maybe a dialect or two. The women eyed him with suspicion, but they were not hesitant to accept his money for their goods. He was a foreigner, but they must have thought he was part of the army due to the red cross on his truck.

He inquired if a local man might be willing to ride on his ambulance as a field guide. At first, no one said a word. A young girl started to come forward, but the older women moved to stand in front of her. She ignored them and pushed her way through and spoke to him. Her long dark hair was held back with a cotton scarf, and her brown eyes looked at him timidly. Nervously, she said that her father might be interested. He had been injured in a farming accident a few years before and now limped. His injury kept him from farming, but he took odd jobs to support his family. Jason offered to drive her home so he could speak with her father, but she flatly refused. He realized his faux pas and quickly asked for directions to their farm instead.

The place had seen better days. A two-story house made of stone with wooden shutters stood at the end of the drive. The roof was a hodgepodge of tile and wood shingles. A run-down barn sat next to a fenced area that held a couple of oxen, a few goats, and some chickens. Smoke rose from the chimney, which hopefully meant that someone was home.

When his truck entered the drive, a man appeared at the front door. He looked to be about fifty years old and held a cane in his right hand for support. His wavy hair, a mix of salt and pepper, desperately needed a trim, and his beard was unkempt. Standing six feet tall, he possessed a muscular frame, albeit with a noticeable paunch that hung over his belt. His tan skin was wrinkled, evidence of a life spent working in the fields.

The man warily watched him approach. Jason brought the truck to a stop and got out. He smiled and said, "Bonjour," but the man only grunted a response he could not understand. Had he been mistaken? Maybe the man spoke Belgian instead of French, but his daughter had understood French. He tried again, explaining that he wanted to do business with the farmer. The man seemed suspicious but eventually introduced himself as Rene Dumont and invited Jason inside.

The house smelled of wood smoke mingled with the aroma of coffee. Its interior walls were covered with smooth plaster separated by open wood beams. The style was rustic, with practical furnishings. Rene motioned for Jason to sit at a wooden table and then offered him a glass of water, which he gratefully accepted. He could see no one else in the home and decided they were all at the market or in the fields. Jason went through his fictitious back story, finally getting to the point of his visit.

Jason explained, "I'm a stranger in your country and I don't know the roads or the landmarks. I need someone to be my guide, someone who not only knows the routes in northern France, but in southern Belgium as well. Without a guide I might end up in the middle of a river or a battlefield and if I'm carrying wounded, that would be disastrous."

Rene remarked, "That could be a very dangerous job."

Jason agreed but stated, "If the Germans aren't stopped, they could easily take Hazebrouck. Providing medical transport for wounded soldiers will be critical to that effort." Still sensing hesitancy, Jason mentioned the payment for Rene's services.

Rene didn't take long to think about it. He felt guilty taking money for something he would gladly do for nothing. He replied, "I cannot accept payment; it is our duty to protect the homeland." Jason didn't argue. Rene was a proud man; he would find another way to pay him. They shook hands on their new partnership.

Jason informed him, "I need to check-in at the field hospital in town and see if they will give us an assignment. If they don't, we'll strike out on our own." Jason smiled and continued, "I'll be back tomorrow to let you know when we will leave."

Rene replied, "I will be ready," then added, "Where will you stay tonight?"

Jason gave him an overview of his trip from Lille to Hazebrouck and how he had been eating and sleeping out of the truck, mainly to keep it safe but also because there wasn't anywhere else to stay.

Rene responded, "What you are doing is very courageous and honorable, please stay here on the farm. You can eat with me and my family, and then either sleep in the truck or in the barn."

Jason chuckled internally; Rene would not allow him to sleep under the same roof as his daughters. He replied, "Thank you, that is very gracious. I will gladly accept your offer." Jason smiled and added, "If our missions are long, you will probably need to sleep in the truck too, but don't worry, it's not that bad." Jason winked at him and left.

Driving into town, he passed farmhouses that looked more or less like Rene's. He had to share the road with oxen-drawn wagons, but he didn't mind nearly as much as the oxen did. As he neared the city, the landscape changed dramatically. From tree-lined drives and quiet country roads, he now saw tall buildings and heard the mechanical sound of trains.

Passing large rail station, he saw munitions being unloaded from several cars. The British had heavier artillery than the French, but he knew they would not match up against the German heavy field Howitzer. Turning away from the station, he saw British soldiers, fresh from the Channel wearing drab gray uniforms and crowding the streets. They stood in stark contrast to the French soldiers who wore bright red uniforms. The gray uniforms would give the British soldiers some measure of cover in the woods, but red uniforms would stand out, just like waving a red flag at a bull.

The sight of British soldiers caused him to question how best to approach the British Command staff regarding his contribution to the war effort. He knew the British desperately wanted the wary United States to support the war. His best chance was to leverage his position as an American journalist and assure Command that writing stories of German atrocities would help build sympathy for the French and Belgian plight. The staff would be too busy worrying about the Germans to check his story.

Eyeing another group of British soldiers, he stopped and asked for directions to Command Headquarters. One of the soldiers pointed south, "It's about three kilometers down there," Jason thanked him. Turning the truck south, he muttered, "No turning back now."

Jason and Rene received their first assignment a week later. While waiting, Jason had spent his days coordinating with Dr. Barton, the head surgeon at the field hospital. Earlier, he had convinced the British Commander that he was also an experienced military medic and had enough field training to take care of himself. With the Commander's seal of approval, he was allowed to consult the British logistic team to determine where casualties would be the highest.

His evenings were spent dining with Rene and his family, and his nights were spent sleeping on a cot in Rene's haybarn. It wasn't a hotel room in Paris but a nice respite from the hard truck bed. The family was becoming more comfortable around him. With a pang of sorrow, he was reminded of Mike and his family.

Rene and his wife, Helene, had three sons and two daughters. His oldest sons, Henri and Andre, had enlisted as soon as war had been declared. Rene thought they were fighting near the Marne River, trying to keep the Germans from taking Paris. His youngest son, Paul, and oldest daughter, Madeleine, looked to be of high-school age. Rene had difficulty keeping Paul from enlisting; he needed him to be in charge of the farm while he was away on the ambulance. The youngest daughter, Marie, had given him directions to the farm on his first day in town.

The family were simple salt-of-the-earth people who didn't deserve what was coming their way. Jason trusted them. This startling self-revelation made him realize how comfortable he had become in 1914. Despite the threat of death from the Black Rose, he could go about his business without worrying that someone wanted to use him or, worse, tear him apart for the tech inside him.

The dinner conversation interrupted his thoughts; as always, it centered around the war. There were rumors that the Germans were marching on Paris, a fight he knew would be known as the Battle of the Marne. The French army would lose eighty thousand men by the end of the battle, so there was a good chance Henri or Andre would be among the casualties.

He brought a copy of the latest newspaper from town, and they were surprised to read that the French government had fled Paris for Bordeaux. With Parisians fleeing the city, General Joseph Gallieni did something that would have seemed outlandish a few weeks ago: he ordered all motorized taxis to transport soldiers to the Front.

With Paris threatened, fear that the Germans would soon take the rest of France was widespread. Helene was worried that the Germans would overrun their town, but Jason assured her that the British would protect the rail hub at all costs. Besides, their farm was south of town, and German artillery couldn't hit them this far away. Even though he tried to reassure them, he also advised that it was good to be prepared and have a plan to flee if necessary.

A few days later, they received word that the Germans had made a huge tactical error while marching toward Paris; they left a gap in the middle of their ranks. The British took advantage, and with French support on their flanks, they drove the German army back across the Marne and prevented the fall of Paris.

In the papers, reports of a quick French victory were replaced by news of the French and German armies entrenching themselves at the Aisene River in what appeared to be a stalemate. The Germans would now try to out-flank them by moving westward toward the Belgian border. The French army would follow suit; it would be a race to the sea. Jason ominously thought, 'The rest of the German army is now coming directly at us."

CHAPTER
44

A WEEK LATER, Jason and Rene reached Arras at about the same time as the retreating French army. Their convoy comprised a combination of horse-drawn and motorized ambulances, and the situation was deteriorating rapidly. The relentless October rains had set in, transforming the dirt roads into treacherous mud trails. The craters left behind by artillery shells only added to the already challenging conditions. Rene was advising Jason of alternative routes should they get cut off by the Germans.

The line of ambulances stopped at the advanced dressing station, where crews began loading the wounded for transport to the mobile field hospital outside St. Pol. The fighting was fierce, and as Jason entered the dressing station, he saw it was overwhelmed with wounded soldiers. He was immediately assaulted by the acrid smell of smoke and blood that filled the space. Men were moaning as their blood dripped onto the floor, creating crimson puddles. Artillery fire rattled the tent as Jason and the medics hastily loaded the wounded.

Jason's rig could easily fit six soldiers, but he carried ten. The ground was shaking, and the noise was so deafening he and Rene could barely hear each other speak. They were in a wooded area, and Jason was worried that one of the trees would be hit by artillery fire, fall, and block the road, or worse, fall on them.

As they got farther from the battlefield, the road wound through open fields, making them even more vulnerable to attack. An ambulance near the front of the line slipped off the road and became mired in mud. Several drivers stopped to help wedge the wheels back onto the road so they could continue on. It was a long, treacherous trip, and many of the wounded had died before they made it to St. Pol.

Jason and Rene made several additional trips to the battlefront, transporting as many wounded as possible. It was dusk, and they were transporting eight wounded soldiers during their last trip of the day. The battle was raging behind them, and the Germans were mercilessly advancing. Suddenly, several German soldiers broke their right flank and began shooting at their rear. Jason called out to Rene, "Take the wheel." Bullets sprayed the truck as he climbed into the rear bed and grabbed a semi-automatic rifle, one of several that he had sent over from the U.S. As he lay on the floor bed, he picked off the enemy, one by one.

In a feeble voice, one of the wounded soldiers said, "My God, I've never seen shooting like that in my whole life." Word of Jason's expert marksmanship got back to Command, and Jason and Rene were given even more dangerous transports to complete.

A week later, while receiving their daily assignment, Jason learned the Belgian capital was currently under siege. The fall of Antwerp would give the Germans access to its ports, enabling them to receive crucial naval reinforcements, shifting the balance of power in their favor.

Recognizing the urgency of the situation, Jason requested that he and Rene be released from their duties in Arras to support the war effort in Belgium. The Commander couldn't afford to let them go, but he also knew that the British would be out-flanked if the Germans took Antwerp and followed the coastline to northern France. He reluctantly agreed to let them go.

Jason and Rene headed toward Lille, taking the road north toward Antwerp. Jason was no closer to stopping the traveler than when he arrived in France. However, he was aware that the traveler would need to delay releasing the virus as long as possible, and the longer it took for the Germans to reach the French border, the more time the traveler would have to wait. This might give Jason enough time to discover his identity and stop him.

As he entered Lille for the second time in less than a month, the city was under evacuation orders. Residents were fleeing with only the possessions they could carry. Most horses had been commandeered, so wagons were pulled by men and women of all ages. He and Rene raced to get through Lille before the city fell.

They stopped long enough to procure fuel from the retreating military, then headed north to Ghent. Rene guided them through county roads to avoid being blocked by refugees packing the main roads. As they drove farther north, they saw fewer refugees and more abandoned homes and farms.

To expedite the journey, they took turns driving. Jason slept in the back while Rene drove, and vice versa. Jason was asleep when the blast hit. The ambulance appeared to roll over endlessly, only coming to a halt when it collided with a tree. Dazed, he managed to crawl out from the rear of the wrecked rig; the cab had been blown apart. He was at the base of a hill alongside a river, and as his ears cleared, he became aware of the distant sounds of artillery and gunfire. He caught movement in his periphery and turned to see the haunting sight of British and French soldiers' lifeless bodies floating downstream in the murky, swollen waters.

Crawling on rain-soaked ground, following scars made by the ambulance as it rolled down, he reached the road. He found Rene near the top; the blast had thrown him from his seat. Tears filled his eyes as he thought of how devastated Rene's family will be. He couldn't leave the body for the crows. The sounds of approaching gunfire forced him to retreat, pulling and rolling Rene's body with him. He wasn't sure why they had been the target of artillery fire. All he knew was that he needed to get out of there fast.

He almost tumbled back down to the overturned ambulance. By the time he reached it, he was completely covered in mud. He thought, "Might be good cover." He cautiously climbed into the truck bed, located his rucksack, and placed Rene's body near the ambulance. Not wanting the Germans to find his stash of weapons or Rene's body, he took a stick of dynamite, lengthened the fuse, then lit it. The Germans would think the truck's gas tank had exploded.

He ran toward the tree-lined river, a knife and handgun holstered at his waist and a smaller knife holstered on his lower leg. On his back was the rucksack containing extra ammo and a small amount of food. The rifle blew up with the rest of the weapons; it would have slowed him down or been too easy for the enemy to spot.

Taking cover under the trees, he followed the river, trudging through the mud for several miles. His objective was to get far enough south to cross over the road without being seen by the advancing Germans. He had a vague idea of where he was, having only a mental map of the area to guide him. Grief struck him with an intensity that took his breath away as he thought, "Rene would know where to go." He shook off his sorrow and reminded himself of the mission, "The Germans are closing in on the border, Hitler will be close." He had to move fast.

BY DUSK, THE sounds of heavy fire had faded, and Jason cautiously climbed the berm toward the road. The river had veered away, leaving more open ground to cross. He crouched below the ridge until dark, then staying low, quickly crossed the road and headed for cover on the other side.

Then he heard it, rifle fire south of his location, "Time for some reconnaissance." Heading toward the sounds, he kept within the tree line. After a few miles, he spotted a farmhouse on the outskirts of a village. The house looked abandoned, sitting so far off the main road that the Germans may have passed without seeing it. Its barn had a hay loft which would provide an excellent vantage point. Approaching cautiously, at times inching his way along, he reached the house's outer wall. After a pause to ensure no one was near, he entered the barn and climbed the stairs to the loft.

Through the hayloft door, he saw a burning village on this side of a wide river. There were occasional rifle shots but nothing to indicate a heavy military presence. The Belgian army had been destroying bridges and rail lines as they retreated toward France. There must still be a bridge over that river, and either the Belgians were trying to blow it, or the Germans were trying to hold it. If it was the Belgians, he would join them. He had to get closer to find out.

In less than five minutes, he was taking cover at the edge of town. There were several German soldiers in the village square, shouting questions at some locals they had rounded up. Wryly he said to himself, "Pretty stupid, I doubt the villagers understand German."

About a dozen villagers stood with the priest in front of the church. Before he could react, the soldiers raised their rifles and mowed them down. Exercising immense restraint, he managed to refrain from retaliating. When his ears stopped ringing, he heard a whimper and a female voice crying, "no, no."

Creeping around a wall, he saw two German soldiers advancing toward a woman, backing her into a corner between two buildings. The menacing scene was bathed in the glow of fire, and he could see the woman was not a villager; she was wearing the apron of a field nurse. She had been backing away from the soldiers but tripped and was now lying on the ground. The men were leering over her. Unsheathing the larger of his two knives, he inched forward, staying in the shadows until the last minute.

Breaking cover, he ran toward the woman. His knife found purchase between the shoulder blades of the first soldier who toppled onto his face, landing inches from the woman. Without breaking stride, he slit the second man's throat with his smaller knife. It was over in seconds, with no sounds except the woman's whimpering and gurgling from the soldier whose throat had been slit. Motioning her to keep quiet, he retrieved his knife from the back of the first soldier, then tried to lead her away from the carnage.

She was biting her lip and flinched as he moved toward her. He mouthed the word "American," and pointed at himself. After what seemed like an eternity, she pushed herself off the ground and moved toward him. Taking her trembling arm, he led her into the darkness. His immediate objective was to get away from there as fast as possible. He thought, "When the dead soldiers are found, the Germans will hunt us down."

He led her away from the village, back to the farmhouse. She had resisted at first, but he whispered that he was an ambulance driver from Hazebrouck and that his ambulance had been shelled the day before. She was still trembling but seemed satisfied with the answer.

Once at the farmhouse, they stopped for a few minutes, listening for anyone who might be following. She looked at him, trying hard to quell her fear. Realizing he was still caked in dried mud from the river, and satisfied that no one had followed them, he used the hand pump at the well to draw enough water to drink, then washed off his mud-streaked face and filled his empty canteens.

He turned to her and said, "I recognize you from one of the advance stations, but I've been to so many lately that I can't remember which one." It was a lie, but he wanted to find out where she had been working.

She nervously nodded, and he continued, "I was driving a motorized ambulance with my partner, Rene, who was killed yesterday by an artillery blast. My name is Jason, Jason Shaw. I'm an American journalist covering the war. I volunteered to transport the wounded because it gives me the opportunity to get close to the Front. I want to report on the German advancements and atrocities which, I hope, will stir up support for the war effort back home."

She seemed to accept his story and nodded a little less nervously this time. He thought about the scene in the village, then added, "You're safe for now, I'm going to get us out of here." He paused and saw her relax a little.

She replied, "My name is Emma Brownfield. I am a medical student working with my father who is a surgeon at the hospital in St. Omer."

A medical student, this surprised him.

"I was working at the field hospital in Poperinge when the refugees started streaming into town saying that the Germans were right behind them. Most of the workers fled south with the refugees, but a driver and I took an ambulance north to evacuate the wounded." She paused and looked as if she was about to cry, "My driver was not very familiar with the area and we got lost. We crossed the river and wound up at the village just as the Germans arrived. My driver was shot, I ran, and well, you know the rest."

He watched her as she was speaking. She was slender, about five and a half feet tall, and carried herself well. Night vision gave everything a greenish hue, so he couldn't tell her hair color, but it was long and plaited atop her head with whisps that had come loose during her struggle with the German soldiers. The fact she was British didn't surprise him, given the growing number of British soldiers trying to prevent the Germans from reaching the North Sea. Once there, the Germans could launch attacks across the Channel directly at Britain.

A question nabbed at him, "Why had she gone toward the Germans when everyone else was running away?" A woman and driver, alone, facing the German onslaught, something didn't add up. "Was she a German spy?" He would sort it out later; they had to find a way across the river before they were cut off.

She sensed his unwillingness to accept her story but knew they didn't have time to debate it. She whispered, "What do we do now?"

He replied, "We need to find a way across the river, and fast. Dawn will be breaking in a couple of hours and once it does, we'll be extremely visible."

He looked her up and down, and she bit her lip again. Her dress was light gray and would stand out in the dark. He said, "I need to search the house and see if I can find something dark for you to wear. You'll give us away in that light-colored uniform."

She looked down and realized what he had been looking at, then nodded her approval. He motioned for her to stay still and quiet while he searched.

One of the back rooms had a bed and dresser. Rifling through the dresser, he found dark dungarees and a flannel shirt. A dark work coat was hanging on the door, and he grabbed that as well. He led Emma into the room and left so she could change. The clothes were a little big on her, but he found a belt and poked an additional hole in it so she could keep her pants up. Looking down at her shoes, he was pleased to see they were lightweight boots. A dark knit cap was sitting atop the dresser, and he handed it to her. She tucked her hair in it, then he touched her arm and motioned that it was time to go.

They were trudging through dense brush as they neared the river's edge. Emma whispered, "I can barely see; you must be part cat." Jason didn't reply; he just put his finger over his mouth and pointed downriver. Emma could now see lights coming from vehicles that were approaching a bridge.

He had to decide, trust her to keep their position hidden, or disable her and continue by himself. He looked at her for a few minutes as if trying to decide. Then he quietly said, "I need to know why you were heading toward the German lines when everyone else was running away."

Her eyes rolled upward, and she shook her head slightly, but she knew he hadn't believed her and decided to come clean. "I know how it looks. My father and I volunteered to come to France, not only to treat British soldiers but to also try and find my brother. He is a member of the British Expeditionary Force under Field Marshall John French. We know he survived the Marne, then we got word he was sent to the Belgian Front, wherever that is."

She tried to decide if he was buying her story, but his face gave nothing away. She continued, "Father and I treated some men from my brother's division at the hospital in St. Omer. When we inquired about him, they said he was missing."

She bit her lip and continued, "He might be wounded, dead, or even captured. My father is sorely needed at the hospital, so I convinced him to let me travel to Poperinge to work at the field hospital. I was trying to find someone who knew more about my brother. When the other medical workers retreated, I knew I couldn't return to my father without news. So, I set off to see if I could find my brother before the Germans did."

Jason thought, if this is a lie, it's the lamest one I've heard in a long time. "What's your brother's name?" he asked, trying to catch her off-guard.

Her voice broke as she replied, "James."

He gently said, "I don't think I've transported anyone named James Brownfield, but I don't always get the names of the wounded I transport."

He looked back toward the burning village and said, "Look, there's nothing more you can do here but get captured, or worse. We need to make it across that river. If you try to give us away, I will not hesitate to kill you. Do you understand?" She bit her lip again and nodded frightfully, thinking how effortlessly he killed the German soldiers.

The river was too wide to forge by foot and too rain-swollen for horses or vehicles. It was probably the only bridge for miles in either direction; they had to get across it. As they inched closer, he could see four German soldiers. He and Emma hid in the thick brush and watched the men while he devised a plan.

He could take two of them without alerting the others, or he could take all four, but one of them might get off a shot that would alert the soldiers in the village. They would have to create a diversion, a reason for two men to leave the others. What he had in mind was risky, very risky.

He turned to Emma and relayed his plan. Now it was time to see if she were really on his side. She shuddered. After her experience with the soldiers in the village, she was terrified to go near them, but she would not survive out here alone. She remembered how fast he had killed the two soldiers in the village and decided to trust him.

Emma stood above the riverbank, her voice echoing desperate pleas for assistance, while Jason maneuvered discreetly, inching closer to the guards without triggering alarm. In a quick hushed exchange, two soldiers swiftly responded to Emma's distress call, leaving the other two steadfast at their post, their watchful eyes tracking the movement. Jason quietly leapt to his feet and lunged toward them, a blade in each hand. They went down quickly and quietly, "Now for the other two."

The soldiers were less than a foot from Emma, who was shaking violently with fear, adding to the reality of the scene. He struck them from behind, his knives penetrating deep into their chests. One went down immediately, but the other, alerted by the shift in Emma's gaze, managed to turn toward him, pull a knife, and twist it into his shoulder. He swept the soldier's legs out from under him and broke his neck with a quick twist.

Emma's knees buckled and he moved swiftly to catch her. Her face was an inch from his chest; she could see he was barely bleeding. She saw the knife enter his shoulder, but he hadn't flinched. That was impossible; she must have been mistaken. She started to say something, but he stopped her.

Before retrieving his weapons, he said, "Cross the bridge now; I need to do something. Don't worry; I'll be right behind you." He went over to the military vehicle and rummaged through it until he found what he was looking for.

Emma hadn't moved when he returned to the bridge, so he grabbed her elbow and forcefully said, "Let's go." She followed, nearly tripping to keep up. They crossed to the other side and he motioned for her to hide behind a stand of trees. Before she could say anything, he was running back to the bridge. He knelt by the base, and fiddled with something. Sparks began flying around his feet, then he was running back toward her. She couldn't believe how fast he was. He made it to the tree line just as the bridge exploded.

Jason knew the blast would alert the rest of the German soldiers, who would soon be firing on them. He took Emma's hand and guided her quickly through the trees. Gunfire erupted from the opposite side of the river. They dodged exploding bark until Emma collapsed next to him. He stopped abruptly, "Was she hit?"

CHAPTER
46

J ASON CAREFULLY EXAMINED Emma but didn't find any injuries. He took out a canteen and held it to her lips, telling her to drink slowly. When her breathing slowed, he said, "I've bought us a little time but we need to get moving, we can rest once it starts getting light." She nodded and slowly got back to her feet.

His night vision directed them as they walked southwest. The railway wound through this part of Belgium, and he hoped to find tracks they could follow to the next town. He estimated they only had a couple more hours of darkness to get as far away from the bridge as possible. Emma was exhausted, so they kept a moderate but steady pace. Talk was kept to a minimum; besides the Germans, any number of predators could be lurking in the woods.

As dawn broke, the mist lay low in the grass, and birds serenaded a new day. Jason scanned the area, looking for thick cover where they could rest for a few hours. He saw a meandering creek at the edge of a meadow. The far side was covered with reeds and thick brush; it looked like an excellent hiding place. To throw off anyone who might have seen their tracks, they crossed the creek about a half mile down from where they planned to stop. He took advantage of the stream to wash away the rest of the mud. He began to unbuttoned his shirt, then stopped in mid-motion, remembering his scars. He quickly buttoned back up. Instead of wash and wear, he would have to wash while wearing.

He cut reeds and laid them down in a hollowed-out area of sand, making a quasi-bed. It was getting lighter by the minute, and he didn't have time to make another one. He pointed at the hollow covered by reeds and said to Emma, "I know that single men and women should not be sleeping next to each other, but I don't have enough time to make another camouflaged pit." He looked into her eyes and declared, "I'm no Boy Scout, but

I promise you two things: I will not touch you inappropriately, and I will never tell anyone about this."

Looking quizzically back at him, she wondered, "What is a Boy Scout?" She was afraid he might leave her if she disagreed, so she slowly nodded.

Before bedding down, they shared a meager meal courtesy of his ruck-sack. It was only a few stale crackers and a couple pieces of cheese, but it eased their hunger pangs. They drank the remainder of the well water, then, risking dysentery, refilled their canteens from the creek. They lay in the hollow and covered themselves with the rest of the cut reeds, lulled to sleep by the sound of water trickling down the creek.

Jason was jolted awake by the sounds of nearby German soldiers. Emma was still asleep. He reached above and repositioned the reeds for better coverage. This woke Emma, who started to speak; he covered her mouth and pointed upward. Her eyes widened with fear, but she kept per-fectly still. His augmented hearing picked up the sounds of soldiers splash-ing across the creek. "I hope I covered our tracks well enough," he thought.

They were close, very close. He heard at least a half-dozen voices, but there could be more. Sweat accumulated on his brow. He could take out two with his knives, maybe a couple more with his bare hands, but he couldn't take out all six without firing; that could bring the whole Ger-man army down on them.

Emma swallowed a gasp; she was trembling. He looked down and saw a long snake slithering over her legs. It wasn't poisonous; he internally pleaded, "Please don't lose it, Emma," as his hand pressed harder on her mouth.

The voices were louder now, and he could make out some of their con-versation. They were complaining about the long hike and how their feet were hurting. He heard one say that he was going to take off his boots and cool his feet in the creek; it sounded like a couple others were going to fol-low suit. They were so close; he and Emma would be spotted any second now.

There was a flurry of activity, and Jason reached for his knife. He heard hollering and thought the men were calling for reinforcements. A smile tugged at the corners of his mouth as he realized Emma's snake had made its way down the creek toward the soldiers. At least one of them was afraid of snakes and was yelling. He heard footfalls heading away from them;

the cowards were running away from a water snake. After counting to a thousand, he peered out from the reeds. The sun had already passed over them, and he guessed it was late afternoon. He scanned the area in search of more soldiers but saw none.

Emma must have sensed they were gone and was soon sitting up. This was the first time he saw her without night vision. Her glistening blond hair had come loose and was partly hanging down her back. She saw him staring, quickly wound it up, and put the cap back on. With her hair no longer a distraction, he noticed her azure blue eyes, filled with intelligence, curiosity, and fear. She was beautiful, then quickly thought, "But she's not Sara." He guiltily began to turn away, but her voice stopped him.

Her eyes darkened with anger as she exclaimed, "What were you doing, you almost suffocated me."

He tersely replied, "You would have given away our position. You could be dead by now, or worse."

She remembered the night before and shuddered. She was still angry but said nothing more as she brushed the dirt off her borrowed clothing. He reminded himself that her story was very weak: "If I hadn't stopped her, would she have alerted the soldiers to their presence?" He remembered the night before when she helped him at the bridge, "No, she was too afraid of them." Still, he thought, "No matter how innocent she seems, I can't let my guard down."

They ate some crackers, washed down with water from the creek, and set off to find the rail tracks. Jason thought about looking for grubs before they left the creek behind them but didn't think Emma would go for it, not yet, anyway.

A couple hours later, they were both itching. Apparently, they had been the dinner special for a thousand bugs while they slept. Emma said something about making a poultice, but he barely heard her. The sight of German soldiers this far south had reminded him how dismally he was failing at his mission. The itching only added to his irritation. He was no closer to completing his mission than when he woke up at the Mont. The traveler was probably preparing the virus, and if that wasn't bad enough, the Black Rose had followed him to Paris. He had to assume they also followed him to the Front.

But why did the Black Rose need to follow him to 1914? They wanted the book, but the book said nothing about a weaponized virus. That information came from the journal. Did they know of its existence? He wasn't sure. Sara estimated that no one had entered the Room of Roses for at least twenty years; too much dirt and debris had accumulated around the door.

The journal indicated that the traveler came here alone, but he had been supported in his efforts by others in the Fellowship. Somehow, the Black Rose learned that he too, was aware of the traveler's plan. He didn't know how, but it was the only thing that made sense. They had been putting obstacles in his path since he left the Mont. They even tried to kill him, and he was sure they would try again. But even if his assumptions were correct, they didn't get him any closer to finding the traveler. He was wandering through southern Belgium, surrounded by the German army, and babysitting a female while the traveler was preparing to kill hundreds of thousands of innocent people.

As they walked, he mentally replayed every interaction he had either personally experienced or witnessed at a dressing station or mobile field hospital. He scrutinized every physician he encountered, but nothing distinctive stood out about them. He sardonically thought, "The guy wouldn't have a sign on his forehead saying, I'm the traveler. No, he'd be more subtle than that." He was hit with the realization that there was no way to find the traveler in time to stop him. "But maybe I can get him to find me." While they continued walking, he ruminated on it.

CHAPTER
47

T HEIR TREK TOOK them through a forested area undulating with small hills, "At least the weather is cooperating," he thought. It was hard to talk because their whispers were drowned out by the sounds of crickets, insects, and nocturnal birds. Jason didn't want to talk to her anyway; he was on alert for sounds of predators, including the Germans.

A few hours later, they came to a rise and heard the mechanized sounds of a train coming from the other side. As a precaution, they laid down flat and inched to the top. A train was stopped at a small station taking on water for the steam engine. At the sight of the first German uniform, they recoiled back to the protection of the berm. It appeared the Germans were also headed southwest and making much better time by rail.

Jason had no idea how they could out-flank them. He motioned for Emma to stay still while he climbed back to the top for another look. He counted at least a dozen rail cars filled with soldiers and munitions. If he could get to one of the munitions cars, he could set a charge and take out the whole train. As he climbed back down to relay his plan to Emma, he heard the steam engine come to life, and the train pulled away from the station. Too late; hopefully, he would get another opportunity.

As the retreating Belgians fled south, they had been destroying rail lines, stations, and bridges. Apparently, the Germans got to this one first. "Damn," he hoped they could scavenge for food once the soldiers were gone. But to his chagrin, at least a dozen soldiers were left to protect the station. He could try to take them out, but if even one survived to sound the alarm, he and Emma would be sitting ducks. They had found the tracks, but following them would only take them closer to the enemy. Jason muttered, "Things just keep going from bad to worse."

Emma cocked her head as if to hear what he was saying. He looked at her, whispered, "Change of plans," and then pointed west. They kept their distance from each other until it was safe to speak. He resignedly said,

"We have to head west and try to get around them. We can't go east; that territory is now in German control. Following the tracks south is too dangerous, and turning back will take us further behind enemy lines." Emma didn't say anything but nodded in agreement.

As they ventured further, the tree line faded, revealing a valley sprawling out ahead of them. Jason's anxiety was triggered when he saw moonlight reflected on a small stream. A full moon with no cloud cover meant they were too visible. Jason walked close to Emma, hoping they might look like one large animal from a distance.

His lingering skepticism urged him to learn more about her. Although she hadn't given them away at the bridge, she might have acted out of fear of death. He internally chuckled; he wouldn't have killed her, but she didn't know that. To assess the risk of her continued presence, he needed more information. Again, he thought, "The more you could get them to talk, the better the chance they would slip up."

Quietly, he asked where she was from. She hesitated, taken aback by his sudden desire for conversation. She kept her voice low, saying, "I'm from Leeds; my father teaches at the University."

Her voice carried the unmistakable undertone of homesickness, "We live in Park Square West; my father has a small medical office on the first floor, and we live above it."

Jason had to be cautious when speaking like this with her. He wasn't sure how single men acted or conversed with single women in this era, so he kept his questions brief, "Is it just you and your father?"

Emma replied, "It is now. James is four years older; he entered the military college after secondary school."

Jason followed up, "No mother?"

Somberly, she replied, "She died when I was six and my father still blames himself; he has never fully recovered. He tried so hard to save her, but she was very ill. We had been living in the country, but after she died father sent James and I to boarding school, then he moved to Leeds."

She paused as if remembering that awful time in her life. "Mother died of pneumonia. Father took a position at the University in hopes of using the research lab to find a treatment for it."

In a surprisingly sympathetic tone, he commented, "Sounds like a lonely childhood."

She nodded, "I made some friends at the school, but the schoolmistress was very strict. I don't think she was interested in teaching us anything practical. Whenever we were allowed visits home, I would sneak books from my father's medical library and try to read them. Every year I found myself understanding more. After primary school, I convinced father that I could help him if he let me come home. By then, James was in military college, and it was just the two of us."

Jason asked, "So you didn't go to secondary school?"

Exasperated, she said, "Father made me agree to attend preparation school for young ladies instead. I went in the mornings when father was teaching, then helped him with his practice in the afternoons. I wasn't very interested in preparing to be a wife because I wanted to be a physician. During sewing class, I would imagine suturing wounds rather than stitching linens."

Without realizing it, he softly laughed. They walked the rest of the night, and Jason learned that Emma hoped to enter medical school after the war. Her father said that with the war claiming so many men's lives, enrollment would be down. St. George's already accepted women into its medical school, and he was sure that Leeds University would follow suit. Until then, her father had been training her. Now, with too few physicians and far too many wounded soldiers, she was often called upon to treat them herself.

Jason mused; instead of tripping her up by encouraging her to talk, he began believing every word she said. "But still..."

He knew Emma probably had a million questions for him, questions that he did not want to answer. He indicated that they should stop talking; he needed to stay alert. This assuaged her. As they walked through small swollen streams, moonlight cast shadows on the outline of mountains to the southwest. He whispered that they were coastal mountains, far away.

Even wearing jackets, the nights were cold; walking kept their body temperatures from falling too low. They needed to find food soon. The growling of their stomachs almost drowned out the buzzing of the insects. Emma was still itching and had found nothing to make a poultice with. She was so preoccupied with this; she didn't notice that his bites had already healed.

Occasionally, they came across an abandoned farm or barn, but the Germans had taken everything of value before burning them down, especially foodstuffs. Sometimes they would find chicory plants and dig up the roots. They weren't very tasty raw but offered some nutrition. They also found a few sugar-beet plants the Germans hadn't plowed over with their vehicles. They gorged on the beets but Emma saved the greenery; she might be able to use it for a poultice if she found additional ingredients.

Fatigue was setting in; Emma's pace slowed, and she unconsciously stopped talking to save energy. Jason wondered how much longer she would be able to walk. His enhanced musculoskeletal system allowed him to walk longer and move much faster than she could. Even with his lingering suspicions, he would never leave her to be raped or killed by the Germans.

On the fourth day, they came across another burned farmhouse. A few of its whitewashed walls were still standing, and they could see the remnants of a red-tiled roof. They walked around back and found a lone goat. It must have run from the soldiers before they could catch it. Now it was looking for its owner and, by the looks of it, needed to be milked. Between the two of them, they managed to corral the goat and milk it, laughing as the milk squirted into their faces as well as their canteens.

It wasn't solid food, but it was nutritious. Jason wanted to kill and dress out the goat, but they couldn't risk starting a cooking fire. The alternative was not cooking it, but they didn't want to get sick from eating raw meat. He grudgingly decided to give the goat a pardon. They tied the poor thing up with a piece of rope that had survived the fire. They would untie it before moving on and leave it to roam. Once the goat's fate had been decided, they hunkered down in a partially intact area of the farmhouse and got the best sleep they'd had in days.

The following day, they found some unbroken bottles in the rubble and collected as much milk as the old goat would give. Jason explored the remainder of the farm and found an old well beyond the charred rear wall of the house. He was able to fix the damaged hand pump and refill his canteens.

Surrounding the well, remnants of burnt structures provided ample cover and seclusion, ensuring both privacy and protection. He let Emma clean up first, then it was his turn. He made sure Emma couldn't see his exposed skin as he washed. Then he used his small knife to scrape the stubble from his chin. "Ah, much better," he thought.

Emma seemed stronger after consuming the milk. He watched as she mixed it with the beet greens and applied the poultice to her bites. She really was an enigma.

CHAPTER
48

THEY STRUCK OUT again at dusk, heading south toward an old-growth forest. Jason wasn't sure if Emma's silence was due to exhaustion, fear of the German soldiers, or even anger toward him. As they approached the forest, he could see trees so tall and thick that they blocked what little moonlight blinked through the swirling clouds.

The trees were of a Chaparral species, and while the thick branches made for a great cover, the above-ground roots made walking hazardous. He took the lead, scanning for danger, particularly for wild boar, known to hunt in these forests. He was unsure why, but her silence disturbed him. "Who knows," he thought, "maybe she's plotting against me?"

He asked, "Are you alright?"

Her brief response was, "You lied to me."

He stopped and peered at her through the darkness, "What are you talking about?"

"You are not a journalist. I don't even think you're an ambulance driver. I think you're a soldier, the only question is, for whose side?"

Jason was blindsided. He had to think fast. What motivated the question? Did she see his scars back at the well? No, that wouldn't have caused her to think soldier; she might have considered injury, but not military. Then a dreadful thought struck him, if she was a spy, this could be a tactic to keep him off guard; after all, a good offense is a good defense. His training officer had advised him, "If you're lying, mix in as much truth as possible and you're more likely to keep your story straight." So, he replied, "I was a soldier in America, but not anymore."

With furrowed brows, she declared, "So you lied."

They stopped walking, and he motioned her to sit atop one of the exposed tree roots.

He began quietly and slowly. "Emma, when this war is over, does James intend to stay in the military?"

She started to say, "He has nothing to do with this." Instead, she replied, "I'm not sure. Before the war started, I would have said yes, but I pray the death and mutilation of so many men will have changed his mind. I've looked into the eyes of the wounded. I've seen their injuries, they might survive, but their lives will be forever changed."

He immediately thought of himself, then Rene, and how his death will change his family's fortune. He quickly put those ruminations aside, "If your brother leaves the military, what will he do?"

She really didn't know where this conversation was headed, and she was taken off-guard by his questions about her brother. "James has a good head for money. I think he would make a good banker," then added, "but I doubt he would agree."

Jason replied, "For the sake of this discussion, let's assume that ten years from now, James is a banker and maybe even has a family. If you were to introduce him to me, would you say, this is my brother, James; he is a soldier?"

Exasperatedly she replied, "Of course not, that was a long time ago. It would have nothing to do with his current status."

Jason then said, "Would you be lying by omitting the fact that he was a trained soldier who fought in the war?"

She was caught in his trap, "Is that what happened to you?"

He noticed her deflection, something a spy would be trained to do. He carefully crafted his response, "In a way, yes. I was a trained soldier, but I didn't fight in a war. We had smaller, more clandestine battles. After a while, I became disillusioned and left the military."

She shifted atop the root, "So how did you become a journalist?"

He looked upward, describing a motivation based on pure truth, "My love of history. I thought that reporting on current events would be observing history in the making."

She began to speak again, but his raised hand stopped her. There was a low growl coming from the darkness ahead. It was getting louder, and now Emma could hear it as well. Instinctively she reached for his arm and clutched it.

Without thinking, he placed his hand over hers and squeezed. Then he took her hand and slowly guided her onto her feet. They had been sitting on the root of a very tall tree. Even with his enhanced vision, he could not see the top of it. Without a word, he hoisted Emma onto one of its branches and told her to climb up as far as possible. He then handed her one of the pistols.

The growling was much closer now. He nodded toward it, "I don't think they can reach you, but if they do, wait until they get close enough so you won't miss. Remember, the Germans are out there too, and the sound of gunshots could lead them to you. If that happens, you decide how you want to use the gun."

Fear gripped her, and she began to protest. But as Jason saw the bared teeth of the first wolf, he urgently cried, "Climb, climb, climb," and then turned to face the wolf pack.

At least six wolves faced him. The alpha advanced while the rest hung back. The animal was enormous; he guessed around a hundred pounds. "Alpha was an adept hunter." He unsheathed the larger of his two knives while keeping the broad tree trunk at his back. He needed room to maneuver but didn't want one of the other animals to circle around behind him. The growling was reaching a fever pitch.

Jason intently studied the giant beast, with its teeth bared and glistening. Saliva was drooling from its open mouth in anticipation of a meal. He knew the others would wait until they were invited into the fight; it was the alpha's kill. He tried to get a bead on the soft spot below the animal's neck, but the wolf was sly and kept his massive head angled down in a protective stance.

Showing no fear, he quickly ran through his options. The animal had a broad, thick skull. Even if he could penetrate it with his knife, the animal could still strike a fatal blow. He could follow Emma up the tree, but despite his speed, the animal's sharp teeth could penetrate his legs and pull him down. If he threw the knife without a plausible target, he would be left without his best weapon, and the animal would pounce for the kill. He could use the other pistol, and alert any German within ten miles. He calculated only one possible chance of survival, and it relied on his enhanced speed and reflexes.

Emma climbed far enough for safety. Gazing through the hushed moonlight, she saw the unfolding spectacle below, watching in terror as Jason faced the pack alone.

He waved the knife at the alpha as if taunting him, then took one step toward the beast. As the wolf lunged, Jason rolled onto his back, plunging the knife into the animal's heart as it passed over him. The wolf reflexively shuddered and fell to the ground. In one smooth movement, Jason retrieved his knife and bounced off the thick carcass onto the tree trunk. Emma looked on in stunned disbelief. As his body hit the trunk, she screamed at him to climb.

The death of their leader had temporarily stunned the rest of the pack, but they were in full attack mode now. As he scrambled up the tree, feet looking for purchase, he could feel the heat of the pack's breath rising toward him. The branch under his foot cracked as one of the pack members tore at it. His hands clawed at the trunk as the branch gave way, his feet dangling.

Just then, a hand came into view above him. He grabbed it, worried he might pull Emma down, but she was solidly locked onto a thick branch. As she pulled him up, he heard the frantic sound of animals yelping as the branch's weight pushed them downward in a domino effect. A rush of wind parted the leaves above, and the moon peaked behind the clouds. They looked down in relief as the defeated pack dragged away the body of their dead leader.

They climbed higher; they couldn't be sure a German patrol hadn't heard the melee. They climbed high enough to be invisible to anyone below. Jason worried that if a patrol got close enough to the tree, they would spot evidence of his fight with the wolf pack and get curious. Just as he was about to share his concerns with Emma, moving lights appeared in the distance.

Jason and Emma silently clung to the tree, watching as the lights drew closer. As he suspected, it was a German patrol. Their vehicles could not drive into the forest, but the Germans could send out a foot patrol for reconnaissance. His worries were validated when the vehicles stopped a few hundred yards from the forest's edge. His high school German classes were coming in handy on this mission. He heard an officer order a pair of foot soldiers to check the forest for signs of Belgian troops.

Moonlight reflected off rifle barrels as the two men approached the trees. Jason internally chuckled as they swore, tripping on roots. Although he and Emma were at least thirty feet above them, he could make out snippets of conversation as words floated upward on the breeze. The soldiers were young; one spoke about missing his girlfriend, who was still in Dusseldorf. The other lamented about his wife and young son in Berlin. Jason was disappointed. He wanted to know where they were headed, not where they had come from. But his disappointment was short-lived as he heard one of them mention joining the battle at the Yser River.

The soldiers were close to their position now. They were navigating the dense forest underground, and he could hear their heavy breathing. Then one said something about a streit, or fight, and suddenly they were right below. He felt Emma tremble with fear. Fortunately, the breeze camouflaged the ensuing movement of the leaves. He reached out, put a reassuring hand on her shoulder, and felt her trembling gradually cease.

The soldiers were looking at the pool of Alpha's blood and noted the disturbed ground surrounding it. One of them pointed at the tree branch that had fallen along with the rest of the pack. They were motioning upward now, pointing at the fresh scars on the trunk. Fortunately, the wolves' claw marks obscured signs of his and Emma's frantic climb. Flashlight beams licked up the tree trunk but could not reach them.

After scanning the area for several long minutes, the soldiers moved deeper into the forest, looking for signs of the fleeing Belgian Army. Jason whispered, "We need to stay put until morning. Do you think you can hold on that long?" Emma nodded in the affirmative, and he mentally prepared for the long night ahead. He couldn't tell what Emma was thinking, but his mind returned to their previous discussion.

When he and Emma started this journey together, he promised her two things: he would not touch her inappropriately and would never tell anyone they had slept beside each other. He never said he wouldn't lie to her. But she had just risked her life to save him, and this excuse was little comfort to him now. He was still in love with Sara, he shouldn't care what Emma thought, but he did. As soon as he got her to safety, he would say goodbye and continue his mission. That would be the end of it.

CHAPTER
49

T HE GERMANS PULLED out before daybreak, and there was no indication they had left troops behind. The clouds had coalesced into grey thunderheads, and it was lightly raining. They cautiously climbed down the tree, clothes soaked and hands bleeding from their arduous climb the night before. Emma looked miserable, and Jason feared she could not walk any further today. She still had the gun, and his first inclination was to hide her nearby while he scouted for shelter and maybe even some food.

She was adamant she would not be left alone, especially now they were sure the enemy was close. He half-carried her through the forest to the edge of a roiling stream. After refilling their canteens, they followed the bank for a couple of miles, keeping within the tree line until the water disappeared over a sharp cliff. It was a dead end, and rain had swollen the stream to the extent that it was too dangerous to cross.

They were now trapped between the raging stream to their west and the German Army to their east. Jason thought about back-tracking; they might find someplace to cross it, something they might have missed. But he vetoed that idea; there was no way Emma would make it. Instead, they veered away from the stream and continued forward, the tree canopy providing a measure of protection from the rain.

They trudged along, soaked to the bone and freezing. He knew Emma would not survive the harsh elements. As he scanned the area looking for something he could build a shelter with, the rainfall gradually slowed to a light drizzle. The trees were thinner here and he saw sunlight ahead. He gently seated an unprotesting Emma, against a tree before heading off to reconnoiter. Staying low, he eventually emerged into a small meadow, sheltered by a rocky wall along its eastern edge. As his gaze swept the perimeter, he caught sight of a rustic cabin nestled within the tree line on the other side.

With his knife at the ready, he continued along the meadow's edge until he reached the cabin. It appeared deserted, but before entering, he thoroughly searched the surrounding area. He found a shed stacked with enough wood for an entire winter, and a tool shed with a ceiling hook for hanging wild game. At the rear of the tool shed, he saw the door to a meat smoker. Realization dawned, "This is a hunting cabin."

He approached the cabin door with a little less trepidation. It was unlocked, not unusual for a place this secluded. If someone wanted to get in, they could just break a window. No sense in risking that. He excitedly searched the cabin. He found wool blankets, extra clothing, and, more importantly, canned goods and dried meat in the pantry. At first, the canned goods surprised him, but then he recalled that the canning process had already been invented, by a Frenchman no less.

Backtracking to Emma, he noticed something glinting up high on the rock wall. He had to ensure it was safe to return to her. Near the bottom of the wall, camouflaged by brush, he found a rough trail leading upward. At the very end, he discovered a hunter's blind skillfully dug into the rugged face of the wall. The cabin's owner must use the blind to shoot game that wander into the meadow. The setup was perfect, but he would use it for a different purpose.

They couldn't risk a fire in the wood stove. Jason judiciously helped Emma peel off her wet clothes, then wrapped her in a wool blanket. They ate a meal of dry meat and canned beans. Even cold, it tasted delicious. After dinner, he tucked her in bed, and she managed a weak "Thank you." He grabbed the rifle found hidden under the wooden floor and climbed to the hunter's blind to watch over the cabin.

Two days later, Emma felt she was strong enough to travel again. Jason wanted to protest, but he knew the window for stopping the Black Rose was closing fast. Until recently, he had one thing in his favor, the rainy season had come early and slowed troop movements. The traveler couldn't risk acting until he was sure Hitler was near the Front. But now, with German troops near the border, the traveler would soon release the virus. He calculated he had less than two weeks to find him. They packed extra food in his rucksack, grabbed some rain gear from the shed, and left the cabin behind.

CHAPTER

50

THEY WERE WALKING through a copse of poplars the following day when they heard artillery fire. Reflexively, they hit the ground and crawled to cover. They were halfway up a ridge that overlooked a wide river. Emma waited while Jason crawled to the top for a better view. A dirigible hung in the partly cloudy sky a few miles west of them. Another round of gunfire caused him to turn and he saw the town. The Germans were clearing it of anyone who might be a threat.

He crawled back down and somberly looked at Emma. "We are definitely behind enemy lines. The Germans are pounding the Belgian army, who are trying to hold their position on the other side of what I believe is the Yser River. I can see a canal system on this side of the river, which is consistent with what I've seen on the map. The bridge puts us at Tervate."

After hearing this news, she anxiously inquired, "So now what, can we get around?"

He somberly shook his head, "There's a dirigible overhead, and I can see dunes to the west, which means we're too close to the sea. If the Germans make it to the coast, there won't be a route around them. We could try to head back to the east, toward Lille, but I think it's probably in German hands by now."

Emma decided days ago that she would not allow herself to be captured by the Germans again. Instead, she would take the handgun Jason gave her and use it on herself. Resolutely she looked at him and replied, "No, let's try to find a way to cross, whatever the cost." He nodded his agreement.

The sight of the canal system reminded him of a small piece of history. During October 1914, the decimated Belgian army fought fiercely to hold a small strip of land in Flanders, south of the Yser River. Although they were dangerously close to being overrun by the Germans, King Albert ordered them to hold their ground at all costs. It took a daring plan to save them.

The Belgian engineers opened the canal locks between Dixmude and Nieuport, flooding the ground between themselves and the Germans. This desperate maneuver kept the Germans at bay until British and French forces joined the battle. Military historians cited the battle as the beginning of trench warfare, as both sides would dig trenches and hold their positions for the next three years.

He and Emma had to cross before the locks were opened, or they would be trapped on this side of the river along with thousands of German soldiers. He crawled back up the ridge and surveyed the battle with a more strategic eye. The Germans were shelling the Belgians, and they were returning fire. Both sides were taking cover behind structures on each side of the river. Buildings were being razed by artillery shells, and the streets were full of craters. The acrid smell of smoke permeated the air.

Movement below caused him to turn his attention to a church on the outskirts of the German-occupied village. The front had severe artillery damage, but the rear was still standing. The movement turned out to be a priest running toward a stand of trees. The priest quickly led two civilians into the church; he repeated this three times. Jason thought, "What is he doing? They will be trapped."

As he turned back toward Emma, he felt a rumble in the ground, followed soon after by the sounds of motorized vehicles coming from the north toward them. A sense of dread washed over him. He thought, "German reinforcements." They would be sandwiched between the two German forces if they didn't move fast. They had no choice; he grabbed Emma's arm and pointed to the church.

They kept low within the tree cover until the last minute, then sprinted toward the church. They ran through the back doorway and were greeted by the Belgian priest, who immediately placed himself between Jason and two terrified children. Jason quickly raised his hands and, in French said, "We're running from the Germans too. There are more coming down the road. Do you have a place to hide?"

Without a word, the priest gestured for them to follow him. They were led to a small alcove off to the right of the vestibule where a few civilians were climbing through the floor to a sublevel, maybe a cellar? They would be sitting ducks down there, but there really wasn't a choice. The priest urged them to get down the stairs with the others. They complied, but the priest didn't follow. Instead, he closed the hidden panel on the floor and knocked some rubble on top of it. Jason thought, "We're trapped," no choice now but to move forward with the rest of the group.

No one spoke, not even the children. The priest must have warned them to keep quiet, then stayed behind to cover their tracks. At that moment, Jason heard loud German voices coming from somewhere above them. As a shot rang out, he knew the priest was dead. He braced himself to fend off the soldiers but heard nothing except footfalls as the church was searched. Within minutes, the sounds of boots on the floor above them faded away.

The air was damp and musty. It was dark and quiet; no one was moving. Jason engaged his night vision and looked around; it was not a cellar but a tunnel. Emma was right beside him, while ahead of him were a dozen civilians lined up against the wall. The oldest was a male who looked to be in his sixties, while the youngest was a girl who was around ten. They were paralyzed by fear. He looked down the tunnel but couldn't see an opening. He took Emma's arm and slowly approached the front of the line where the elderly man stood.

In whispered tones, Jason asked him where the tunnel led. The man replied in Belgian, but Jason only understood a few words. One of the women spoke up, "Do you speak French?" Jason nodded yes.

"My name is Celia; I can translate for you. This is my father Gerrard. He says this is an escape tunnel built many years ago for a different war. It used to lead to the river's edge, but no one has been down here for many years. He doesn't even know if the river entrance is still open. However, the priest just told us that the canal locks have been opened in Nieuport, so within a few hours this tunnel will be under water. We need to get back into the church as soon as it's safe."

Jason shook his head, "Please tell these people that we cannot go back. The priest covered the entrance to prevent the Germans from finding the tunnel. We need to go on and see if we can find the opening before the tunnel fills with water." Peering ahead, he said, "I see very well in the dark, so I will take the lead. Tell everyone to take the hand of the person in front of them and walk slowly."

She nodded and did as he asked. He moved them as fast as he could. This tunnel would be their watery grave if the wave hit before they got out. Dirt from the tunnel roof rained down upon them every time a German artillery barrage went off. It was difficult to breathe. Jason doubted if there were any intact air shafts, oxygen would soon become an issue.

The farther they walked, the damper the tunnel became. After they had walked a hundred feet or so, the ground became muddy. Emma whispered, "I don't know how you are doing it; I can't see a thing."

He replied, "I've always been able to see well in the dark. It has something to do with my rods, or is it my cones? Anyway, my father was the same way, so it must run in my family." He hoped the lie would satisfy her but didn't think it would.

The tunnel was sloping downward now. He grimly thought, "If the opening is below the river, the next section will be impassable." He hoped they would be in luck. But luck was not on their side. There were too many people breathing too little oxygen. They dropped to the wet ground one by one, unable to go on without fresh air. Jason lowered his metabolism to decrease his oxygen consumption, but Emma also struggled. He helped her to the ground and placed her back against the tunnel wall. Reluctantly he left her and headed for the entrance, he had to get oxygen into the tunnel, or he would lose them all.

He mucked through a couple hundred feet of mud and thought, "I must be getting close; the river wasn't that far from the church." The tunnel started gradually sloping upward, but he still couldn't see light ahead, and then he discovered why. The tunnel roof had caved in, maybe from the shelling or the battering of river water; it didn't really matter. He knew that with every artillery burst the tunnel behind him was at risk of collapse. He had to get it open.

He started up the debris pile but thick mud and rock debris caused him to slip backward. He frantically kept at it, and when he finally found a foothold, he climbed as close to the top of the pile as he could get. He pulled out the larger of his two knives and began digging. He had no idea how deep the mound was; he just kept stabbing away at it.

Two more took its place for every handful of mud and debris he removed. It seemed to be taking forever. He had no idea if Emma or any villagers were still alive; he lost all track of time. Suddenly his knife poked through an opening, and he breathed fresh air. This reenergized him, and he dug even faster. Eventually, he was able to get his entire body through the opening. As his head poked through, he was slapped in the face with waves of water. He exclaimed to no one but himself, "I have to get the others out before the waves erode the opening and collapse the entrance again."

The villagers were coughing and sputtering as he neared, but they were alive. Light now streamed into the tunnel, and the group moved faster. Starting with the old man, he lifted each villager up and out of the opening. Emma was last, followed by himself. Once outside, he found the group in terrified silence, hiding near the river's edge in the reeds. He thought about collapsing the tunnel again but worried they might have to retreat back into it.

It was now dusk; the artillery fire would soon cease. If they could find a way to cross the river, the darkness would shield them. A river crossing would be hazardous, especially with the flood waves coming, but it would be certain death to do nothing and wait for the Germans to find them.

Jason looked around and saw Gerrard inspecting two old wooden boats in the reeds. The old man pulled a small knife from his pocket and began cutting the reeds. As Jason watched, he gradually understood what Gerrard was doing. The old man was planning to lash the boats together to make a single boat large enough to carry all of them.

Inspecting the boats, Jason realized they looked worse than they really were. The bottoms had been coated with tree resin, so they were in good shape. Boards were missing from the hull, but there would be enough by lashing the boats together. They had to work fast. Jason wanted to push off in two hours. He looked at the group, at the terrified children. There was a dismal chance of survival, but they had no options. If the boat sank, he could swim across, but the others wouldn't make it.

The boat was ready by dark. Two salvaged boards served as paddles; Gerrard would take one and Emma the other. The rest of the group would lay low on the bottom of the boat while Jason watched for floating debris and directed them across.

Before they set off, Emma stood close to Jason and whispered, "Thank you for all you've done to help these people, not to mention how many times you saved my life. You could have made it faster alone, but you've risked your life for us." She paused as she looked toward the river, "It doesn't look good, does it?" She looked back at him with eyes that were pleading for reassurance, but he had none to give. Instead, without thinking, he bent down and kissed her, and to his surprise, she kissed him back. They clung to each other for a few seconds, then he pulled back and walked toward the river.

He and Gerrard steadied the boat while the others climbed in. The children were exhausted and scared to death. A couple of women soothingly talked to them while placing the children's heads in their laps. He was unsure, but he thought they told the children to keep their eyes closed until the boat reached the other side. One of the teenage boys found a stick in the water. Then one of the women tore off a piece of her white petticoat and tied it to the end. This would be their flag of surrender; they would take it out and wave it low to the water as they neared the opposite shore. Hopefully, this would stop the Belgian army from blowing them out of the water.

It had stopped raining, and the air was still. The half-moon was obscured by clouds, making it more difficult for them to be seen. Jason gave directions to the oarsmen, trying to keep them from drifting sideways and being toppled by the current. Water was leaking into the bottom of the boat, and the women were working hard to keep the children calm. He gave a couple of the younger men his empty canteens and motioned them to start bailing; they quickly obliged.

Jason heard rifle shots and felt water spraying around the boat. The shots were coming from the northeast side of the river, from the Germans. The sounds caught the attention of the Belgians, who began shooting. He wasn't sure if the Belgians had spotted them or if they were just returning the German fire. Neither side had night vision, so it would be a random shot if they hit the boat.

He wasn't sure how long it would take to get out of German rifle range or if they ever would. They had passed the halfway mark, and he was beginning to see the human shapes on the river's southwest side. More shots rang out from the north; Gerard's head flung backward, and he disappeared over the side of the boat. Celia muffled a scream and looked overboard but saw nothing in the dark water. She hesitated momentarily before picking up his oar and carrying on.

The children were crying now and could not be comforted. One of the women picked up the flag that Celia had dropped. She began waving it towards the shore. Shots hit their boat, and water began streaming into their makeshift vessel. Jason could hear Belgian voices now, and it sounded like they were urging the boat toward them. The soldiers were shouting something about "water coming." With a sense of foreboding, he looked upriver and saw a wall of water approaching them.

CHAPTER
51

As he urged the men to bail faster, Jason jumped over the side of the boat. Emma was frantic and felt sure he would drown. She looked over the edge, peering into the darkness until she saw him. He wasn't drowning; he was pushing the boat toward shore. If she hadn't been so terrified by the sight of the wall of water coming directly toward them, she might have wondered how he was doing it.

Several soldiers frantically waded into the river as the boat neared the shore, grabbing their bow and pulling them onto a rocky beach. They began grabbing people, getting them out of the boat as fast as possible, and pushing them up the bank. Emma felt cold hands pulling her out of the boat and looked up to see Jason, dripping wet but alive.

The Belgian soldiers led them over the rail tracks, then through a series of trenches until they were safely away from the river and under cover of a dugout. One of the French-speaking soldiers, Luca, told Jason that they were just outside Pervijze, a village that had been bombarded with artillery fire. Their position was tenuous, as the Germans outgunned and outnumbered them.

Jason advised him of the German reinforcements streaming down from the north, and the soldier relayed that information to his commanders. Luca turned back to Jason and said, "We will not retreat, the French will arrive soon, and we will hold the southwest side of the river." Luca continued, "The engineers opened the canal locks at Nieuport, and even now, the water is pushing the Germans back." The soldier pointed toward the river and said, "The land between the Germans and the railway embankment will be inundated with water, swallowing the bridge. The rail berm creates the higher ground, so we will stay dry."

Jason knew the peril these men faced, but he could not stay and help. The consequence of a weaponized virus was far worse than losing one battle. Historical records were sketchy on Hitler's whereabouts before the

Battle of Ypres, so now would be the most likely time to release the virus. He still hadn't come up with any ideas about how the traveler could be sure about getting the virus across enemy lines; he must be using a carrier, but who could it be, the traveler himself?

After what he had seen of the German destruction of Belgium, it would be unlikely that the virus carrier would be positioned in Ypres before the arrival of Hitler's regiment. Another thought struck Jason, "The Germans were taking prisoners of war. What if the traveler were a soldier?" Being taken prisoner would expose him to hordes of German soldiers. "Too many ifs," he had been in this century for almost six months, and he still had a lot of questions but no answers.

He glanced at Emma, speaking with another soldier across the dugout. He painfully thought, "She had been behind enemy lines; did she really have a brother? How plausible was that story? Could she be the carrier? She had held up well during their arduous trek, was that normal for a female in the twentieth century?" He scoffed at himself; he was just exhausted and not thinking straight.

Once he convinced Luca and his superiors that he had credible intel about the Germans, intel that would be beneficial to their offensive, they agreed to send word to the British headquarters at the Hooge Chateau in Gheluvelt, a village on the outskirts of Ypres. But then he second-guessed himself, "Had he blundered, did he just change the tide of history," but he couldn't dwell on that now.

Emma had already left the dugout when Jason heard a voice calling, "John Smith, John Smith!" Jason almost forgot it was the name he used in Pontorson. He looked through the crowd of soldiers to see who was calling. He couldn't believe it; Jules Arnaud was coming toward him with a huge smile. They shook hands, and Jason said, "Jules, what are *you* doing here?"

Jules lowered his head and replied, "You think I am too old to fight, but I have connections in the military, and they couldn't say no." Jason tried to recover and deny those thoughts, but Jules continued, "This is my homeland, and my King has asked us to hold this piece of land, no matter the cost. I have no family; it is my honor and duty to serve my country this way. We *will* hold this land until reinforcements arrive, of this I have no doubt."

Jason smiled and nodded, "You are a brave man. I have been in many battles myself, and I have never met a soldier with as much conviction as you. I wish you well my friend. I would stay and fight with you, but I must prevent a disaster that would take thousands of lives."

Jules shook his hand again and said, "Then you must go. I wish you Godspeed and hope to see you again my friend."

Jason gave him a hug, then turned to catch up with Emma. Just before reaching her, he turned back and gave a final nod to Jules. He knew they would not see each other again.

Emma waited for him to join her, "I must get back to my father in St. Omer. Luca told me that the British are suffering heavy casualties near Ypres, he will need my help." She paused, looking thoughtfully, "The Belgians will be transporting their severely wounded there tomorrow. I will go with them and tend to their medical needs during the journey."

There was no way that Jason would let her make that hazardous trip without him. He didn't have another plan anyway. They would leave at dawn.

CHAPTER

52

THEY TOOK A horse-drawn ambulance to Bergues, where they would board a southbound train to St. Omer. The roads were in a deplorable state, and they got bogged down several times. Jason's role was rearguard, to jump out and place a plank under the wheels when they got stuck. This happened several times during the journey, and his shirt and pants' front became spattered with mud.

The tortuous ride increased the soldiers' suffering, and their moans heightened the tension. Without a surgery suite, there wasn't much Emma could do. She had procured a small amount of laudanum at the bunker and doled it out as judiciously as possible. She did not fit his idea of a twentieth-century woman. She was not dependent or submissive but rather assertive and independent. Weren't these attributes of women in the twenty-first century? He thought, "No way, it can't be her."

Despite his attraction to her, his nagging suspicions just wouldn't go away. Ever since he woke up in Landstuhl, he had trust issues. When he told Mike about his decision to leave the military and live off the grid, Mike's response was, "Not everyone is out to get your tech, you will live a very lonely life if you can't trust anyone."

The benefit of being in 1914 was that no one knew about his tech; they wouldn't understand it even if they knew. And they certainly didn't have the knowledge or resources to reverse engineer him. That could be why he trusted Rene and felt comfortable with his family. Perhaps that's why he really wanted to trust Emma.

It was dusk when the train pulled into the station at St. Omer. They were at least fifty kilometers from the Front, distant enough from the battlefield to evade artillery shells yet near enough to promptly receive wounded soldiers and save them. He and Emma rode in one of the transport wagons with the wounded. Along the way, he saw soldiers everywhere—wounded coming and new recruits going. He also saw pilots from the British Royal Air Force, headquartered at the Bruyères aerodrome on the outskirts of town.

As they rode, he surveyed St. Omer. It was full of activity and much larger than he expected. Its location near the Aa River and the canals gave it an industrial advantage. It had become a major rail hub for northwestern France, which made it a strategic location for the Allies. Lining the roads were attractive homes with smooth plaster facades and wooden shutters. Their tidy appearance looked oddly out-of-place, so near the Front. In the town center were tree-covered public squares and imposing gothic-style buildings. Surprisingly, many civilians were on the sidewalks; the sizeable military presence must make them feel safe. He was also sure that some were getting wealthy by selling their goods or services to the soldiers.

The wagon pulled up to a large three-story brick building with a hip roof. A newly painted sign read, 10 Stationary Hospital, a former boarding school now allocated to the military. Orderlies emerged from the building and carried the wounded into a large triage hall where a physician quickly sorted them to the correct wards. Emma grabbed the physician's arm and said, "I'm Emma Brownfield. I need to find my father. Is he still here?" The physician said something Jason didn't quite catch, and Emma practically ran through a doorway to their right.

He followed her down a long hall with classrooms on either side. Where desks had once stood, there were now rows of wounded soldiers lying on cots. The rooms on his right had tall windows facing the front of the building, while rooms on the left faced a rear courtyard. Radiators lined the outer walls, and he wondered how efficient they would be when winter finally set in.

As he followed Emma, his mind wandered again. He knew two things for sure: first, he signed up for a one-way trip, and second, he had to be careful not to influence the historical timeline. But the longer he was here, the more vested he became in the fight. There was death and misery everywhere, "Hell, I'm looking at it right now."

If, by some miracle, he found the traveler and stopped him from releasing the virus, should he join the fight? He would likely not survive, but maybe that's how it should be. He didn't belong in 1914. However, looking at Emma's silhouette ahead of him, he mused, "Maybe I could."

She stopped at the room near the end of the hall; it appeared to have been some kind of assembly room or large parlor. Again, he saw rows of wounded soldiers. Emma called out to a man tending to one of them, "Father!"

The man looked up; he didn't recognize the person in oversized dungarees and a dark cap. She called to him again, and a look of recognition and confusion crossed his face. They hugged, and he began showering her with questions. She answered as succinctly as possible, then turned to Jason and introduced him as "Jason Shaw, the American who rescued me from the German soldiers."

His name was Dr. Arthur Brownfield, and he looked to be somewhere between fifty and sixty years old. He was thin and stooped as if he had spent his life bent over patients. His eyes were the same color as Emma's, but his were tired and concerned. His white coat was smeared with blood, and he spoke softly, "Thank you for bringing my daughter back to me, sir." He wiped his hands on his coat and held one towards Jason, who shook it. He continued, "I've not had the opportunity to meet many Americans. Perhaps you could tell me about your home when there's time."

Jason nodded, then replied, "First, I must return to Hazebrouck; I have unfinished business there. I should be back in a couple of days; we can talk then." Emma's father smiled and nodded in agreement. Jason turned to Emma, saying, "I'll look in on you when I return." He walked back through the door and disappeared into the crowd of orderlies and wounded soldiers.

CHAPTER
53

O**N THE TRAIN** to Lille Jason heard disturbing news from the soldiers crammed in his railcar. The city was under heavy bombardment, and the soldiers were part of a last-ditch effort to save it. A familiar urge to join the fight hit him strongly. He was increasingly becoming vested in the fight, but only he knew of the traveler and his plan, and only he could stop him. Instead of joining the effort to save Lille, he disembarked at Hazebrouck and made his way to Rene's farm.

The constant muted sounds on the train had been like a lullaby, luring him into a deep sleep. Without the fog of fatigue and the distraction of Emma's presence, he analyzed the situation. A feeling of unease swept over him as he fought his ongoing suspicions of her. He and Sara had projected a viral incubation period of three to seven days. If Emma had gone behind enemy lines to infect the Germans, she should have infected others by now, but she hadn't.

A wave of relief swept over him, "It couldn't be her; it has to be someone else, and that someone is probably in St. Omer getting ready for the offensive at Ypres." He should be back there trying to figure out who it was, but he was compelled to take care of Rene's family.

As he neared the farm, the ground shook under the weight of artillery fire and the sky was obscured by smoke. Many of the farms were now abandoned. In less than two weeks, the Germans had made significant advances in this part of the country.

The farmhouse looked even more neglected than before. "What if Helene and the kids had already fled the Germans?" No, not without Rene. The farm door squeaked opened and he saw the figure of Helene waiting for him to approach; her expression was unreadable.

He recounted Rene's heroism in the face of fire and the many wounded men they had safely removed from the battlefield. Helene was stoic, but the children cried. Her voice finally broke when she told him Henri and

Andre were listed as killed at the Marne. Then she thanked him for making the trip to personally tell them about Rene.

Jason's furrowed brows raised, and his jawline tensed. He emphatically said, "Helene, you need to take the children and go to your cousin's farm in England. The Germans will be here soon, you need to leave tomorrow."

She looked at him in disbelief, "We cannot prepare that soon, there is much to do, our farm, our animals, and we do not have money for the passage."

Leaving them to process their situation, he retrieved some gold coins from the trunk hidden in the haybarn. He returned to the kitchen and handed her the coins, "This is the money I owe Rene; it is yours now. There is enough for passage and for a new start in England."

Helene began to protest, but his determined voice dissuaded her. "Don't worry about the farm. I will talk with the military commander and make sure the animals are cared for. They probably would have confiscated them soon anyway." He paused and looked sternly at each of them, "Pack tonight, tomorrow I'll get you on a train that will take you to Le Havre where you can board a ship to England."

She looked at him as if in a daze but slowly nodded. Turning to Paul and Marie, he told them they must pack lightly. Marie asked if she could take her cat, and Jason nodded. The following morning, he yoked the oxen to the wagon, loaded his trunk and the family's bags, and headed to the station. Tearfully, they said their goodbyes, and Jason watched as they walked climbed the platform. Silently, he prayed they would make it safely to England.

CHAPTER
54

THE OFFICER IN charge of the train back to St. Omer had initially refused to let Jason load his trunk on board as space was needed for wounded soldiers. Jason finally convinced him that he was working with Dr. Brownfield at the hospital in St. Omer and that the trunk contained vital supplies for the hospital. "It wasn't really a lie," he told himself. The trunk did hold clothing and hygiene supplies, "along with a hidden compartment of weapons," he sardonically thought.

He found a quiet corner in one of the rail cars and used his trunk as a seat. Time was running out; he had to find the traveler and stop the virus attack. If the traveler was a physician, which was his best guess, he would stay close to St. Omer and use his journalistic cover to contact as many physicians as possible.

Stationary Hospital 10 was only one of several hospitals in St. Omer. How many physicians could there be between all of them? Another thought hit him, physicians didn't go to the front line, but ambulance drivers did. What if he were looking for a driver instead?

Another, even worse, possibility occurred to him. The Royal Airforce was in St. Omer, what if the virus were going to be delivered by air? He went through a mental exercise, trying to figure out how something like that would work. The planes were mainly used to spot German troop movements, not to drop weapons. However, if a pilot had an infected dead rat or something like that, he could toss it out over German lines. He would check out the aerodrome tomorrow.

At St. Omer, he hoisted his trunk onto a wagon carrying wounded soldiers to number 10 Stationary Hospital. Engaging the driver, Emile, in conversation he discovered that most drivers were not local; they had traveled from other parts of France. Most were disabled or too old to join the military, and, like Rene, this was their way of helping the war effort. He doubted any of them had heard of the Rosicrucian order, let alone were members of it. "No," he told himself, "The driver idea was a dead end."

That thought led him to another possibility, what if the traveler were receiving help from members of the 1914 Order? After all, the Rosicrucian origins supposedly went back to Atlantis; surely, there were groups all over Europe by now. Discounting this possibility almost immediately, he reminded himself that the traveler was a member of a rogue group that sprung up after World War II. If a member of the Black Rose showed up on their doorstep and told them about a plan to unleash a weaponized virus, they might think he was crazy. No, the traveler had to be working on his own. It would be too risky to share the plan with anyone.

He wanted to hide his trunk and work on a plan before seeing Emma or her father again. He asked Emile if space had been set aside for the drivers. Emile replied, "We are sleeping in an old gymnasium behind the school." Jason explained that he was a journalist and needed a quiet place to write, "Are there any barns or outbuildings that might have some unused space in them?"

Emile thought about this, then replied, "There might be some room in an old shed behind the gym, near the property's rear boundary."

They helped the orderlies unload the wounded soldiers, then Emile drove them back to the shed. It was pretty dilapidated and full of discarded furniture and probably some rats, but no one else was staying there, and he would make do. Emile helped unload the trunk, and they shook hands. Jason said, "Thank you, let's have coffee sometime," then smiled and added, "I'd like to interview you for one of my articles." Emile smiled broadly and shook Jason's hand again. Jason wryly thought, "I'll bet he has some unique insights about this mess."

He spent the next hour trying to make the shed somewhat habitable. He unrolled his sleeping bag onto an old bedspring, then searched for a table for his lantern. To support his journalism ruse, he cleaned off an old desk and made it appear that he was using it. He could not lock the shed, so he hid his trunk among the discarded furniture and covered it with dust. This served two purposes: one, it would appear to be just another discarded item, and two, if the dust were disturbed, he would know someone had been poking around.

As he was leaving, he noticed something. There was a disturbance in the dust on the floor toward the right side of the door. He investigated and found it went almost to the shed's outer wall. Following it to the end, he stopped and looked around. At first, he didn't see anything unusual, but he pushed a few items aside and saw a wooden box.

The box was covered in dust but not nearly as thick as the surrounding items. As he picked it up, glass rattled inside. Using a knife, he wedged the lock open. At first, he wasn't sure of the contents, but then understanding engulfed him. He was looking at chemistry equipment, things that could be used to reproduce or weaponize a virus. The traveler *was* here.

He relocked the box, replaced it, and ensured the thin layer of dust was intact. He would use it to trap a different kind of rat than the ones scurrying around the shed. With all the hospitals in St. Omer, Emma may have led him to the exact place he needed to be. Breath catching in his throat he thought, "Was that just coincidence?" He left the shed and walked toward the hospital, ready to bait his trap.

CHAPTER
55

THE HOSPITAL WAS divided into wards; each treated a different type of injury and was supervised by a specialist physician. Three wards were set aside for battlefield injuries, such as amputations and penetrating injuries. Two wards were reserved for medical conditions such as dysentery, pneumonia, and skin infections. Dr. Brownfield had dictated that these were housed in buildings adjacent to the main structure to prevent the spread of disease to post-surgical patients.

Dormitories on the second floor housed the largest of the wards, the amputee ward, with the common rooms utilized as surgical suites. The first floor, which Jason saw on his first day, was utilized for penetrating wounds. The small school chapel had been designated for soldiers with brain injuries. It was the smallest ward; he decided to start there.

Tall stained-glass windows depicting biblical events, were at odds with the scene facing Jason as he stood at the door. Men strapped to beds were moaning, crying, and calling for their mothers. The doctor was bent over, examining one of approximately fifty patients crammed into the relatively small space. Dr. St. Claire was one of the most eminent physicians at the hospital. Before the war, he worked in the renowned neuropsychiatric teaching center at the Pitié-Salpêtrière University Hospital in Paris.

The scene was so horrific he wanted to turn away, but forced himself to remain, planted in place. While standing in wait, he took note of the doctor's appearance. His thick hair was gray and matched his trim mustache and goatee, while wire-rimmed glasses framed his hazel eyes. While his hair color and glasses made him appear to be a man in his sixties, his posture and movements belonged to someone at least ten years younger. "His age looks right; maybe he works on staying in shape," Jason thought.

He stood unmoving, until the doctor had finished. His presence was finally acknowledged by St. Claire, who now approached him. Jason introduced himself and explained that he was there to interview the physician about his work. The doctor motioned him to an alcove behind the nave where he had a small office.

St. Claire looked tired but perked up as he discussed his work, particularly about his research on shell shock. There was controversy among physicians regarding the etiology of the condition. Some felt it was caused by emotional or psychological trauma; however, Dr. St. Claire disagreed and believed it resulted from concussive forces that affected the brain. Listening to him talk, Jason felt he had been transported to the dark ages of medicine, just like Bones in one of the Star Trek movies.

Dr. St. Claire himself would probably be shocked if he knew of Jason's neurological enhancements.

During the interview, he played the role of a professional journalist, asking the types of questions his readers would be interested in. As the interview concluded, he mentioned that he was staying in the shed behind the old gymnasium. If the doctor had any further information, he could send word through an orderly.

As he imparted this last piece of information, he looked closely at the doctor for any sign of anxiety or fear but saw none. If St. Claire had placed the wooden box in the shed, he showed no indication that he was worried about Jason finding it.

He repeated the interview ruse with each of the remaining physicians at the hospital, but so far, none showed any indication that they had hidden the box in the shed. He saved Dr. Brownfield for last; he hoped they, including Emma, might have dinner together afterward.

He found Emma's' father in one of the classrooms on the first floor, tending to a gunshot wound. Emma was assisting. The sight of her bending over the soldier, working diligently to remove the bullet, almost took his breath away.

"What is wrong with me?" he asked himself. "I barely know her, not to mention that she could be the very person I came here to stop!" He could not afford to get close to anyone, especially someone as astute as Emma; he might inadvertently give himself away. She was already questioning his night vision and that he had barely bled when the knife cut into his shoulder. Luckily, she was too scared to notice when he used his enhanced speed and reflexes to kill the soldiers about to rape her.

As he waited for Emma and her father to finish treating the soldier, he again wondered if being condemned to live out the rest of his life in 1914 would be such a bad thing. Even though he was stalking a potential mass murderer, his post-Iraq anxiety was gone. He wasn't living each day fearing that he would be captured by some foreign government to live the rest of his life in a cage.

He had been here for only six months but had made a few friends, something that wouldn't have happened back home. And while he worried that getting too close to Emma would be a personal risk, he didn't fear that someone would kidnap her to get to him. There was something else; seeing all these wounded men trapped in broken bodies for the rest of their lives gave him a different perspective on his enhanced body. He had always felt that he would rather die than be enhanced, but now he saw worse outcomes than death.

His interview with Dr. Brownfield went well. The doctor's story of working at Leeds University jived with what Emma had already told him. The doctor discussed new surgical techniques for treating gunshot wounds and the advent of tetanus toxoid to prevent wound infections that were invariably fatal. He also spoke about the availability of solutions, such as Dakin's solution, to clean out wounds and prevent infection. He proudly stated that, unlike field hospitals, "This stationary hospital has the capacity to implement aseptic techniques in the surgical suites." As the interview concluded, he pointed toward Emma, who was initiating a blood transfusion. He stated, "This wasn't possible until just recently."

Emma's father appeared to be a knowledgeable and caring physician. Jason had difficulty envisioning him as the traveler but had to remain objective. All the physicians interviewed that day were about the same age, so no one could be excluded on that count.

As Jason put his notepad away, he felt a shift in Dr. Brownfield's demeanor. He looked at Jason knowingly, "My daughter insists that you behaved honorably during your flight from the Germans, and I believe her. She has a promising future ahead of her." He beamed proudly toward her, "She will be one of the first women admitted to medical school in England, a well-deserved honor." His eyes danced as he declared, "She's a brilliant surgeon, much more so than I was at her age."

Jason squirmed in his chair; he had a feeling about what was coming next. Emma's father confirmed it by saying, "I would hate to see anything interfere with her life's dream."

Jason nodded in agreement and replied, "Neither would I," he meant it. The doctor then asked where he was staying. "Here it goes," he thought. He explained that he needed a quiet place to write up his interviews and that one of the drivers had directed him to a storage shed behind the gymnasium.

Then he saw it, a flicker in the old man's eye. Was it recognition, fear, or something else? The doctor quickly recovered, and Jason wasn't even sure he saw anything. He continued with the same basic story he had told all the other physicians. "I will be at the aerodrome most of the day tomorrow, interviewing the RAF Commander, but if you have any additional information that you would like me to use in the story, you can send a message through Emile."

After Dr. Brownfield's subtle warning about Jason's relationship with Emma, he decided not to mention dinner. Instead, he walked to the old school's dining hall outside the kitchen, picked up a bowl of soup, some bread, and wine, and then headed back to the shed to eat alone. The trap was set; would the rat take the bait?

The following morning, he went through the motions of leaving for the aerodrome but then circled back and waited in the woods behind the shed. He had taken a horse from the ambulance stable, and it munched quietly beside him, thankful for a reprieve from pulling wagons. He planned to stay hidden and watch the shed all day, if necessary, to see if one of the physicians would come for the box.

He didn't need all day. About an hour before lunch, he saw Dr. Brownfield openly striding toward the shed. He knocked briefly at the door, then opened it and walked in.

Jason quickly strode to the door and peeked in. Emma's father stood in the middle of the room, looking around at nothing in particular. Jason cleared his throat before entering, then said, "Can I help you find anything, sir?"

Arthur Brownfield's forehead was creased, and his eyes were distant; he blurted out, "Where is Emma?"

He was taken aback, "Emma, I haven't seen her since last night at the hospital when I was speaking with you, why?"

Arthur replied, "She's gone, no one has seen her."

Jason's chest constricted, and his palms began to sweat, "What do you mean she's gone? Why would she leave, where would she go?"

Arthur sat in the only chair in the room, the one at Jason's makeshift writing desk. Jason, trying to calm his fears, sat on the bed, and tentatively asked, "What happened to make you so worried?"

Arthur tried to maintain his composure, but Jason could tell he was rattled. Arthur softly said, "We rarely disagree, but last night we argued about you. Emma is special, and after our discussion last night, I realized you know it too. She got angry when I told her I thought it was best if you two avoided each other. She said she knew her own mind and wasn't some silly schoolgirl with a crush."

Jason began to smile at this revelation but stopped himself.

Arthur was agitated and spoke rapidly. "She's never talked that way to me before, then she stormed off to her room. I hoped to smooth things over this morning, but she wasn't in her room when I checked. I started searching all the wards thinking maybe she was just trying to avoid me, but I couldn't find her. In the amputee ward, one of the soldiers called my name. I went over to him, and he said he had been in my son James' regimen. He asked if Emma had given me the message that he saw James less than a week ago in Poperinge and that James was headed to the Front. I fear that Emma has gone to find him."

Jason immediately stood and grabbed his rucksack. Arthur also stood and asked, "What are you doing?"

Jason replied, "I'm going to find her and bring her back."

Arthur said, "I have always been very protective of her, but she is not a girl anymore, she's a woman, and I should have trusted her belief in you." He shook Jason's hand and whispered, "Godspeed," then walked out the door.

Jason barely heard him. His breath was coming fast, and despite the cold air, he was sweating. He grabbed a handgun and a rifle from the trunk, then ran for the horse he had left in the trees. By train or roadway, it was almost thirty miles to Poperinge. He could shave off some time by taking a more direct route. If he needed a wagon for Emma, he would confiscate one when he got there. Right now, his need to find her outweighed his need to find the traveler. He prayed he would be in time.

CHAPTER

56

I T WAS DUSK when Jason arrived in Poperinge, or Pops, as the British had named it. He left his exhausted horse at the cavalry barns and quickly made for the casualty station. He had ridden through a foot of mud, which had slowed him considerably; "God I hope she's still alive."

Poperinge was the gateway to the battlefields north of Ypres. Five main roads led into the center of town, like hubs on a wheel. It was bustling with military traffic, soldiers, and civilians who had stayed on to support the war effort. He stopped to ask one of the soldiers for directions to the casualty station, then hastily ran to find it. It was large, the largest he had seen so far. The nurses were too busy attending to the wounded to notice him as he ran from row to row looking for Emma.

Finally, one of the nurses stopped and asked him who he was looking for. When he replied, "Emma Brownfield," her expression revealed her concern. Emma had left for the Front at Ypres a few hours ago on one of the ambulances. He barely mumbled, "Thank you," before sprinting outside and jumping aboard the next ambulance heading to the Front.

Artillery shells landed ahead of them. The wagon swerved violently, trying to avoid the dead soldiers and horses littering the ground. The driver kept tight to the tree line, taking as much cover as possible in this wasteland of humanity. The battle was so close they could see soldiers shooting at one another from behind trees. "Could Hitler be one of them?" he thought.

They pulled up to a bunker where the wounded were being triaged. He didn't wait for it to stop. He jumped off and wove his way into the bunker. Emma was bending over a chest wound, so immersed in her work that she didn't notice him rushing toward her. He breathed a sigh of relief and gently touched her arm.

The soldier was bleeding profusely, and Jason could tell he would be gone soon. As she irritatingly jerked her arm back, he calmly said, "Your father and I were frantic when we found you were gone. The Germans are right on top of us. Let's take anyone who can withstand the ride to Poperinge and get out of here."

She had been prepared to argue, but his calm tone seemed to defeat her. She looked at him with teary eyes, "I thought my brother was here; that's why I came. He's not among the wounded now, but he could be soon. I don't want to leave if he's fighting near here."

Jason took a deep breath before replying, "Emma please think, if he does get wounded, they will take him to Poperinge, where we will be waiting. Now, let's go before this bunker gets hit by artillery, the Germans are too close."

She initially said nothing, then slowly nodded. Urgently he led her to a wagon where the wounded were being loaded. She got in the back with the soldiers, and Jason took rear guard, his rifle at the ready.

As they rode, he saw that the Allies were dangerously close to being outflanked on the right, the side closest to them. Artillery fire was directly overhead; he looked back as the triage bunker exploded. Just then, he spotted a rifle barrel sticking out from behind a tree. The weapon fired, and their driver went down.

The horses continued, pulling straight ahead. He climbed over the wounded men to reach the front bench, pushed the driver to the side, and regained control of the horses. He pulled them to the left and veered between trees. Tree bark was splintering around them as more German soldiers joined the assault. He shouted at Emma to get down on the wagon floor.

As the Allied soldiers pushed the Germans back, artillery fire faded. "Thank God," he said, "we just might make it." The words were barely out of his mouth when he felt pain in his right upper chest and saw blood oozing from a gunshot wound. Remarkably, he kept hold of the reins and remained conscious until they were back in Poperinge. As the horses stopped in front of the casualty station, everything went black.

CHAPTER
57

J ASON AWOKE TO the smell of ether. He was lying on a hospital cot, and Emma stood over him looking horrified. "What are you?" she whispered tremulously.

He struggled to focus, but was too groggy to fully comprehend what she said. He thought he heard her say, "How are you?" He saw the tube snaking from the blood bag into his arm, then blackness encompassed him again.

As the anesthesia waned, he saw Emma still beside him. Her face was drawn, and she looked exhausted. As the fog cleared, he thought, "How long had he been like this?"

She said coldly, "I'm putting you on the next transport to the hospital in St. Omer. You need more advanced medical care than I can give you here. You might have severed arteries or a punctured lung; you need a surgeon." Her eyes avoided his, "I'm also worried about infection. My father will know how best to help you."

Realization hit, and he looked at her knowingly, "You're the one who removed the bullet, aren't you?" She bit her lip and looked away. He continued, "Emma, I'm not some kind of monster, I told you I was a soldier in another war, during another time. I was severely injured. I can't explain it to you now, but I promise I will. This just isn't the right place for it." He paused, "You know, it's ironic. I'm the one who usually doesn't trust anyone, now I'm asking you to trust me."

Emma thought about his request. Despite everything, she wanted to trust him. He could have left her in the village with the Germans. But instead, he had risked his life repeatedly to save hers. And he had behaved honorably during all the nights they spent together fleeing the Germans.

He felt her soften a little and quietly said, "Emma, I'm not leaving you here. If you stay, I stay." He thought for a minute and continued, "I will be up and around in no time, and don't worry about infection; I have a very healthy immune system. I would like us both to go back to St. Omer. There is something important that I was sent here to do, and I need your help."

He was telling her the truth about his immune system. After the severe burns he suffered during the blast in Iraq, infection was the biggest threat to his life. DARPA had been working on a "smart" vaccine for quite some time. Their first human guinea pig was Jason.

The concept behind the vaccine stemmed from the mRNA vaccines developed during the coronavirus outbreak of 2020. During the pandemic, scientists had to pre-program vaccines to detect specific RNA codes. Scientists at DARPA eventually utilized mRNA technology to create a vaccine that would detect and copy any foreign RNA or DNA sequence. Before the host even realized they were infected, the body would detect the invader. The vaccine would trigger the immune system at that point, empowering it to initiate a swift and lethal counterattack. The vaccine saved Jason's life then and would do the same now. But if he told Emma about this, it would sound like science fiction, so he omitted the details.

Less than two days later, he was out of bed and walking around. Emma was amazed; he was doing well, with no sign of infection. She told herself the bullet must not have done as much damage as initially thought. Her curious expression told him she wanted an explanation, but he just thanked her. He was anxious to return to St. Omer to see if anyone had disturbed the box. There would be time for explanations later. With no sign of James, he convinced Emma to leave.

Three days later, they boarded a train headed back to the stationary hospital. Emma kept her medical bag close in case she needed to tend to Jason's wound during the journey. As the train began to move, Jason's gaze fell upon the initials embroidered on the bag: ERB. A cold chill ran down his spine. He couldn't help but ask what the letters stood for, though he already knew. She replied, "Emma Rose Brownfield. Rose is my middle name."

CHAPTER
58

E MILE WAS DRIVING one of the many ambulances waiting for them at the station. Instead of riding to the hospital with the wounded, Emma asked that she and Jason be dropped off in the retail district to purchase supplies for the hospital. Jason began protesting; he wanted to return to the shed. But Emma was adamant, so Emile obliged and dropped them at an intersection about a block from the local mercantile. He would take the wounded to the hospital, then come back and pick them up. Jason was perplexed by Emma's actions and wondered if she was purposefully delaying him. But if so, for what reason?

Soldiers and civilians filled the bustling sidewalks. Some strolled leisurely, while others savored meals at sidewalk cafes. The enticing aroma of freshly baked goods and coffee tempted their appetites. He pushed aside his suspicions, and they decided to take a few minutes to eat. They located a cozy table outside a bakery and ordered brioche and coffee. The prices were steep, but Jason didn't mind. For the first time in years, he sat outdoors with a beautiful girl and didn't watch his back.

He was on the verge of locating the traveler, and he couldn't help but feel that it would strain his relationship with Emma once he did. At this thought, a pang of guilt about Sara immediately gripped his heart. He still loved her, but it felt like a lifetime ago, over a hundred years in the past. Emma was in his life now, and she was an exceptional woman. Her intellect, curiosity, and adventurous spirit reminded him so much of Sara.

Emma sensed that, even though he displayed no outward signs of the injury he had sustained a week earlier, he wasn't yet prepared to open up to her. To keep the conversation going, she shared stories about her life in England, describing the picturesque park square that lay opposite their house and how its colors transformed with the changing seasons.

When Jason inquired about her plans after medical school, she hesitated before responding, "Right now, it's difficult to envision a life beyond this war. Despite our unwavering efforts to repel the Germans, I've been to the Front. I've seen the lifeless bodies and the wounded; it feels as if life will never be the same. Look at the villages with buildings that have endured for centuries; they've all been reduced to rubble. How can one ever rebuild that? Even more disheartening are the countless men we've already lost; this will undoubtedly have a profound impact on society for a generation or more."

She paused, sipped her coffee, and continued, "It's odd that without the war, I wouldn't be allowed to enter medical school, but with the war, I'm not sure what the future will bring."

He nodded; his understanding unspoken. In that moment, he longed to forget everything—the mission, the war—just to sit there with Emma forever. It was the hundredth time since they'd met that he found himself deeply impressed by her intelligence, maturity, and insight.

They finished their coffee and walked down the street to the mercantile. Clouds were gathering, and it looked like a storm was heading their way; they hurried to complete their purchases and return to the shelter of the hospital.

The large store had two floors above street level and a basement below. As they stepped through the door, the wooden floors creaked in protest under their weight. Fabric was in short supply, but they managed to find four bolts of white linen suitable for bandages. Emma sighed in frustration at the dwindling inventory. "I'll need to have a talk with the Commander in charge of the hospitals," she remarked, "and request more supplies to be sent from England."

Before leaving the store, they made a quick stop at the sundries section to purchase soap and astringent. They would have bought more supplies, but they were already carrying all they could manage. As they exited, Jason emerged with his arms full of fabric bolts and spotted Emile waiting for them. He quietly requested Emile to drop them off behind the hospital and then deliver the supplies to the orderlies at the hospital entrance. Emile was instructed not to mention Jason or Emma and simply attribute the donation to a local benefactor. Emma began to voice her protest, but Jason gently touched her arm, silently reminding her of their need for discretion.

They hid in the tree line watching the shed. Although it was lightly raining now, they had to ensure no one was nearby. As they entered the old shed, Jason was relieved to find that nothing was out of place. The dust sat on his trunk undisturbed, but when he checked on the box of chemistry equipment, it was gone. He was now sure the traveler was one of the five hospital physicians.

Jason recognized that he could identify the traveler more quickly with Emma's help. He motioned for her to take a seat at his desk, the same desk her father had occupied just a week ago. So much had transpired since then. He settled on the bed, gazing at Emma, wondering how she would react to his story. Clearing his throat, he began, "Emma, I understand that what I'm about to tell you may sound unbelievable, but I ask that you keep an open mind. You're already aware of the unusual anatomical features of my body, so please consider that as you hear me out."

Then he began. "I came here to prevent a horrific tragedy. There is a German soldier named Adolf Hitler at the Front in Ypres, destined to become one of the leaders of post-war Germany. He fervently believes in racial purity and the superiority of the Germanic Race. Once he gains control of Germany, he will persuade others to adopt his beliefs and eventually lead a formidable army. Under his leadership, six million Europeans of Jewish descent will be systematically executed—a genocide that will wipe out entire generations of families. It will be known as the Holocaust." Jason paused, studying her reaction, and saw a profound sense of horror in her eyes.

She bit her lip and said, "How do you know this, no one can tell the future."

He disregarded her question and continued, "There is a small group of people who believe that if Hitler is eliminated now, before his twisted views take hold of an entire nation, the genocide can be prevented."

Emma, though skeptical, inquired, "What's wrong with that? Why would you want to stop it?"

He answered, "Because many innocent people will be killed along with him. This group plans to release a nasty virus, one that could kill even more people than the Holocaust; more importantly, they would change history from this point on."

She stopped him and said, "That's ridiculous, who could possibly change history like that?"

Jason took a deep breath before continuing, "Here it goes. The individuals who engineered the virus aren't from this time. They're from a time that hasn't occurred yet. In their pursuit of preventing the Holocaust and the persecution of thousands of families, including Jewish people, they discovered a way to alter the course of history."

She looked at him in disbelief and said, "You're talking about the future, do you really expect me to believe that people can travel backward through time?"

He looked into her eyes and said, "I know it's difficult to believe, but that's exactly what I did."

She replied, "How?"

He struggled with this part of the story, "I can't explain it because I'm really not sure myself. The science is very advanced, even for my time. I just know it *is* possible because I am here." Before she could interrupt, he said, "You saw my special anatomy when you removed the bullet, think about it. Your father is a surgeon and you're his student, have you ever seen nanorods that can strengthen muscle or help bind regenerated tissue to bone?"

She bit her lip and began to nervously fidget. She looked at him and said, "Your outer skin was hard to incise and your muscle tissue was so dense that I went through three scalpels just to cut down to the bullet. Then I saw the worms." Her face contorted.

He laughed, "Those aren't worms."

She replied, "Then what are they? They were moving, but with a purpose. They appeared to be moving toward each other. I thought you might be infected with something."

Jason became serious again, "I told you that I was a soldier in another war. I was injured in an explosion and had deep burns on my arms, legs, and the upper part of my chest, down to the bone in some places. My eardrums had been blown out, and my retinas were permanently damaged by the bright light of the explosion. I would have died without extraordinary medical treatment."

He paused to let her absorb this, then continued, "As a soldier, I had signed over the rights to my dead body to the military. I had no family, so it really didn't matter what they did to me after I was gone. What I didn't read in the fine print was that I also gave them the right to use experimental treatment options to keep me alive if there was no alternative. And that is precisely what they did. In the place I call home, my time, we have advanced science to the point where doctors can actually manipulate genes."

He paused again, "You have probably heard of the molecule discovered by Fredrich Miescher in 1869. It's the blueprint for how to build every cell in our bodies. The blueprint tells cells what type of tissue they will develop into or what kind of tissue they can regenerate. For example, our skin. If it's not too badly injured, it can repair itself. But some cells, like cells in our nervous system, cannot regenerate."

She replied, "Yes that makes sense. I've seen patients who have sustained nerve damage; they never improve."

"The proteins that make up all these cells are called genes. If the body needs to repair itself, certain genes must be activated by specific stimuli. In my time, physicians have mastered the art of not only activating genes but also deactivating them. This field of science is known as epigenetics. Imagine patients who are paralyzed; their nervous system cells have suffered irreparable damage. However, if we can find a way to stimulate these cells to divide and repair themselves, patients could regain their mobility."

She said, "That's amazing, I would have never imagined anything like that."

"Currently, your technology and scientific equipment haven't reached the level where you can achieve this. You're limited to using microscopes that can only magnify small microbes. In my era, we have what's known as the electron microscope. It generates images of specimens by utilizing a beam of electrons, similar to cathode rays, rather than beams of light. This breakthrough enables us to visualize objects as minuscule as viruses."

Jason was expanding on the state of current science to explain advanced concepts. This wasn't quite as high a leap for Emma to make. Some of his words made sense, but other things were beyond her imagination.

She said, "What does this have to do with your worms?"

He laughed and said, "You mean my nanorods? Well, they do move, just like worms do, but they are man-made. Scientists created them to perform continuous functions in the body, like grouping together to form tissue so dense that a knife can barely penetrate it."

She remembered the knife jab and said, "So that's why you barely bled from your shoulder."

He nodded, "My nanorods can also augment my own muscle fibers to increase my strength when my adrenal system is activated."

Emma was stunned, "I have studied the adrenal system, but I don't remember anything about muscle activation."

He explained, "The adrenal gland has many functions, one of them is called fight-or-flight. It's a physiological response to danger. Let's say you were walking in the forest and came upon a wild bear," he grinned, "or a pack of wolves. Your heart would beat faster, your breathing would increase, and you would probably start sweating. The metabolism in your gastrointestinal tract would slow down, while the metabolism in your musculoskeletal system would increase. Even your eyesight and hearing would become more acute. All of these changes would increase your ability to run, to escape the danger. In most people this system is automatically activated by a danger stimulus, but I am able to manually control mine when I need to."

She asked, "So, is that how you are able to see better in the dark?"

He shook his head, "No, my retinas were damaged beyond repair. They were replaced with a neural implant, or artificial connection in the brain, linked to an artificial lens. The lenses are an upgrade of our natural ones; mine are capable of night vision, which you've seen in action. They also have a function similar to a metal detector. The lenses can penetrate clothing and other thin materials; this allows me to detect weapons that might be hidden."

She nodded, and he continued, "Everything that was done to me was to enhance my value as a soldier, they didn't necessarily have quality of life in mind when they did it."

She ignored his last comment; she was still stuck on the lenses. She asked, "Could they could use the science to help blind people see again?"

He nodded, "Yes that was the original purpose, and that is exactly what they're doing, except for the night vision of course."

Emma said, "That's amazing and wonderful. I would really like to visit your time, to learn about the science and its medical applications."

Jason shook his head, "Sorry, this was a one-way trip. Something about the human body not able to withstand more than one trip through time. So, there's no going back, I knew it when I started."

Emma gasped, "You can't go back. What about friends or family?"

His voice lowered, "I have no family, and this group of bad people I told you about, killed everyone I cared about just to prevent me from stopping them. So, you see if they win, my friends died for nothing. I have to use everything at my disposal to stop them, to prevent them from killing millions of people."

He did not tell her about the natural-occurring Spanish flu that would kill tens of millions of people just three years from now; there was no reason to.

CHAPTER
59

EMMA TOOK IT well. Jason wasn't sure she believed it, but she agreed to help him anyway. They both stood, and she walked over to him. He bent down, and they kissed deeply, longingly. He held her for a few minutes, not wanting to let go. At that moment, he knew he would do whatever it took to spend the rest of his life with this woman. She pulled back first and said, "What do you need me to do?"

Jason explained his theory about the five physicians. She looked at him, "My father would never intentionally hurt anyone. It has to be one of the others."

Jason replied, "I'm running out of time. Let's go see him and let him know you're safe, then we can come up with a plan."

It was midday, but when they emerged from the shed, it was dark, and the sky was black. The wind was whipping the tree tops, and debris flew everywhere; winter had violently arrived at St. Omer. Jason covered Emma with his coat as they raced across the field and into the hospital.

Emma's father was in his office on the second floor; he had just operated on a soldier with a gunshot wound to the abdomen. He beamed when he saw Emma and thanked Jason for her safe return. Emma asked about the soldier's condition, and he replied, "The intestines were perforated. I repaired them but left the abdomen open. I have ordered Dakin's solution rinses four times a day, but he will likely die from peritonitis." Her father sounded hopeless, but then he smiled and said, "We do the best we can, don't we?"

Her father continued, "Now my dear, any news of James?" Then somewhat anxiously, he added, "Did you make it to the Front?"

Something clicked inside Jason. That last question suddenly made everything clear. "Sir, is that what you wanted, Emma near the front lines at Ypres?"

Arthur looked aghast and replied, "Why would you say such a thing?"

A clap of thunder muffled Emma's protests, and Jason ignored her. "Because I think you wanted Emma to spread the virus. She's a carrier, isn't she?"

The room darkened, and rain pelted the windows. Arthur indignantly replied, "Carrier of what? I have no idea what you are talking about." He looked at Emma, then back to Jason, "I think you should leave right now and never approach me or my daughter again."

Jason looked at him knowingly, "It's not going to work, sir. You told me that Emma spoke with one of the men in the amputee ward and was told that James was at the Front. But Emma never spoke with a soldier there; you lied. I'm not sure what kind of story you cooked up about James, but somehow you got her to the Front to find a brother who was never there."

Jason's accusation was punctuated by another clap of thunder, closer this time. Emma looked at her father in disbelief as he sat down defeatedly. "I'm sorry, Emma, I had to do it. You see, they have James. They said they would kill him if I didn't go through with the plan."

Jason understood now. Arthur *was* the traveler. He must have had second thoughts about releasing the virus, but the Black Rose sent someone to ensure he followed through.

Emma's thoughts swirled like the leaves outside the window, caught in a gusty wind. She struggled to make sense of her father's unexpected revelation. She looked at him and said, "Why, why would you do it?"

Arthur looked at Jason and asked, "Does she know about the device?"

Jason nodded, "Yes, but not the specifics."

Arthur sighed, seemingly resigned to tell Emma the whole story. He began, "My parents were both chemists who worked for a large pharmaceutical company. They were a career couple who put off having children until their forties. I guess they waited too long because I was an only child. My mother was German-Swiss, and my father was English. They worked for Roche, so I grew up in Switzerland. I inherited my parent's love and aptitude for science but didn't want to spend my life in a lab. I was more interested in science's impact on helping people, which led me into medicine."

He continued, "I attended the University in Zurich where I received simultaneous degrees in biology and chemistry, then went to medical college at Oxford. I wanted to stay in Switzerland with my parents, but I had received a Rhodes scholarship. My roommate at Oxford was a Rosicrucian. He didn't discuss his mystic beliefs at first, but as a result of our scholarly discussions, he realized that I was trying to resolve my belief in God with my belief in science. He provided me with thought-provoking reading materials and, after a year of preparation, he invited me to the Temple. I met men of science who, like myself, were looking for answers to existential questions."

He paused for a moment as if deciding how to continue, "In addition to my studies at Oxford, I studied at the Societas Rosicruciana in Anglia, the Rosicrucian Society of England, and attained the Second Order grade of Adeptus Exemptus. I was pursuing both my scientific and metaphysical passions and thought I was completely fulfilled. That's when we found the book."

He then described the book's contents and explained how he and his friend, Andrew, created a time-travel device by following the instructions in the book. He looked at Jason and said, "And you must already know about the portals?"

Jason nodded, and Arthur continued, "I grew up hating Hitler and all he stood for. Most of my mother's family had been executed by the Nazis for helping Jews cross the border into Switzerland. The loss haunted my mother, but she never spoke of it; the horror was too great. I initially posed the weaponized virus plan to Andrew as a mind exercise, positing that if Hitler had not survived the first world war there wouldn't have been a second. Preventing Hitler's rise to power would spare the entire world from the rath of a madman, including my mother's family. I realize now how wrong I was. Hatred, anger, revenge, these are not Rosicrucian tenets, we abhor violence. But that was part of the hook, by stopping Hitler we would stop his tsunami of violence upon mankind."

Emma interrupted, "Wait a minute. Jason told me there was another war after this one, what does that have to do with releasing a virus?"

He replied, "You will need a short history lesson to understand that."

Arthur educated her about Hitler's rise to power and the political climate that supported him. He then turned his attention to the effect Hitler's regime had on the Order. "Modern Rosicrucianism began with a German, Christian Rosenkreuz, who discovered and learned the Secret Wisdom on a pilgrimage to the East in the fifteenth century. He returned to Germany and began to gather like-minded men of science into a Fellowship based on that wisdom. One of the Rosicrucian's earliest manifestos was first published in Germany, the Fama Fraternitatis R.C. The publication was intellectually stimulating and significantly increased the number of believers in that country."

Emma started to interject, but he said, "My dear, this is my story and its complicated, please let me finish before you pass judgement on me."

She bit her lip, and he continued, "Hitler was an occultist; he believed in the power of mythical artifacts such as the Holy Grail and the Spear of Destiny. He felt the possession of these holy artifacts would confer the ability to control the world and create his Aryan Master Race. Hitler's loyalists took advantage of his beliefs to gain favor with him. Enter the Thule Society."

He paused to get a drink of water. "A Hitler loyalist, Baron Rudolf von Sebottendorff, portrayed the Thule Society as the custodian of ancient wisdom and led Hitler to believe that the Society knew mystical secrets, secrets that would lead him to the artifacts he was searching for. But the Rosicrucians had also claimed to be the possessors of ancient knowledge and therefore came under scrutiny. As an established mystic order, they posed a threat to the Thule manifesto. As the Nazis rose to power they imprisoned and executed many Rosicrucians."

Emma couldn't help herself; she blurted out, "I understand why you would hate such a man as Hitler, but are you asking me to believe that you built a device that allowed you to travel back through time?"

Arthur replied, "My dear, the fact that Mr. Shaw and I are here proves it is true." He looked at Jason questioningly and said, "I'm assuming that Shaw is not your real name."

Jason nodded and said, "Jason Falcone, and yours?"

Arthur said, "Josef Blackwood, but I gave that name and that life up long ago. Please don't use it."

Jason thought, "So that's where the name, Black Rose, came from."

Emma was still shocked and decried, "What about your parents, my grandparents? You just left them."

He replied, "As I mentioned, my parents were in their forties when I was born. Ironically, my mother worked on the first small molecule inhibitors to treat cancer, but the treatment couldn't cure hers. My father died less than three years later, probably of grief. So, you see, the only family I had left was the Order."

He looked at Jason and said, "I arrived at the Mont in 1888. Unable to pose as French, I crossed the channel to England. I came prepared with enough gold to purchase a home and set up a little medical practice. Before my journey, our splinter group, the Black Rose, hacked into the archives at Leeds University and created a transcript of my medical studies there. Everything went as planned," he looked at Emma, "until I met your mother."

"Evaline was a beautiful young woman like you, Emma. She was married to a village shopkeeper and had a young son, James. Her husband, Byron, became ill, and I treated him for several months before he died. That's how I came to know her. Between my medical and mystical studies, I hadn't paid much attention to women. The Order believed married men could not devote the time needed to obtain true enlightenment, and I agreed. But after a couple of years away from their influence, I was lonely, so she arrived at precisely the right time in my life. I fell madly in love and pursued her."

He looked at Jason and said, "In the future physicians and scientists are held in high esteem, but in the 1880s it was a different story. Most physicians were paid in trade, so they were cash poor. But Evaline didn't care about that, she was poor as well. Women didn't have many rights back then and Bryon's family took the shop from her. They doled out just enough money for her and James to survive."

In hushed tones, Emma said, "So James is not my brother?"

To this, Arthur replied, "He's your half-brother. Your mother and I married after her compulsory year of mourning, and you were born less than a year later. After I married your mother, James' family abandoned him. I was the only father he knew and never told him any different. For the following six years, I lived a life of sublime happiness, then your mother became ill. It had been a horribly wet and cold winter, and respiratory illnesses gripped the village. You and James became ill, but your young immune systems fought it off. I had immunity from the vaccines I received before my time journey."

Emma asked, "Did mother ever suspect the truth about you?"

He replied, "No, I gave up all thoughts of the Order and the virus and committed myself completely to her. Once she died, I transferred that commitment to you and James. I had absolutely no intention of ever carrying out my original plan. Besides, I began to seriously question the morality of it. I had become socially conscious; there was no way to ignore the severe poverty and disease that plagued the unfortunate. I decided to dedicate myself to the eradication of disease, not the spread of it. But the Order didn't believe that was my choice to make."

Jason interrupted, "So the Order didn't trust you would implement the virus. Is that what happened?"

Arthur admittedly said, "Yes. About a year ago, someone from the Order used the portal to travel here and monitor my activities. Just before the war was declared, he approached me at the University and identified himself. He said he was here to help me with my mission. I told him that I had changed my mind. When his attempts to convince me didn't work, he appeared to accept it and left. But something about the man's demeanor made me uneasy, and I kept Emma close. I tried to stay close to James as well, but before I knew it, he was shipped off to France. I thought he would be safe from the Order, but I was wrong. They found him soon after the Battle of the Marne."

Emma blurted out, "Father, I love James too, but you can't justify trading one life for millions. Besides, how could you be sure that James or I wouldn't get the virus and die anyway?"

He replied, "Because I made sure you wouldn't. As a contingency, I developed a vaccine against the virus; you and James were vaccinated before he shipped out." He looked again at Jason, "I needed the chemistry equipment to develop more doses. I kept the box hidden, so the Order wouldn't find out what I was doing. I was trying to buy time to produce enough vaccine." He looked back at Emma, "That is why I didn't stop you from going to the Front. I wanted the Order to believe I was using you to implement the plan. To protect you, I made sure Jason followed."

Jason interrupted, "But you must have thought I was a member of the Order sent here to watch you?"

Arthur suppressed a laugh, "Oh I knew you didn't belong in this century; I could tell by your demeanor. Even posing as an American, you're far to informal and familiar around us. But when you followed Emma and brought her back from Poperinge, I knew you were trying to protect her. If you wanted her to infect others, you would have left her there."

Jason was nodding his understanding when he caught movement out of the corner of his eye. He was so engrossed in Arthur's story; he had suspended his situational awareness.

CHAPTER
60

J ASON TURNED AND saw St. Claire standing in the doorway, holding a pistol aimed directly at him. Jason looked at him without a hint of surprise and said, "So you're the other member of the Order. I thought your neurologic treatment center seemed slightly advanced for this period. I'm guessing you got yourself assigned to this hospital to ensure Dr. Brownfield knew he was being watched. Clever of you."

It was St. Claire's turn to speak now, and his voice was cold and hard with the hint of a German accent. "We have also been watching you. You managed to evade us every now and then, but your actions were predictable, and we always found you again. When our efforts to halt you in Paris fell short, we decided only to observe and assess your subsequent actions. We had not anticipated that you would find Joseph, but regrettably, we underestimated your abilities. No matter, your interference is at an end."

Jason replied, "We? How many of you decided to make the one-way trip to Wonderland?"

St. Claire replied, "Now you're being clever, trying to deduce how many of us are here. Two of us came through; Brother Charles spotted you in Pontorson."

Jason replied, "Let me guess, an overweight bald man? You have it wrong; I was the one who spotted him."

The windows trembled with the storm's ferocity, and Jason wondered if they would hold, "No wonder I didn't hear St. Claire's approach," he thought. He was desperate to keep him talking, to direct his attention from Emma, "So what's *your* motivation for killing millions of innocent people? What would cause you to break your oath to do no harm?"

Thunderclaps erupted overhead, and the lights flickered. If they went out, Jason would have the advantage.

St. Claire looked at him with disdain, deciding if he would answer. In a patronizing tone, he finally replied, "Germany is my homeland. You have no idea, nor do you have the ability, to conceptualize the damage done to my country by that mad man."

Jason caught an undertone of emotion in St. Claire's response and knew it went much deeper than that. He replied, "Your country is doing fine now, it's well-respected, has good leadership, it's leading the European green energy movement, so what's so bad about that?"

St. Claire's face distorted in disgust. His lips curled downwards as he exclaimed, "Did you forget about the millions who died under his cruel regime? The families that were torn apart, the genocide of an entire ethnoreligious society, the loss of intellectual capital as scholars fled the country rather than be forced to work for the Third Reich."

Andrew began to interject but was silenced by a fiery glance from St. Claire. Beside him, Emma stood frozen in disbelief and shocked horror. Her widened eyes were trying to make sense of the scene before her.

Before St. Claire could catch his breath, Jason replied, "Is that what happened to your family, is that why this is so personal for you?"

St. Claire's eyes narrowed into fiery slits, and his jaw clenched with visible tension, "My family was forced to flee their homeland in the middle of the night, to seek refuge in a country that made them ashamed of their heritage. My grandfather was detained by the SS before he could flee; he was never seen again."

Jason's mind raced. St. Claire's demeanor had rapidly changed from smug to irrational. Sacrificing millions of lives to stop Hitler was not a detached, intellectual calculation for this guy. It's a personal mission, something that he is compelled to do; the man is insane. He'd better change the subject before St. Claire completely loses it. Sardonically, he said, "So, what's the play here. You must have heard there's no weaponized virus; you made the trip for nothing."

St. Claire paused, appeared to refocus, then grinned manically, "So did you, Mr. Shaw, but we know that's not your real name."

Jason quipped, "And what's your real name, Mr. Black? And, oh yeah, now that you've dropped the phony French accent, I recognize your voice from our near meeting at the mansion."

St. Claire replied, "Since it won't matter now, it's Karl, Karl Braun."

Jason mockingly said, "So what's your game, *Karl*?"

With a condescending tone, Karl replied, "The Order is full of physicians and chemists. Do you really think I would have made this journey without bringing the virus with me?"

Jason was afraid of that, "You know it's a one-way trip. You're going to live out the rest of your miserable life here, alone."

Karl exclaimed, "No one ever proved it was a one-way trip. Besides, I won't be alone, I will join one of the Orders and live out my life peacefully surrounded by the Fellowship with the knowledge that I eliminated the most evil man the world ever produced."

Jason began to respond, but Karl snarled, "Enough talk, we're going to walk out of here quietly, we don't want to attract any attention, do we. Josef will walk first, followed by you. Emma will be right beside me, with the barrel of my pistol dug into her side."

Jason gave Emma and Andrew a look that told them not to move. Resolutely, he turned back to Karl, "No, we're not going to make it that easy for you. If you fire that gun in here, you'll be surrounded by soldiers in no time. Let me make a counter-proposal, put the gun on the desk, turn around, and walk out."

Karl sneered at him, "We both know the outcome of your last counter-proposal, four charred bodies; that was the outcome. How does it feel to have that on your conscience? No, I won't hear of any such thing. I have the upper hand, Falcone."

Jason tried again, "You have my word that we will not follow you. Get on the next train to nowhere and leave these people alone. You've lost; there's no reason for you to die. Think Karl, shooting us is suicide."

Karl took a menacing step forward and said, "It's not suicide to shoot a German informant. How many times have you been behind enemy lines? Do you really think anyone would believe you over us?"

Karl's comments and their eminent danger jolted Emma from her state of shock. She began to object, but Karl hissed, "Shut up, foolish girl. Your father will help me finish the plan, or he will see you tortured. You think the attempted rape by those German soldiers was bad; you don't know how bad it could get. Your father looked horrified when he told me about it, so I'm willing to bet he will do anything to prevent it."

Jason saw Karl suddenly turn the gun toward him; he had to take him out before he could turn the weapon back on Emma. But before he could move, Emma threw herself in front of him. The bullet meant for him hit her instead.

The unexpected events caused Karl to hesitate just long enough for Jason to act. He flew across the room, simultaneously pulling out his knife. He sliced Karl deeply across the throat before he could get off another shot, leaving him to bleed out on the office floor. Immediately he turned back toward Andrew, who was cradling Emma in his lap. Her eyes fluttered open; she looked at her father and said, "I forgive you."

Jason reached her and took hold of her hand. She looked at him; her voice was fading, but she managed to say, "I love you, please go back and save your friends."

Her voice trailed off, and she was gone. Jason couldn't believe it; he looked pleadingly at Arthur to do something. Then he saw the pool of blood growing larger underneath her. At the site of it, he uttered a haunting moan, and as the thunder waned, he held onto her, sobbing deeply into her motionless figure.

CHAPTER
61

T HE FOLLOWING DAY, Arthur left for England to bury Emma next
to her mother. He hadn't heard from James but was hopeful he was
still alive. Before leaving, he stopped at the shed to speak with Jason.
When he sat down, Jason asked, "Is it possible? Emma told me to go home
and to prevent my friends from being killed by the Black Rose. But I was
told that it was a one-way trip."

Arthur thought momentarily, then said, "I believe you have abilities
I do not understand. The speed with which you dispatched Karl was
remarkable, to say the least. While it's true that for an average person, time
travel can only be done once, who is to say the same applies to you."

He patted Jason's knee and said, "Good luck, but if you decide to stay,
you know where to find me, I'll be right here."

Jason stood, shook his hand, and said, "Thank you, goodbye."

Arthur turned and, with head bowed, walked out the door. He had
paid dearly for his mistakes, and Jason felt sorry for him. He picked up his
rucksack and headed for the train. With Emma gone, it didn't matter if
he died trying to get home. She had given him so much; even with her last
breath, she had given him hope that he might save Mike, his family, and
Sara.

He avoided Paris. If either hotel porters, Jean or Marcel, survived the
war, they could take whatever he left behind. From the train's window he
witnessed how much the world had changed in just a few months. Everything, including food, was being rationed. Rather than delicate dresses,
the women who braved the streets wore rags and stood in soup lines with
gaunt children clutching their skirts. The only civilian men he saw were
either disabled or too old to fight.

The train was full of wounded soldiers. Jason had his fill of death; he
knew what the next few years would bring and was helpless to stop it.
He didn't even feel the accomplishment that completing a mission usually

brought him. But this wasn't a completed mission; it was an unnecessary one. This thought filled him with guilt; Emma would be alive if he hadn't traveled here. But coming here allowed him to meet her. These paradoxical thoughts were tearing him apart.

He arrived at the Mont just before dawn, slipping in through the back and into the crypts as he had done eight months before. Everything was in the niche, just as he had left it. He changed, grabbed his backpack, which still held the book and the journal, and picked up the device. It took him a few minutes to remember how to adjust the time dial to find the right entangled particle.

He stopped and thought for a minute. He was returning to a date before Sara found the book. Would it still be in his backpack when he arrived? Would two copies of him be in the present? No, he didn't think so. The questions were mind-blowing, and he had no answers.

Deciding to play it safe, he set the return date to roughly twenty-four hours before Sara found the book. After removing it from the Pithos jar, he would travel back to his cabin, timing his arrival a day before Mike called him about the package.

Three days later, his flight arrived in Greece. Sara told him how and where she had found the book, leading her to the device. He just had to get there and remove them before she did.

He anchored off the island and waited until dusk. He swam to shore and then proceeded to the cave where the book was hidden. It was there, in the pithos jar, just as Sara said. He had already decided that since no one would find the journal without the book, he wouldn't bother looking for it. He placed the book in his waterproof backpack, retraced his steps to the boat, and sped away.

CHAPTER
62

J ASON FINISHED HIDING the book and the device in separate, secure locations. As he walked away, a quote from the "Butterfly Effect" popped into his head, "Change one thing, change everything." He hoped that wasn't a portend of things to come, that he hadn't inadvertently changed history by traveling to 1914. However, he thought, "Maybe a little change in my life wouldn't be so bad."

He recalled his conversation with the doc while he and Sara were at Landstuhl. His life was his own, and the events in 1914 made him realize that he could only control what he did, not what others did. His experiences and the relationships he formed while there made him realize how lonely he had been.

He swung the axe down on the round of oak. It was the same day and time he received the phone call from Mike, the call that changed the course of time and would reshape the rest of his life. He took out his cell phone to watch the minutes tick down. If Mike called, it would mean he failed to stop Karl. He thought about the movie, "Ground Hog Day," and hoped that his phone would not buzz.

But it did. The caller ID read Mike Miller. With an overpowering sense of dread, he answered. His chest tightened, and he barely heard Mike say, "Hey man, Nicole and I are heading to the cape with the girls. I'm on my way home right now to get them. We rented a beach house with plenty of room, and the girls would really like to see you. I know you're into your reclusive lifestyle and all, but I'd like you to join us. What do you say, brother?"

Tears filled his eyes as he let out a sigh of relief. He smiled and, with a thick voice, said, "Give me a few minutes to shower, I'll meet you on the Tern." He pocketed the phone, looked upward, and said, "Thanks Emma."

EPILOGUE

J ASON COULDN'T STOP himself; his curiosity finally got the best of him. It had been three months, and he swore he wouldn't google Emma's father to see what had become of him. He sat before his encrypted laptop and typed in Dr. Arthur Brownfield. Surprisingly, more than one physician with that name was found. He scrolled the list, looking for someone the right age.

His eyes latched on to "Dr. Arthur Brownfield, a field physician in WW1 who significantly advanced the use of aseptic technique during surgery." The article mentioned that he invented "eyeless needled sutures," made of a single strand of sterile material, significantly decreasing post-operative infections. He found the last sentence in the article ironic, yet it touched him in a way he couldn't describe; "He is credited with saving thousands of soldiers' lives during the First World War."

He tried looking up James Brownfield but found nothing. For Emma's sake, he hoped that James had survived the war. Then, fearing what he might find, he thought, "Oh, well. While I'm at it, I might as well look up the other guy too."

He punched in the name Roger Carroll and found one listing for a man of the right age. The article said, "Roger Carroll was involved in the discovery of the neutron in 1930." He thought, "This can't be him," but then he saw the accompanying picture and immediately recognized Roger's bald head.

He sat back and reflected on what he had just learned. His second objective had been to protect the timeline, to prevent the Black Rose from changing the future, but had he succeeded? Time will tell.

Printed in Great Britain
by Amazon